Judith Cutler, like her h̶ ̶ ̶ ̶ ̶ ̶ ̶ ̶ ̶ ̶ ̶ ̶ ̶
Birmingham. She taught̶ ̶ ̶ ̶ ̶ ̶ ̶ ̶ ̶ ̶ ̶
but is now a part-time lectu̶ ̶ ̶ ̶ ̶ ̶ ̶ ̶
Continuing Studies Department. ̶ ̶ ̶ ̶ ̶ ̶
Birmingham Symphony Orchestra's Benevolent ̶ ̶ ̶ ̶
committee of the Birmingham Chamber Music Society. ̶ ̶ ̶
also the Secretary of the Crime Writer's Association.

Judith has enjoyed considerable and popular success with her first four novels featuring Sophie Rivers. DYING FALL, DYING TO WRITE, DYING ON PRINCIPLE and DYING FOR MILLIONS all have a Birmingham setting. She has also written a number of short stories, most notably for the BBC Short Story slot. She is currently working on a new Sophie Rivers novel.

Dying For Power

Judith Cutler

PIATKUS

First published in Great Britain in 1998 by
Judy Piatkus (Publishers) Ltd of
5 Windmill Street, London W1

This edition published 1998

The moral right of the author has been asserted

A catalogue record for this book is available from the British Library

ISBN 0 7499 3081 0

Set in Times by Intype London Ltd

Printed and bound in Great Britain by
Mackays of Chatham PLC, Chatham, Kent

I would like to thank: Paul Mackney of NATFHE, for background information without which this book could not have been written; the men and women of the West Midlands Police Service for their patient help; Edwina Van Boolen and Frances Lally for their invaluable support and criticism; Robert Kornreich for being there when I needed him; and Flossie the Cat for the gentle pleasure of her quiet life.

For Janet
and for Farat and Simon
who succeeded where Sophie
and Afzal failed

Prologue

Berlin on a baking Friday afternoon. The Turkish market. I wanted to dive into the cascades of fresh coriander, embrace the unleavened bread. The tomatoes glowed in the sun; the velvet of the late peaches gleamed. I had another half day before I had to return to Birmingham, two and a half days before I was once again incarcerated in William Murdock College. And I was thinking about falling in love.

As if he were thinking about exactly the same thing, Greg touched my elbow. He smiled down at me, his eyes very blue against his tan: 'I reckon you could use a beer.'

'I reckon you could, too.'

Some of the little bars had not awnings but vines to shield the tables from the sun. He steered me into one, and sat me down. He did that sort of thing: elbowed his way to bars, organized taxis, selected the best but cheapest imbis for lunch. If you didn't watch him he'd also decide what you ate and drank and where you went. And he would insist on taking me by the elbow to help me cross the street. Perhaps that was why I was only thinking about falling in love, not going ahead and doing it. In any case, it was, as I told myself, only a holiday romance. I was staying over here with Courtney, a friend of mine who'd had a terrific critical success with a screenplay based on his life in Durham Gaol. One of his new media friends had lent him his apartment, and Courtney – lonely for all his cheerfulness – hadn't managed to think of anyone else to invite. I'd jumped at the chance: the holiday company I'd booked a fortnight in

1

Greece with had failed the day I was due to fly. So Courtney and I had travelled out together, but we weren't inseparable.

'The thing is, dear, it'd cramp my style dreadfully if we stuck to each other like glue,' Courtney had said. 'I suppose bi- is pretty chic, but—'

'You're not bi- any more than I'm gay. Point taken,' I'd said. So we tended to sight-see together during the day, and I didn't ask about his nights. There wasn't anything to ask about mine. Not that they were dull. For what greater pleasure is there than to sit on a balcony on the edge of a great city watching life pass beneath your feet, with a pile of new paperbacks and a bottle of chilled wine at your elbow?

A week into the holiday Courtney'd been drooling over the men's undies in the window of Ka De Ve when someone had picked his pocket. I'd given chase, yelling in English, and cannoned into Greg, who kept his hands on my arms a second longer than was technically necessary and turned out to be good-looking in a rugged sort of way. When Courtney caught up with us he found he hadn't lost more than a few marks; he even claimed he'd enjoyed the frisson of being groped by a stranger. His eyes meanwhile were gleaming: almost as much as mine were. It was natural for the three of us to have a beer together and Greg's favourite bar was just across the road. Over cool beers the talk turned to cricket – Greg hailed from Sidney, and was desperate for someone to chew over the latest gossip with.

'What are you doing over here?' Courtney asked at last, trying to change the subject.

'I'm living here for a bit. It's my work – I'm an engineer. You know they're rebuilding half Berlin for the Millennium? I'm involved with the concrete distribution over in Pots-dammer Platz.'

'The biggest building site in Europe?' Courtney was impressed. 'The one you look at from the Info Box?'

'That's the one.' His smile managed to convey that he was proud of the project while remaining modest about his own achievements.

'With Hitler's bunker tucked away in the corner?' Courtney had taken photographs for his grandfather, whose

2

landing in Berlin had been bumpier than ours – he'd parachuted from a bomber.

'That's right. Don't know why they don't open it to the public.'

'But—' I began. Then stopped abruptly. I didn't know Greg well enough yet to be confrontational.

Greg seized the glasses. 'I'll get another round in, shall I?'

As soon as Greg's back was turned, Courtney scrabbled for his Ray-Bans and his camera.

'Hey, where d'you think you're going?' I demanded.

'Look, Sophie, we've never fallen out over a man yet and I don't want to start now. See you when I see you!' And he slipped out into the street.

I wasn't sure about having him go all self-sacrificing on me. I was too fond of him for that. And I wasn't sure I liked being shoved down Greg's throat, either. I wondered whether I should leave too, but stopped myself. Greg might manage to down three beers, but it would be ungracious, indeed rude, to expect him to tackle four.

So Greg and I spent five days together. He took some time off and squired me to all the touristy things, since it was my first time in Berlin. Courtney and I had already done the bus trip round the city, and some of the museums, so Greg took me to the places we hadn't seen, like the Museum of Applied Art, where we laughed over the Habitat chairs and the red typewriter I'd bought second-hand with money from my first Saturday job. We were beginning to feel comfortable together.

And, though neither of us had said anything, we were wondering about going to bed together. We might have been a textbook illustration of body language and meaningful eye contact. It was just a matter of the right moment. Any moment now. In the little bar, in the greenish light under the vine awning, he was smiling, and I was smiling back.

Since he'd paid a lot of money for some wonderful meals my salary wouldn't run to, and I love food, it occurred to me that I could return the compliment with a nice ethnic meal at his apartment or ours. It wouldn't matter if it were a touch on the al fresco side. All I needed was in the market

3

– I'd head back there when we'd finished the beer. No need to tell him why.

He gestured to the now empty glasses.

'No thanks. I'd like to go back to the market.'

'More photos? Jeez, Sophie, you got shares in Kodak?' He laughed at me indulgently and took my hand.

'No,' I said, squeezing his lightly. 'To get some food.'

'You must have bloody hollow legs, that's all I'll say. Not that you look bad on it.' We were definitely one conversation nearer to bed. 'But don't buy food there, sweetheart. I mean, the hygiene! And those women give me the creeps, all covered up. Damn it, they're living in a civilized country and they creep round swathed in black from head to toe. In this heat, for Christ's sake! Why can't they behave like ordinary decent people? Fit in. But they have to be different. No wonder the Krauts burnt down that Turkish hostel. Now, *that's* more like it.'

I followed his eyes. Two very beautiful young women strolled past, arms round each other. Both wore shorts so truncated you could see the rise of their buttock cheeks; tops so brief their nipples were almost exposed. And each had her hand tucked inside the back of the other's waistband, fondling the flesh beneath.

'Fancy being three in a bed with them,' he said. 'Say, Sophie, you don't ever – er – do you?'

I most certainly didn't.

'Come on, don't look so po-faced! I was only joking. Come on, let's go and get that food. And have one last photo-opportunity with those refugees from the Arabian Nights.'

So that was that. I trotted out the usual speech about people's rights to live their own lives; he agreed, but laughed, clearly thinking about the lesbians. It was too hot for a row, and it wouldn't have changed anything anyway. In any case, there was more to a holiday than romance. I hailed a taxi, said goodbye, and left him on the pavement.

'Sophie, love, you'll have to tell me all about it.'

Courtney stroked my hair and smeared a tear away with

4

his outstretched thumb. He poured me another glass of wine and sat beside me on the balcony.

'Nothing to tell. I just decided I didn't like him.'

'Not even enough for a quick fuck?'

'Not even enough for that.'

'What a waste. But at least you're getting better.'

'Better?'

'I thought you'd never fancy anyone again, not after Whatshisname. You know, the one we both fancied on that writing course. You've been like a nun ever since.'

I shook my head. Despite myself, my eyes filled with tears again. But not for Greg.

'Someone else? Another one that didn't work out?'

I nodded; he hugged me.

'At least you fancied Greg. Like I told you, you're on the mend. You wait till next time. Go on, put some more mascara on and we'll paint the town red. I know just the place if you promise not to be shocked. There's this wonderful queen, must be all of six-three, will *insist* on wearing a tutu and fishnet tights. Six-inch heels, too! He'd be so dishy if only he waxed his body hair. Come on, now, sweetie – trust your Uncle Courtney!'

Chapter One

So here I was again, suffering a dreadful sense of déjà vu. Another academic year; another GCSE English resit class.

The September sunshine streamed through the windows, remorselessly highlighting the thick patina of dirt. Years of economies imposed on the college meant that cleaning windows was not a priority. The mote-filled light fingered posters and wall-charts from last year – or maybe the year before. I really would have to make an effort to tidy up if this was to be my regular room for teaching this group. And, come to think of it, to find an overhead projector that worked – and to persuade someone to clean that palimpsest of a whiteboard. The only chemical that would shift the layers of board marker was rumoured to be carcinogenic, and since even the most cavalier of the caretaking team would always insist on donning a mask and heavy-duty gloves to use it, that was one job I wouldn't volunteer for.

The room was uncomfortably hot already. It would be far worse when filled with the twenty or so bodies which had toiled up fifteen flights of stairs for their first repeat GCSE class with me. I'd already tried to open the windows – being a believer in fresh air – but last year a passion had developed amongst some of William Murdock's more enterprising students for dropping items out of the window: possibly in the spirit of Galileo Galilei. My knowledge of physics is lamentable, but even I know that anything dropped from the fifteenth floor can do an amazing amount of damage to anything – or worse still, anyone – that happens to be in its path. It was hardly surprising, then, that Management had come up with a prompt solution: all windows were to be 'controlled'. A controlled window was one that henceforth would open no more than two inches at the top or two inches at the bottom. So far the only windows to be controlled were those overlooking the newly designated senior staff car park – until now parking had been blessedly, if chaotically, democratic. As luck would have it, the senior staff car park was on the south of the building, and if autumn sun made the rooms that side like a greenhouse, goodness knew what it'd be like in high summer.

Sufficient unto the day, no doubt.

I wiped a light slick of sweat from my upper lip and looked at my watch. There was still a supplementary strap around my wrist where the skin was white against my Berlin suntan.

Seven minutes late.

I'd chosen my clothes to show off the rest of the tan: my usual short skirt and a T-shirt. All that energetic sight-seeing had counterbalanced the food and wine. My heart was beating away in my chest, showing no signs at all of having been broken by Greg. There were moments when I still wondered if I should have tried to take him in hand. But there'd been other sexist or racist observations, before the one which proved the final straw. I'd pretended to myself I could ignore them – just because the old hormones were getting excited. No, it would never have worked.

Anyway, I was looking better than I'd looked for months. And feeling fitter: I could truthfully tell the recalcitrant students, when eventually they arrived, that it was possible to use the stairs. All of them.

I wouldn't start off in heavy mode, though. I'd remind them gently that they had a syllabus to finish in nine months, rather than the two years they'd had at school. Five minutes lopped off here and there and they'd miss vital work. Kind but firm: that would be my tone. *When* they finally arrived.

At last Brummie voices echoed round the corridor outside. I popped my head round the door, then emerged a little further to tap my watch meaningfully. Predictably the group was almost entirely male; women seemed to find it easier to pass first time, though I had a fair success rate with all the youngsters who came to me for a second attempt. In fact, there was only one young woman in this group, an Asian in standard student gear – jeans and T-shirt. She was the first into the room, with a quiet, 'Hello, Miss,' and planted herself quickly at a front desk.

Then came an uneven procession of young men, swaggering to desks at the back. Most of them carried enormous bulky sports bags, despite the fact that William Murdock was a college with very few sports facilities. Perhaps the exercise lay simply in carrying the bag.

Only one young man – a very handsome one – headed for the front. He smiled at the girl, and sat next to her.

There was an immediate silence.

Everyone looked at him, and at me, then back at him. The tension was palpable. Despite fifteen years in the job, I was completely at a loss. Eventually I found something to say. 'Students sit where they want in my classroom.' I drew myself up to my full five foot one. 'So long as they come on time.'

The lad smiled at me, but then found the sun was in his eyes, so he moved further from the window. The others watched. At last one or two shuffled to their seats, and a couple more actually sat down. But they left their bags on the desks. Their quiescence was only temporary. So who was the king-pin in this group? Who might I have to take on in order to keep control? As I called the register I stared at each face, implanting them on my memory. 'Amjad Akhtar? Mohammed Ali?' One or two seemed embarrassed, and dropped their eyes; the majority folded their arms and waited for what I feared was the next act.

Most were Asian, the majority in jeans and T-shirts, but a couple sported Bangladeshi clothes – appropriate enough on a day like this. One or two more wore the check scarf I associate with Arab leaders such as Yasser Arafat.

'Guljar Singh Tamber?' That was the young man who'd sat at the front. So he was a Sikh, was he? I wasn't surprised he wasn't wearing a turban: most Sikhs at William Murdock tended to have their hair cut to whatever happened to be the fashionable length at the time.

A few more names. Then, 'Zia Yamin?'

8

'Yes. Miss.' He raised an eyebrow, and seemed poised to say more.

Since I didn't like the tone he'd used for those two syllables, I decided not to give him the opportunity. I plunged straight into my introductory spiel, continuing even when the door was flung open and another lad appeared, hot and bothered and clutching a skull cap. If I wasn't careful we might have another of those silences.

'Right,' I said, 'the place for your bags is on the floor. If you want to pass these exams we'd better start straight away – and that means note-pads and pencils at the ready.'

As if in answer to my unspoken prayer, the Jewish youth sat right by the door – and no one turned to see what he wore on his head. Neither did I draw attention to his name. They'd find soon enough he was Sam Jacobson.

One of the things I'd always liked about William Murdock was its easy racial mix. It gave me great pleasure to watch Northern Ireland Catholics discover that a Protestant can become a friend; a Hindu share a joke with a Muslim; an Afro-Caribbean go off to the canteen to eat with a Sikh. I'd been prominent on our Equal Opportunities committee, an organisation which had hitherto had very little in the way of conflict to resolve. I did recall noticing, however, as I'd steamed up the stairs, a clutch of posters recruiting for Student Union clubs, and not the usual football and indoor cricket ones: the Sikh Society; the Hindu Society; the Muslim Society, which already had a series of meetings to advertise. Nothing for a Christian Union, but as my religious commitment was conspicuous by its absence I could hardly complain.

Usually teachers try to make the first class a relaxed affair with the aim of encouraging the students to get to know each other. But not this afternoon. Under the pretence of making up for the time they'd wasted, this afternoon I'd opt for firm, with the possibility of kindness at some future – unspecified – date.

Having worked them very hard, and right up until the last minute, just to establish that they went home only when I said they could, I smiled – firmly, of course. 'OK. You'll prepare that exercise for next week. And you'll be here *on*

9

time. All of you. The class starts at three-fifteen, not three-thirty.' I made eye contact with as many as possible, including Zia Yamin, and nodded their dismissal.

I was in the corridor locking the classroom door when a man of about my age came up to me.

'Ah! Miss – Miss – er—' He smiled with rather more confidence than the situation perhaps warranted and stuck out a hand to be shaken.

'Rivers. Sophie Rivers.' I smiled at him, assuming that he was a new colleague I'd not yet met. Communications at Murdock were slow and uneven; this was partly because of the buildings, the taller of which had lifts most kindly described as intermittent. On the other hand in recent years Management seemed to have made a concerted effort to make things worse by re-allocating all the public rooms to other – 'priority' – areas such as administration suites. This term some of Senior Management had purloined the nicest teachers' workrooms for their individual offices. The more cynical amongst my colleagues alleged that this was a divide and rule policy – I more temperately suspected mere lack of imagination. Then for some reason Management had contrived to forget about calling a staff meeting for the new year, a fact even I found worrying since we had a new principal, as well as some new heads of department.

This young man had pale carroty hair, with white eyelashes and eyebrows. His complexion was wraith-white. He made up, however, for his general insipidity with a bone-crushing and protracted handshake. I immediately suspected the worst: he must be a new Senior Manager.

I tried to withdraw my hand.

He responded with a further shake and a wide smile. If I'd been him I'd have spent some of his doubtless obscene salary having those teeth capped: I'd never seen such narrow, rat-like specimens.

'Now,' he said, releasing me, 'let me see. What's your role?'

'I teach English,' I said, more abruptly than I'd intended. The class must have been more stressful than I'd realized. And this was only the first week! Another thirty-seven to go ... 'And you? You're new, aren't you?'

'Edwards,' he said. 'Financial Services.'

So what was he doing up here? The highest administrators ever got was the seventh floor – and then only because the conference room was located there. No doubt there was insufficient oxygen for them at our level.

'Welcome aboard,' I said, vaguely nautical on account of our Principal having been an ex-Naval captain. Ex-Principal, come to think of it. He'd suddenly resigned at the end of the summer term: on the grounds, it was claimed, of ill-health. On the other hand, one of the secretarial staff had seen him completing his fortieth length at her local baths, so his health couldn't have been too precarious. Interesting things, rumours.

Edwards smiled, revealing those teeth again. 'Now,' he said, leafing through the pages of a file he was carrying, 'how many students did you have this afternoon?'

'Twenty-three,' I said.

'Twenty-five is the target. We may have to merge.'

'Merge? With what?'

'Another group. Mr Foster's is – let me see – only twenty-two.'

'Teach forty-five people in one class? You've got to be joking!'

His green eyes expressed little humour. 'I take it, Miss Rivers, you are on the old contract,' he said, jotting something in his file and walking away.

Damn right I was. Being on the new contract meant the penalty for cheeking Those Above was summary dismissal.

I watched him to the end of the corridor and headed back to base. Sharing my office with twelve other people, I was sure of a sympathetic response when I regaled them with my story.

But there was to be no regaling anyone at the moment: the room was in uproar. It didn't take me long to work out why. Three more desks, three more chairs and three more filing cabinets jostled each other by the table we'd set aside for our kettle and cups. The senior caretaker was gesticulating with a calculator and a tape measure, presumably to demonstrate that, even with the extra furniture, we were maintaining our legal minimum of space. Then a squad of

11

his acolytes strode in and one by one all our cabinets were herded together and placed in a solid phalanx at the far end of the room. The desks were rearranged in solid blocks, four abreast facing another four. The chairs – old local authority green rexine armchairs – wouldn't fit. No loss – they weren't comfortable. But to my horror they were replaced, not by new ergonomically sound seats, but with plastic stacking chairs from a classroom.

I managed to corner a hot and embarrassed caretaker as he retreated down the corridor.

'I thought we were shedding staff, not taking on extra?'

'That's right. But we're rationalising the staffrooms. Maximising the space.'

'So you end up with fewer staffrooms? What'll happen to the empty rooms?'

'God knows,' he said. 'But I bet it'll mean me having to move more filing cabinets.'

Chapter Two

Aggie, my next-door neighbour, was laid up with a bad toe. Since I was cooking what she admitted was a decent meal for myself I made enough for her too and took it round. She peered doubtfully at the sauce – honey and mustard, with a little white wine – but agreed that it tasted good. 'Not like some of your foreign muck,' she said.

'Foreign muck' was much in evidence at the meeting Shahida, one of my favourite William Murdock colleagues, had organized, in the form of cocktail-sized delicacies brought by several of the women present. And we'd all brought an item for a mini bring-and-buy sale – as Shahida said, in a fund-raising campaign every penny counted.

'It's quite clear,' she said, 'that we won't get planning permission to convert the garage to a room for the crèche—'

'Garage!' I echoed. 'You mean—' A service station? somewhere to park the family car?

'It runs the whole side of the house so it's quite large,' someone said. Not a service station, then.

'It's the only room remotely big enough. If women want to work to support themselves and indeed their children, then we have to provide a crèche while they work. We did hope that if we decorated the garage properly, we'd get permission, but the councillor we spoke to said we hadn't a prayer. Not until we'd got enough loos and proper heating.'

'It always comes down to bogs and boilers,' said an Afro-Caribbean woman.

I didn't know any of the members, and had rather hoped Shahida would have made proper introductions before the meeting got under way. But since most of them knew each other already, and she was clearly nervous at chairing a meeting for the first time, I didn't press the matter.

'So what do you – we – need to do?' an elegant woman in a sari asked.

'Oh, Baljit, I'm sorry. You and Sophie are in the dark, aren't you? Ladies, I do apologize. Baljit is – Why not introduce yourselves, and then we'll all do the same.'

I grinned at her, and raised a discreet thumb in approval. There were some intriguing women: the sari-wearing woman was a barrister; there was a doctor, originally from Ghana. The Afro-Caribbean was an architect who'd once been a victim of domestic violence herself.

'Later, perhaps, we can involve men,' said Jasmine. 'But first we need to establish our credentials, as it were. To prove – as much to ourselves as to anyone else – that we can do it.'

A hum of approval.

'Are you objecting to men on principle?' I asked. 'Do you want the campaign kept secret?'

Lucilla shook her head. 'It's not a safe house, not the sort of place women in real danger would need.'

'No, that sort of thing is usually organized by the police. Somewhere completely anonymous where vengeful male relatives – it invariably *is* the males – can't find them.' Sammie, a painter and decorator, nodded emphatically as it dawned on me that she and I were the only white women in the room. 'This is for all women, regardless of race or creed, who need to protect themselves and their children from violent families. And to do that, sisters, we need to raise a great deal of dosh. Quickly.'

And we got down to business. Once over her nervousness Shahida chaired the meeting lightly and efficiently, and jobs were allocated with the maximum of speed. A network of contacts was to be established, charities were to be approached – and all before the next meeting. Having no expertise in that area – but, I asked myself humbly, in what area *did* I have any expertise? – I was afraid of becoming a passenger. But then I discovered a talent I didn't know I had – Shahida suddenly roped me in to auction the little items we'd brought. Perhaps the capacity for playing one person off against another is not one the average fairy godmother would bestow, but at least it raised twenty-seven pounds, and I would go home with a whole tin of Shahida's mother's pakora.

Shahida took me to one side before I left. 'Could you do me a big favour?'

'Of course.'

'Well, it's this Saturday evening – someone's coming to dinner and I need an extra body.'

I looked her square in the eye. 'You're at it again, aren't you?'

Happily married herself, and the proud mother of a delightful daughter, she wanted me – and, indeed, any other of her friends who happened to be single – to be in the same blissful state. There was no doubt it was blissful: the glances she and her husband exchanged when they thought no one was looking suggested they shared a great deal, from political opinions to sexual fulfilment.

I played hard to get. 'Depends who else is coming.'

'Two business colleagues of Tanvir's. And Afzal – I think you've met him before.'

I had. We'd got on well enough, though neither had been sufficiently attracted to contact the other afterwards. At least, I hadn't – I'd been too preoccupied by the problems surrounding Andy, my cousin. But those were over now.

'Of course,' I said. 'No problem.'

Until Saturday evening, that is, when Shahida confessed that Tanvir's colleagues had cried off. Which left me wondering aloud about her plans for me and Afzal.

'Come on, you know you liked him,' Shahida said as she poured me a drink. 'And he certainly—'

'Certainly what?' I sloshed my gin and tonic round idly, grateful that, although Shahida didn't touch alcohol herself, she never showed any signs of disapproval when others did, and as a result of her husband's regular trips abroad, she had an excellent range to offer. If there was any wine –

15

possibly opened specially for me, since Afzal was also a Muslim – I knew that it too would be excellent.

'He thought you were very lively and attractive,' she replied, censoring something, I was sure.

'And unmarried. How come he's not married himself? Thirty-whatever seems quite old for an Asian over here to be free.'

'Hmm,' she said, censoring something more. 'William Murdock parents want to marry the kids off before they've cut their teeth, poor little dears. I lost another one over the holiday, Sophie. Yasmin. Out in the sticks in Pakistan with a brand-new husband who doesn't speak English. And I had such hopes for her . . .'

'The trouble with you teachers is that you want to run everyone's life,' said Tanvir, her husband, bringing in dishes of nuts and crisps. 'Maybe they'll be happy.'

'Typical engineer! Humans aren't Lego pieces to clip together and unclip if things don't work out. Which reminds me, Sophie's brought a box of Duplo – you'd better work it out before you let Maria loose on it.'

So here I was, wearing a pretty blouse, a long linen skirt and my best suntan, waiting to charm and be charmed. And to eat. Shahida wasn't the greatest of cooks, but she had a mother who cooked the meanest samosas I'd ever tasted. If chicken was on the menu Tanvir might well have cooked it, since Shahida, although no longer a vegetarian, preferred not to be too heavily involved with meat of any sort.

Azfal arrived on the dot at seven-thirty. I'd arrived earlier to help Maria – pronounced with the stress on the first syllable – with her bath, a community affair generating a change of clothes. Afzal flourished a bottle, a large bunch of roses and a box, the rattle of which suggested further Duplo. Perhaps small children have radar instead of ears . . .

'Maria! What are you doing? You're supposed to be asleep!'

'Discovered life after bed, has she?' Afzal asked. 'Come on, Maria, come and sit on my knee and see if you can open this.' He hitched her up and peeled back the start of the Sellotape.

There are never, of course, enough bricks to build the

ambitious construction one has in mind, particularly when this is designed by a committee comprised of a lawyer, an engineer and two lecturers, so my present had to be opened too. What this was doing to poor Shahida's cooking schedule I didn't like to ask, but, politely she refrained from giving little glances at her watch to suggest she was anxious. At last, Tanvir looked at the clock. 'I'm afraid it's this young lady's bedtime. Sophie, will you carry her up? Afzal, I can't see us separating her from this castle, so could you carry that up? I'll read her to sleep while Shaz sorts things out down here.'

'There's nothing to sort,' Shahida objected.

'Yes, there is. Your orange juice.'

It was kind of Maria to fill her nappy: even kinder of Tanvir to wave us downstairs while he dealt with everything. And since Shaz still had half an inch of orange juice to finish, Afzal got himself a gin and refreshed mine. We started to gather up the spare bricks; he clipped some together.

'What's that?' I asked.

'A bird. Can't you tell? OK, it's got a bit of a flight problem—'

'It certainly has. Can't flap its wings. But my fish'd have a few difficulties too.'

'Fish? Call that a fish? Come on, Sophie—'

And so we became friends. We all liked cricket, and there'd been plenty to talk about in the season just finished.

'What we really need is a couple of bowlers who can manage pace and accuracy.'

I'd rather thought that Pakistan had some of the finest bowlers in the world and would have said so, until I realized – I hoped they wouldn't notice my blush – that they had passed Lord Tebbitt's cricket test with flying colours. But then talk drifted to Imran Khan, and thence to Pakistan politics, and it was clear that they were as expert in that area as they subsequently proved to be in English politics.

Then we got on to the theatre: a new production at Birmingham Rep. The reviews in the *Birmingham Post* were excellent – Tanvir pushed away from the table to read them out to us – and it seemed natural for us all to team up to go together.

'What about Maria?' I asked. 'Will you be able to find a sitter?'

They laughed. 'Is it my mum's turn or yours?' Tanvir asked.

'Yours, I think. Mine'll swear it's hers, though. We're more or less driven out every week so that the grandmas get a good dose of her. They don't reckon a full day each is enough.'

'I'm not surprised – she's an absolute sweetie. A real delight,' Afzal said, with rather more emphasis than I expected. And there was a little silence I didn't feel qualified to break.

Tanvir got up to clear the plates, I gathered the casserole and chutney dishes, and followed him into the kitchen. While he unwrapped clingfilmed cheese, I scraped the plates and loaded the dishwasher.

'Will you be going to see the Albion play this season?' he asked.

'Might do. Can't break the habit of a lifetime. What about you?'

'It's a bit rough on Shaz. Now I'm doing all this travelling, it leaves a lot for her, despite the grandmas. And – it's a funny thing – I actually like staying in and playing with Maria. Has Shaz told you what I found the other day?'

I shook my head; I knew Tanvir was in the habit of finding all sorts of irresistible toys.

'Come on, and I'll show you. Can you bring the bread?'

'Sure. Though I don't reckon I shall ever be able to eat anything again.'

'Well, mind you eat some of that applewood smoked. Shaz got it specially for you. And then,' he continued, raising his voice, 'she ate the lot, so I spent a most enjoyable half-hour fighting my way into and out of Safeway's car park. Not to mention the longest checkout queue in the western world. I'll show you what I found – Afzal might like it too.'

Shahida watched with amusement.

'What is it?' Afzal asked.

'Just you wait. I'm not spoiling the surprise.'

18

We didn't have long to wait. Tanvir returned with a rectangular cardboard box, which he laid on the table and opened with a flourish.

'There!'

'Goodness, man, you're starting her young!' Afzal fished out a miniature cricket bat.

'I always wanted to play,' Shahida said wistfully. 'I reckon England would be doing a lot better if they'd only let me bat at school.'

'A most elegant right-hand bat,' Tanvir chimed in, squeezing her hand. 'And your daughter will have the proper gear right from the start. None of your plastic stuff. Feel this.'

'And the pity of it is,' said Afzal, weighing the little bat for balance and playing a cover drive, 'she'll probably prefer tennis.'

'Well, we could do with some decent female tennis players too,' Tanvir said, laughing. 'How long is it since Virginia Wade?'

Arun, Shahida's brother-in-law, was due to drive me home. Apart from the fact he'd failed in his ambition of being an Afghanistan freedom fighter and occasionally drove as if he were late for tea in Kabul, I'd rather he drove me than I risk my licence. Anyway, he needed the money.

I was just about to phone for him, when Afzal turned to me. 'Can I give you a lift home?'

'Oh, you don't need to go yet!' Shahida said, a mite less enthusiastic than she meant to sound.

'You two keep early hours – what time did you say Maria wakes you up? Seven? Well then.' Afzal grinned at me. 'Sophie and I, on the other hand, don't have any such problem. So – maybe Ronnie Scott's?'

Tanvir and Shahida winked. I'll *swear* they winked. But I didn't call Arun.

The crowds of teenagers swarming along Broad Street put us off. We were at least fifteen years too old to join them, and much too sensibly dressed. Making no concessions to the late evening chill, the men strolled in shirtsleeves, the

19

women in sleeveless tops cut deep front and back. Goodness knows how they sat down in those lycra-tight skirts.

There was nowhere to park. We sat in the traffic, exchanging mutters about the future of the world if there were solid jams at eleven on a Saturday night. Then there was a sudden flurry as four or five white kids sprinted from the car park at the side of the Mondiale, and slipped into the milling crowds, quickly lost in the mass.

'What d'you think all that was about?' I asked.

'You're not asking me to be heroic?'

'Just suspicious. And if there's nothing—'

As soon as he could, Afzal signalled and pulled over into the car park. Someone was just pulling out of a slot, so he waited to reverse in; some kid in a tarted-up Metro tried to get in first, but Afzal kept his head and his line and gave a lesson in parking. The Metro driver spat at him. Literally. Afzal shrugged.

'We're here. Now what?'

'Let's just walk round the perimeter,' I said, 'where it's not so well lit.'

The groaning was audible from about twenty yards, which we covered at a sprint. A young man lay halfway across an Escort's bonnet, bleeding badly from his arm.

Afzal produced a mobile phone and dialled. 'Do you know any first aid?' he asked.

'Not enough – I don't even know how to take off his coat. And there may be other injuries.'

Afzal touched the youth's good arm, and leaned to peer into his face.

'Fuck off! You fucking Pakis have done enough, haven't you?'

I joined Afzal. 'What's up?'

'Bloody jumped by a bunch of Pakis, wasn't I? Took me money and me cards. Bloody hell.' He put his head back on the bonnet, and groaned into semi-consciousness. Afzal whizzed back to his car, returning with a travel rug. 'You'd better do the honours,' he said.

I obliged.

And then the first police car arrived.

* * *

Afzal started yawning.

We'd talked to the two young officers, explained why we'd come looking, while the victim surfaced periodically to mutter expletives about Asians before being popped into an ambulance. The woman officer suggested we might like to cruise round the streets looking for the young men; Afzal gestured at the swarms still filling the pavements and the road.

'In any case,' he said, 'we saw no more than these young men running.'

'And you say they were white – and he swears they were Asian. Probably not connected. OK. We'll send officers round to interview you tomorrow. If you could just confirm your addresses?'

That seemed good enough for us. Afzal picked his way wearily round the back streets, and headed towards Harborne. It was clearly time for bed. Separately. This time I wasn't even going to think about rushing things. As he pulled up outside my house he yawned again. I hoped it was genuine fatigue.

'I was going to suggest coffee—' I said – hesitantly, for me.

'Let's take a rain check.' He yawned again. 'I'm sorry.'

But I'd already joined in. 'This is catching!'

'I'd like – shall we do lunch one day next week?'

'You think William Murdock allows lunchtimes? I'm not joking. Shaz will tell you.'

'She has but you won't be working on Saturday? Good. Twelve? Excellent.' And we exchanged chaste kisses on the cheek.

As I cleaned my teeth, I found myself smiling at myself in the mirror. On the whole I was glad William Murdock hadn't – yet – asked me to work on Saturdays.

Chapter Three

I spent Sunday morning mowing lawns – mine and Aggie's – and generally making the gardens presentable. My diligence was born partly from a delight in the present weather – I could top up my suntan, remembering to be sensible about UV filters – and partly from a desire to do something useful. The chicken I was roasting could look after itself, and I was happy to obey Aggie's instructions to pick enough runner beans for the pair of us from the wigwam of plants in her garden. I knew of old she didn't trust me not to use garlic when I cooked courgettes (I'd stuffed a couple of cloves I wouldn't tell her about inside the chicken), so I'd bought a few late-season peas for her. And to my astonishment she had produced a gooseberry pie, the pastry ready-glazed, for me to add to the oven.

'Don't need to stand to top and tail a few gooseberries,' she said. 'And any fool can make pastry in two minutes with one of these.' She flourished what looked like a wire knuckle-duster.

The promised visit from the police – an African-Caribbean woman called Maxine, whom I'd met when I was going out with a detective based at Rose Road, and a very young man I didn't know – happened just as I was taking Aggie's tray round. I'd meant to eat my own meal with her but had the chagrin of watching it chill and congeal as I talked. I knew it would microwave later, but it wouldn't be the same. And I was worried about the gooseberry pie overcooking . . .

In the end, I was forced to interrupt the constable – Ges, apparently – as he wrote assiduously, and send him round with Aggie's portion. She always enjoyed ten minutes with a good-looking young man: community service, he could describe it as, if challenged. Meanwhile, I made Maxine a cup of tea and gossiped about some of the people I knew at Rose Road Station. Ian Dale was still on annual leave, apparently. And Tina Reed, who'd only been a sergeant five minutes, was applying for secondment to a Third World force.

'I think she's had a love affair go wrong,' she sighed.

I sighed too, but didn't enlighten her. Tina had stuck by Courtney Walsh, my holiday companion, until he was released from prison. He'd told her gently but repeatedly that he could offer her no more than platonic friendship, but she'd clung to the belief that he could 'recover' from what she insisted was the mistake of his homosexuality, just as if it were a minor illness. Needless to say, he hadn't.

Maxine flicked a glance at her watch. 'D'you think the old lady's eating him for pudding?'

'Instead of the gooseberry pie? Anyway, there's not much more I can say to either of you, Maxine. All I saw was four white youths haring into the crowds on Broad Street and then slowing down. Their speed, and then what looked like an attempt to blend in, rang a few alarm bells. We looked for a crime – and found a victim. Does he still insist that his assailants were Asian?'

She nodded.

'Anything else useful?'

'Says they smelt funny. I suppose he means the curry spices – they get into your skin, don't they, if you eat enough?'

'Are you sure that that was what he meant?' There I was, a teacher even on Sunday. I smiled apologetically. 'Well, I've no idea what the white guys smelt like, so that's no help. And I never saw their faces. They all had very short hair, though. Short back and sides – like soldiers.' Or, come to think of it, like policemen.

She shook her head. 'Clothes?'

'Something dark. Maybe those hoodie things. They certainly weren't distinctive. But I'll tell you one thing, Maxine – neither of us saw any Asians.'

At this point Ges returned, carrying empty plates. And I packed them both off, no further forward at all in their investigation.

I spent most of the afternoon in the garden trying to prepare classes. But I couldn't stop thinking about the crime. The young man wasn't seriously ill, he'd been very unpleasant to Afzal – and if it were just another unsolved crime, what the hell? But I didn't convince myself. I knew I had to do something. If only I were on better terms with the policemen and women I knew! Chris Groom and I had hardly spoken recently; Diane Stephenson and I had never liked each other; Ian was unavailable; Tina might well be upset, to say the least, to discover that Courtney had chosen me to accompany him to Berlin. There was a guy in the Fraud Squad, but a street assault was beneath his notice. I was stuck.

There was nothing for it but to cycle over to the Mondiale and have a sniff round on my own. I toyed with inviting Afzal, but it was such a wild-goose chase I decided against it. I didn't know what I was looking for, exactly – but I took some rubber gloves. And a roll of freezer bags. Just in case.

In case of picking over litter, sifting through waste bins. For that's what I ended up doing. And I found something so interesting in the ninth that I finally did what I should have done in the first place: called into Rose Road and asked to speak to the Duty Inspector.

I suppose it would have been possible for the civilian receptionist to show less interest, but I'd have awarded her an NVQ in bored insolence. I was unpleasantly surprised – most of the men and women I'd come across at Rose Road had been friendly and helpful, and surely not simply because of my relationship with Chris. Relegated to a plastic seat which rapidly became sticky in the wrong places, I looked at a copy of yesterday's *Sun*. When that intellectual stimulation was exhausted, I stared at the notices about Neighbourhood Watch, car theft and rabies.

Forty-five minutes.

A woman came to report a missing watch.

24

I thought of my garden and my prep and phoning my friends. I looked at the notices again.

An hour.

For the last fifteen minutes my glances at my watch had been increasingly ostentatious, and they were now accompanied by gusty sighs. No doubt they irritated the receptionist as much as her nail-filing irritated me. I expect she had no idea why I wasn't favoured with anyone's company, but she gave the impression that she didn't care.

Eventually I got to my feet. 'Look, I can't wait any longer. Let me write down my name, address and phone number. There. Now, when he or she is free, maybe the Duty Inspector could contact me. It's information about a crime committed last night which they're investigating.'

'OK. You off now, then?'

'Yes. But I shall be available on that number for the rest of the day. I'll write down my work number too, just in case he's really, really busy. But he'd be wiser to try me at home.'

She nodded vacantly.

I nodded back. And left.

Not a peep from the phone all evening.

My conscience started to twang. What should a good citizen do? I phoned again, leaving a message for Maxine or Ges, asking them to contact me urgently when they returned for their next shift. Perhaps that would get results.

Chapter Four

The weather broke overnight. I awoke to rain, the sad Monday morning sort that makes the world appear bedraggled and forlorn. The lawn didn't look so much revived as drowned, and the car reminded me it hadn't been cleaned – the dust of the last few weeks had curdled in depressing little runs. The obvious thing was to turn tail and go back to bed. But that wasn't an option. The traffic would be awful too. Half of me wanted to go by cycle, to bowl smugly past the stationary cars – the other half pointed out the disadvantages of splashed tights and blind motorists. The dry, comfort-loving half won. And regretted it. It took no more than twenty minutes to cross the Hagley Road.

As I got out to lock the staff car park gate behind me – William Murdock, it went without saying, wasn't able to afford high-tech automatic barriers – I found a beat-up Maestro already halfway through. He'd only stopped because he'd have had to shunt me to get any further in. I didn't recognize the face. But then, there might be new staff whom I'd never met. But there was no scarlet and black parking permit stuck on the corner of his windscreen. Bending, I peered in at the driver's window.

'Excuse me,' I said, gesturing that he should roll it down, 'but are you a member of staff?'

The window shuddered downwards, stopping halfway. A burst of halitosis emerged. 'What's it to you?' demanded a sallow, acned young man with a Glaswegian accent.

'This is the staff car park.'

'So?'

26

'If you're not staff, you can't park here. You'll get locked in. There's a student car park two hundred yards down the road. Or if you're just visiting, the security staff will show you where to park.' I smiled helpfully and straightened.

'What's to stop me parking here if I want to?'

The fact that my car was three inches from his front bumper? On the whole, however, I felt it wiser not to point that fact out to him. He did not appear to be a respecter of other people's bumpers.

'As I said, you're likely to be locked in.'

By now there was a queue of staff cars stretching thirty yards down the road and I was soon joined by the driver of the first. 'Problem?' he asked me.

'This silly tart won't shift her arse,' said the Maestro driver, spitting two inches to the left of my foot.

'And *this* member of staff is pointing out to you that you're not allowed to park here. So get into reverse, sunshine, and get the hell out.' Carl always did have a way with words. But I wouldn't have used those particular ones – not if I owned a memorable car like Carl's red Alfa Romeo, not with the car park open to any stray pedestrian. Nor would I have added, 'And we expect students here to be able to read. Cast your eyes over that notice – the one that says STAFF CARS ONLY. Now hop it.'

The Maestro driver got out, five foot eight and fourteen stone of truculence. 'And who's going to make me, *sunshine*?'

Blessedly on cue, two security guards arrived.

'If I move my car,' I said, 'it'll be easier for you to move yours, won't it?'

He spat again, but got back in, and started his engine. I moved sharply into a distant slot. The queue could clear itself without my assistance, and I had a class to teach at nine. But when a plane slid overhead, I wished I was on it, wherever it was going.

Janet, a historian new to William Murdock but a seasoned campaigner elsewhere, was boiling the kettle when I arrived in the staffroom. Without asking, she reached for my mug,

27

popped in a tea-bag and sloshed on the water. 'You've been climbing those stairs again,' she said.

'Only two lifts working,' I said. 'But it's good for the health, isn't it?'

'Not mine. Not until I've lost a couple of stone.' She patted her hips with the air of one resigned never to using the stairs. 'So I prefer the lift. Though not with the sort of company I had this morning. This kid had only brought his ghetto-blaster with him! You know – the walk as if his balls are too big, the Essex accent: "Wo's it to do wiv you if I wanna play me music?" Except it's not music, it's that bloody techno stuff.'

'Blasters are banned, anyway, aren't they? College rule number ninety-something. And one I heartily approve of!'

Janet nodded. 'I always want to retaliate to other people's music with a quick burst of Bartok, just to make a point.'

At this point we were joined by Sarah Robertson, the new French lecturer. 'You'd be taking ever such a risk. I tried complaining about noise when I was on holiday. I was afraid I'd end up in the swimming pool! And I can't swim.'

'What happened?' If there are natural victims Sarah was one of them. Although she wasn't yet thirty her shoulders were already slightly hunched, and there was something about her wispy fair hair and pale skin, exacerbated by her tendency to droopy floral skirts, that brought out the maternal in me but exasperation in other, more hearty, colleagues. Her legs apologized when they appeared in mini-skirts – unlike mine which tended to yell, brazenly.

She measured her coffee to the last granule, added a sweetener, and poured on water. 'They catcalled. Muttered things. It was like being in the playground.' Although her shudder was exaggerated, it looked horribly genuine. She looked up. 'I hated school. That's why I'm in further education. Couldn't stand the thought of going into a school every morning.'

Janet grinned bracingly. 'There's this joke, isn't there? "Son, get up, it's time for school." "I don't want to go to school. The teachers all hate me and the kids all bully me." "Son, you've got to go to school – you're the headmaster!" '

It was hard to believe that Sarah was amused, but she smiled.

'What are you expecting to find here?' I asked.

'Well, it isn't a school. The students *want* to come here, don't they? And those I've taught so far have been quite nice.'

'That's A-Level, isn't it?' Janet observed, looking serious, knowing Sarah could be in for a series of unpleasant shocks when she confronted less committed students.

'And the travel agents. Very pleasant girls. Beautifully turned-out.' She smiled apologetically. 'I always try and look smart when I have them.'

How long had she been here? A week? I hoped she would keep her illusions a little longer.

Shahida joined me for coffee at break, looking troubled. She didn't say anything, but distractedly pushed back the scarf she always wore over her hair – it was so much a part of her I never thought about it, except when I bought her a silk square for her birthday. If she wore a skirt it tended to be long, but she usually wore jeans or trousers, both of which suited her.

'You OK?' I asked.

'Fine.' She pushed at the scarf again.

'Or?'

'Or what?'

'Or how not-OK are you?'

'It's just this Access class.' Another push.

'I thought you liked Access teaching. Older students, all keen and hard-working—'

'I do. But there's this guy. He sat glaring at me all through the first session last week, while I was explaining the syllabus, and then when I asked if anyone had any problems, he put up his hand and said, "When are we going to have a proper teacher?"'

'Jesus! What did you say?'

Her hand went to her scarf again. 'I said I was their teacher for the year. Everyone else seemed embarrassed, so I left it at that. Only this morning he asked again. And he said women should be at home, looking after their kids.'

'And you said?'

'I said my childcare arrangements were my own business, and if he had any complaints about the quality of my teaching he should take them to Roger, since he was in charge of the Access programme. He said he'd do just that.'

'Silly sod. These blokes with their male menopauses! Brummies always did get them badly. Take no notice. You know Roger will back you up to the hilt. All he has to do is wave your results under the guy's nose.'

'There's just one problem, Sophie. It's not male menopause. He can't be more than twenty-five. And he's not your native-born Brummie. He's like me. He's a Brummie from Pakistan.'

The highlight of the afternoon was to be a twilight staff meeting, the opportunity for us to meet our new head of department and no doubt be treated to a pep talk. We'd seen glimpses of him during enrolment, but he seemed to spend most of his time in meetings of the hierarchy to discuss enrolment numbers, class sizes and closures, and all the other theoretical issues that conveniently prevent the upper echelons from being involved in the joys of non-stop interviews and form-filling for prospective students.

'God knows why we have to come along now,' Shahida said, looking ostentatiously at her watch. 'What's wrong with lunchtime meetings?'

'Not enough lunchtimes,' I said. 'I've got a meeting every lunchtime this week. Two on Wednesday. But I don't like five-thirty – that's going-home time in my book.'

'Lucky you. I'm on till nine,' Janet said. 'If there are enough students for the class to run. It was touch and go last week. Ah, here's the great man.'

This was likely to be embarrassing. In my first year teaching, I'd actually taught our new boss. He'd been a mature student – older than me, as it happened – and I'd helped him towards a grade A pass in his English A-level. Very gratifying. But less gratifying now to see that his career had swept onwards and upwards, compared with mine. OK, I hadn't been prepared to sacrifice the whole of my personal life to ambition – though it sometimes seemed as if all my spare time were devoted to marking and preparation. But when I looked at his pay scale compared with mine I felt less content with my mundane lot.

'God, that suit must have cost him a bob or two!'

'Not to mention that haircut.'

Teachers could make very bad audiences.

'All very well for him,' Janet said, 'but this is the first pay-rise I've had in three years.'

'You're joking!' Even little Sarah sounded horrified.

'Wish I were. At my old place it was the management's ploy to encourage us on to the new College Employers' Federation contract—Sorry!' she muttered, as our Head caught her eye. At least he'd achieved some teaching skills as he scrambled up the promotional ladder.

'Good afternoon, ladies and gentlemen. I'm Dan Godfrey and I'm—'

'Your pilot for this trip.'

Dan flushed. He had the sort of complexion that darkened rather than reddened – very Latin-looking, as another voice remarked. His profile was uncomfortably like Rudolf Valentino's, I had to admit. Age had definitely improved his appearance, and he'd had every woman in my class slavering over him. He emphasized his facial bones by encouraging a heavy wing of hair to flop forward; he would throw it back every so often with a gesture that showed the elegance of his hands and encouraged the diamond in his signet ring to glint. Still, perhaps it was natural to be vain if you were as handsome as he was.

'I'd hoped to meet all of you informally before today, but since enrolment was so busy—'

'And you were so busy hobnobbing with Senior Management—'

'I've obviously not been able to. Actually, I would like to formalize the procedure. I would like to meet each of you for a half-hour discussion of your present function at William Murdock, and, more importantly, what you can do for the college in the future. This will form part of your normal appraisal pattern.'

'Excuse me – isn't appraisal done by your line manager?'

'It still will be. But I will be involved too.'

He was on dangerous ground here; policy had been agreed between the Governors and the union.

'Now, I don't want to keep you more than another five minutes – I know you're all dying to plunge into the rush-hour – so let me quickly say what I want to say. All further education funding depends on three elements: recruitment, retention, and successful completion. I'm pleased to report that the college has almost met its recruitment target, set by the late principal, Mr Worrall—Yes?'

He was really rattled now. But the question Bill asked was fair. 'When are we going to meet our new principal? All we know is, it's a woman. Shouldn't we have been introduced?'

'I believe Ms Fairbairn will be calling a meeting shortly. To continue – we had a target set by the Further Education Funding Council. Eight per cent growth – no mean achievement. And much of the extra recruitment was done by my department.'

'You mean by us.'

'Congratulations.' His smile clearly tried to conceal his anger at the *sotto voce* interruptions. Presumably those responsible were on the old contract – either that, or they were taking a terrible risk. 'Now the next part. Retention. We must do our very best to make sure every one of those bums on our seats stays there. So every student absence must be reported, and every absence followed up. Each time a student misses your class you report him to his tutor, and you phone him or write to him personally. At once. That very day. Is that understood?'

There was a shocked silence. If you taught twenty-four hours a week, what with the marking and preparation involved, there weren't many hours left over for phoning recalcitrant kids, however much you might want to. If, indeed, they were on the phone anyway . . .

'We contact and follow up and keep in touch and *we don't lose that student.*'

'But—'

'We keep every student. By whatever means.'

A hand shot up. 'Dan—' We were all on first-name terms at William Murdock, always had been. So why did the speaker quickly substitute, 'Mr Godfrey? What about the odd student that William Murdock doesn't want?'

'Didn't you hear me, Robert? There is *no* student that William Murdock doesn't want.'

As one, we bridled at that. Janet raised her hand. 'Every college has its ne'er-do-wells, surely. The ones who don't attend, the ones who sit in the canteen and smoke pot and—'

'I don't know where you've been teaching, Janet, but at William Murdock no one will be smoking pot in the canteen.'

Janet flushed, but stood her ground. 'And how do you propose to stop them?'

'You are the professionals. It's up to you. What is certain is that we need every single student to complete the course and sit their exams. And pass them. How we achieve that depends on you.'

'Do you mean,' Janet persisted, 'that the department will have a disciplinary policy without any sanctions? In this part of the city, where petty crime is endemic? What if someone nicks my car – do we keep him on?'

'I'm sure every sensible motorist makes sure that his or her car can't be stolen. But we're talking hypotheses here. The fact is that we lose money for every student we lose. And ultimately that means we lose jobs. Thank you, ladies and gentlemen. My secretary will arrange your individual interviews, starting tomorrow.'

'*My* secretary! She's the departmental secretary!'

'Did someone wish to say something?'

But no one did. We left the conference room in cold silence.

'Look,' said Shahida, 'why don't you come back to my place and eat with Tanvir and me? And you can tell me how you got on with Afzal. I forgot all about you two going off clubbing together.'

I was tempted. It would have been cathartic to share anger over Dan's meeting and if I'd revealed my part in his career she'd have honoured my confidence. Goodness knows why I didn't want it to be a topic of general discussion – was I protecting his ego or mine? But she saw little enough of Tanvir as it was, and I ought to pop round to see Aggie . . .

I meant well, but I probably sounded ungracious. 'I'd love

to. But I really need to get stuck into my marking - I want to keep it under control this year.'

'In other words, mind my own business!' She was laughing: clearly I hadn't offended her.

'We never got to a club, Shaz. We found this bloke who'd been beaten up and wanted to blame Afzal. On account of Afzal was Asian, you understand, and the man thought his assailants were Asian.'

' "Thought"? Wouldn't he know?'

'Not if they were in disguise,' I said.

I saw Janet at the bus stop and pulled over to see if she needed a lift.

'Only to Five Ways,' she said, hitching her coat round her hips more tightly so the seat belt would fasten. 'I know I ought to walk, but it's uphill all the way. Hey, that's one cool boss we've got! How did he get away with it? Hell, Sophie, I wouldn't have expected *you* to take all that lying down.'

I wouldn't either. Embarrassment at my colleagues' childish rudeness shouldn't have stopped me. 'I don't know that he's got any choice,' I temporized. 'I think all colleges are more or less constrained to do the sort of thing he was outlining. And many of us do it informally anyway, don't we? But it was the way he said it that was the problem. Hell, why on earth don't they cross at the crossing?' I braked hard and slapped the horn for good measure; when you're doing forty in the outside lane of a dual carriageway your options for dealing with errant pedestrians are limited. For my pains I got fistfuls of obscene gestures and a mouthful of abuse in which the word 'fuck' figured prominently but not exclusively.

'Why on earth don't they look before they jay-walk?' Janet asked. 'That'd be more to the point. William Murdock students, no doubt?'

'No doubt. Look at that tailback! I'm afraid you'd have been quicker walking.'

'Quicker, maybe. But a good deal wetter.'

Chapter Five

'I did it!' Janet announced, triumphantly breaking open a Kit-Kat – well, it was eight-thirty on Tuesday morning, and no doubt she needed to keep her strength up. 'I kept the class open! I said, "It's the mark of a civilized state to have A-Level History available to all who want to study it," and he's kept it open!'

Sarah looked awed. 'You said that to Dan?'

Janet looked her straight in the eye and nodded triumphantly.

'And you had how many in the class?' I asked.

'Fifteen. Spot on.'

'Well done.' And then something nagged me to ask, 'How did you get that many?' Janet had the good grace to look slightly shifty. 'Actually, I enrolled my two younger daughters and their boyfriends. They're all on the dole so it doesn't cost them anything.'

'Are they,' I pursued, as delicately as I could, 'going to come to classes?'

'Well, one or other of them will pick me up after each class. Turn and turn about.'

'Are you on the new contract or the old?'

'The new, of course. All us new recruits are. Why?'

'Let's just say, don't for goodness' sake get caught. I suspect forging registers may be a capital offence.'

'Sophie! You're serious, aren't you? Oh, not about the hanging – but you don't approve.'

I stirred my coffee. 'It's not approving or disapproving,' I said slowly, 'it's the risk of being found out. They're

35

swarming all over the place doing spot checks on room use. If you claim students are there and they're obviously not, you could be in for it. And if you enrol them then mark them absent, Dan'll get you to phone them, and chase them. He won't take any excuses. How about persuading them to sit in the class every other week? They might even enjoy it.'

'Since when were Oasis on the history syllabus? OK, Sophie. I'll think about it.'

'It's none of my business,' I said, belatedly. 'I'm sorry.'

'You won't say anything?'

'Cub's honour,' I said.

'Or you, Sarah?'

Sarah shook her head, her fine hair flying.

So I was in sombre mood when I went off to my A-Level English group. Sixteen second-year students – the equivalent of an upper sixth in a school. We were to tackle *Beloved*, Toni Morrison's novel about Black Americans. I was afraid they would find it difficult, but I'd done all I could to make things easier for them, and went down to the classroom staggering under a load of notes I'd word-processed myself and had photocopied. The pile represented a disproportionate amount of my summer holiday, come to think of it; all I'd asked the students to do over the break was to read the book.

I'd always got on well with this particular group, finding them pleasant if immature – well, they were only sixteen last year – and hoping that the leap to a big grown-up seventeen might make them more rewarding. This would be the first time I'd seen them this term. So it was time for a general catching-up: how'd they got on in any GCSE's, any news of siblings I'd taught who'd gone on to university. All very congenial.

Except it wasn't.

There was an atmosphere, no doubt about it. And it was nothing to do with the tightly-closed windows, which no one had got round to controlling yet – possibly because they only overlooked the hoi polloi's car park. At last, after a buzz of whispering, Ferhana stood up. I noticed that she had newly acquired a headscarf.

'Sophie—' she began, flushing scarlet.

36

'Take your time,' I said. 'And if you want to sit down, that's OK.'

She looked round desperately. The consensus seemed to be that she should remain standing.

'Sophie – it's this book.'

'*Beloved*?'

She nodded miserably.

'Are you finding it tough going?' I asked disingenuously, already suspecting what the problem was. And it was nothing to do with the difficulty of the text.

'No. Well, yes, a bit. But it isn't that. It's my cousin, Sophie. I was reading it, like you said—'

I nodded encouraging. 'Did you enjoy it?'

'It's great, Sophie. I mean, it's – I just cried.'

I nodded again. I'd cried too.

'But my cousin, he says – well, there's that word. It's rude. And they're doing it with *calves*, Sophie!' she concluded desperately, sitting down hard.

'Well done,' I said. 'That took a lot of doing, didn't it, Ferhana?'

She half-smiled, nodding quickly.

'What about the rest of you? Ahmed?'

If anyone in this group was going to get to Oxbridge, it was Ahmed.

'The woman's a Nobel Prize winner, Sophie. She didn't get that for writing rubbish.'

'But it's rude, innit?' This was Shafiq, who was not likely to trouble the Admissions department of any of our universities. 'It's that word, miss, innit?'

'Yes.'

'So these girls shouldn't be reading it. It's fucking swearing, innit?'

I kept my face straight. So it was all right to use the word, provided it didn't mean what it was meant to mean.

'It's OK for you blokes, is it? And for Ferhana's cousin?' Velma was an African-Caribbean Brummie, likely to have other feelings about the book.

'That's nonsense, isn't it?' This was Noreen, quiet in normal circumstances but gratifyingly roused. 'Look, we've all read the book. Prepared it. So have you. It's the best text on the syllabus. Why should one bloke who isn't even part of the group lay down the law?'

'He'll tell my dad, Sophie. And my dad'll take me away from college.'

One or two other veiled heads nodded.

'How does he feel about the other texts? I mean, *Dubliners* is quite a strong attack on religion.'

'But it's not Islam it's attacking. And – it hasn't got that word in it.'

'So what have you settled?' asked Shahida, while we brewed our breaktime coffee.

'A compromise. Doesn't it always come down to that? They'll keep the texts here in college, in their lockers, and I'll talk to Sean – there's an English team meeting this lunchtime – about issuing a letter saying that the texts are prescribed by the examination boards for the highest literary reasons. Sign it, "Head of English". That should crack it.'

Shahida laughed, but then looked sombre. 'I'm afraid Ferhana's right. Her father could pull her out of college. And what do you think Dan prefers – literary merit, or bums on seats? Do you really expect him to back you against a father threatening to remove one of those bums? For a streetwise woman, Sophie, you can be pretty naive.'

Complacent was the word I'd have used. I'd got all my marking out of the way and had a jog. In fact, I was so pleased I treated myself to a lager while I watched the *Nine O'Clock News*. I'd missed most of it, but I was in time for the closing headlines and then the local news. A lump of concrete dropped on a police car from some high-rise flats; a pensioner raped and beaten before being robbed of seventeen pounds; and late reports of a fire in a bed and breakfast hostel in Moseley – no casualties.

And then, gasping at my efficiency, I toddled off to prepare my sandwiches for tomorrow's lunch.

I was thinking about the people in the Panda car, wondering what sort of person could be capable of such a cold-blooded attempt to hurt two innocent humans, when I remembered my business with the law. The polythene bag containing my find was still stashed in my garage. I phoned again, leaving yet another message.

I'd just settled down in bed with *Jane Eyre*, having reached the place where the mad wife in the attic tries to set fire to Mr Rochester, when the phone rang. Heart pounding, shocked back to this century, I grabbed it.

'Shahida? What on earth's the matter?' She'd never phoned this late before.

All I could hear was sobbing. I reached for my clothes. 'Hang on, Shaz. I'll be round in ten minutes.'

'No. No, it's all right. Nothing you can do.'

'Is it Maria? Or—'

'No. We're all fine. It's our hostel, Sophie.' I could hear her controlling her voice. 'We're going to have to work a hell of a lot harder. There's been a fire. The police have called me—'

The report from Moseley that I'd seen on the news. 'I'll see you there. I'm on my way!'

What sort of thing would people need when they'd been smoked out of a place that was their home, albeit a temporary one? I'd got spare blankets – I'd meant to get rid of them when I'd bought duvets – and some sheets. A whole bag of old clothes destined for the Oxfam shop. Some chocolate I was hoarding. Biscuits. Hmm. I had a feeling they might need a bit more than that.

The police weren't keen on letting me through the cordon.

'I'm on the committee that runs the place,' I said. 'Look, there's the chair – Shahida!'

In response to my yell, she ran over, flinging herself into my arms. The officer she'd been talking to followed more decorously.

'Don't know why I got so hysterical. Sorry.'

'I'm not surprised. My God, what's been going on?'

I'd never been that close to the scene of a fire before. All that water! What had been a lawn and play area was awash, and feet were churning it into mud. They'd left the appliance lights flashing, so all the colours were ghostly impressions of themselves. The women were in a stunned knot, many carrying children woken from sleep and inadequately wrapped against the chilly autumn night.

'What'll happen to all these women?'

'Social Services are sorting out something. Oh, Sophie, what a cruel thing to happen! They had so little in the first place—'

How could I distribute my car-load without looking like Lady Bountiful? 'Would it be OK if I handed out a few blankets? And there's some clothes – I don't know what would be suitable—'

For the first time Shahida managed a smile. 'It depends on the length of the skirts, Sophie. Tell you what, why not pass the stuff on to Social Services so they can sort it out? And they'll be able to come back tomorrow to pick up their things which aren't damaged – maybe later tonight, once the fire service gives the go-ahead. But the blankets – let's pass them round now. Those children look frozen.'

Through the cordon to the car and back again. The blankets took on a life of their own, slithering towards the mud, but we got them there. Some of the women were pathetically pleased, others surly. Shahida had been right about the distribution of the clothes.

But then the proceedings took on a bizarre, carnival twist; an ice cream van, heralded by 'Jingle Bells', arrived. Unencumbered by children and drooping blankets I made it to the van first.

'It's not ice cream we need so much as hot tea. Know anyone who could help out? Of course, we do need ice cream too – for the kids.'

I found a tenner. He found his mobile phone. 'What about burgers and hot dogs, too, love?'

For Hindus? Muslims? They'd just have to sort it out themselves. 'Brilliant,' I said. 'And if you can rustle up some hummus kebabs, even better.'

Shahida was going to talk to the police. 'To check residents, talk about insurance, that sort of thing. Don't worry – everything is paid up to date. No problems on that score.'

'So there are other problems?'

'The Fire Officer isn't happy about the origins of the fire. He thought at first it was a chip pan, but now he's not so sure. There's going to have to be an investigation.' She yawned, tears filling her eyes.

'Ready, Miss?' A uniformed sergeant touched her elbow solicitously. 'There's a minibus on its way for the residents. The fire service will make sure everything's safe. It won't take any longer than we can help, I promise you.'

She sighed wearily.

'Do you want me to come too?' I asked.

To my relief she shook her head. 'Go home. It's Wednesday tomorrow, remember!'

'That's your bad day.'

'That's right. I'm teaching straight through from nine till nine. With a Law team meeting at lunchtime and late enrolment duty from five till six.'

And she wasn't even on the new contract.

Chapter Six

'Tell the snotty bastards to go fuck themselves. We choose the syllabus round here. We're the teachers, if that still counts for anything.'

This cultured exchange took place at the English team meeting. Sean had called it last week to discuss next year's set texts – the financial climate being what it was, we were worrying about our budget already. I'd just raised the problem of Ferhana and her family.

'It isn't as simple as that, Bill,' I said. 'I agree that we shouldn't choose books simply to suit someone else's prejudice – we can't anyway, since the syllabus is dictated by the examining board – but we do have choices within that framework. Perhaps we should consider other people's sensibilities when we make those choices.' Sounding too pious and PC for words, but nonetheless sincere, I continued. 'There are some problems we can anticipate and overcome before they arise. Like rescheduling exams for when the kids aren't fasting. It doesn't put other people at a disadvantage and it levels out the playing field for Muslims.'

'I don't have a problem with that,' Sean said. 'I'll put it to Malcolm – any changes in the A-level programme are up to him. OK, folks? I've got to go and talk to Dan in two minutes to justify my existence.'

'Just watch it if he starts talking about re-rating your future to meet market imperatives. Sodding Managementspeak! Orwell was right! Now, *that's* what should be on the syllabus. Orwell's essays. *Politics and the English Language . . .*'

42

'OK, Bill. Get a copy and we'll appraise it for next year. Meeting closed. Dan, here I come.'

I would wait for Dan to mention our previous relationship, I decided, as I sat twiddling my thumbs in the corridor outside his office, on one of a row of plastic stacking chairs. It was too like the rows in the old, unfriendly sort of hospital waiting room to encourage hopes of a comradely discussion – though I would have welcomed a pile of old magazines. I'd already been perched here for ten unproductive minutes. I had a horrible suspicion that Dan's lack of punctuality was intended to emphasize his power – otherwise he'd surely pride himself on his efficient time management.

'Ah, do come in!'

He'd popped his head round the door; there was the same bland and meaningless smile he'd worn on those splendid features as when he'd addressed the staff meeting. There was no glimmer of recognition in his eyes, though I would have said that the years had been kind to both of us.

He returned to the far side of what was indisputably a new desk, bought by the acreage. Richard, the previous incumbent, had managed with the standard issue, even if he had occasionally resorted to using the floor as a pending tray. Gone were Richard's homely railway prints; academic year-planning charts filled their place. Also new was the cup he was drinking fresh coffee from: fine bone china. I sniffed appreciatively – indeed, hopefully – but he was too busy looking me up and down to notice.

'Old contract,' he said, 'I presume.'

I gaped.

'The suntan. It hasn't yet started to fade. New contract people have been back four weeks already. Don't you feel guilty?'

'Guilty?'

'That they work so much harder than you.'

'Longer, perhaps, but not harder. And they get paid more than me. We had a choice: Mr Worrall was so equivocal about the new contract he let people choose freely, without

43

any pressure either way. Of course, things may be different now.'

Without biting, he opened my file. 'You were responsible for work experience liaison last year. Not this year?'

'Last year there were two separate departments: A-Level and GCSE, which Richard ran, and GNVQ. So there were two distinct jobs. Now there's one giant one, given the GNVQ emphasis on work placements. Not to mention ASDAN—'

'ASDAN?'

Fancy his not knowing that! Managers were usually hot on acronyms. 'The new academic equivalent of the Duke of Edinburgh's Award. To qualify for an award in that you need to see Real Life. Mr Worrall wanted to establish a new post responsible for it all. I've no idea what Ms Fairbairn plans to do.'

'There'll be no new posts, that's for certain. A leaner, fitter establishment – that's what Fairbairn wants.'

'What's she like?' It was a legitimate question: we were, after all, colleagues.

'What do you mean?'

I'd reckoned without the gulf he wanted to create between us. 'What's she like? You know, as a person, a human being,' I pressed on, regardless.

'I can't answer that.'

'Well, perhaps I'll be able to answer it myself when I meet her. Soon, I hope. She is planning a staff meeting?' I remembered, too late, that Dan might have reason to dislike staff meetings after his experience with us. 'Or something less formal? A cup of coffee or something?'

'You don't expect the Managing Director of Cadbury's to meet the man stirring the chocolate.'

'Cadbury's have always had a name for benevolent paternalism. But in any case, I reckon we do more than stir chocolate. We can change people's lives.' Another mistake: somewhere in my memory glimmered a recollection that it had been Dan's probation officer who'd dragged him along to enrol for my evening class. And I seemed to remember that it wasn't a trivial crime he'd committed.

He fiddled with my file. 'What with one thing and another,

you seem to have lived a charmed life,' he said. 'Perhaps *your* life needs changing.' His smile, if it was a smile, was singularly opaque.

'What sort of change did you have in mind?

'Taking on the whole of the work experience liaison. You've got the contacts.'

'Couldn't be done on top of the teaching I'm committed to. It has to be a full-time post.'

'Drop the teaching.'

'Who'd look after my students—'

'*William Murdock*'s students. An agency teacher. We'd find someone.'

'But all the best ones will have been snapped up for the start of term.'

'Tough.'

'Tough on Murdock's reputation! Ours are deprived, inner-city kids. They need the very best of teachers, not other people's leavings!'

His voice dripped with pedagogic sarcasm. 'And you are the very best of teachers?'

'You got a grade A with me all those years ago!' I'd done it now. 'You should know.'

'My God,' he said. 'Little Running Rivers. I wouldn't have known you.'

I wouldn't ask why not. But he was determined to tell me.

'I mean, you've lost all your puppy fat. And your hair wasn't blonde back then. Long mousy rats' tails. Coffee?' He pressed an intercom button on his new phone without waiting for a reply. 'All those years! And you're still teaching.' He sighed.

'I enjoy teaching. And I've got better at it.' Damn – I didn't want to sound defensive. Neither was I fishing for compliments, though I got one.

'So you're a very good teacher indeed. But those skills are transferable.'

'I know. My insurance broker used to teach. And the woman that runs the local deli. And – come to think of it – a bus driver I was talking to the other day.'

'Exactly. Interpersonal skills. I'll put you down for an interview for staff development.' He started to fill in a form.

'Hang on, Dan! I *like* teaching, remember. I like the kids. I like my subject.'

'But you're not highly qualified enough. You need an MA for today's market.'

'I'm happy here,' I enunciated very carefully.

'All the same—' He broke off as the door opened, ushering in the aroma of good coffee. 'Ah, thanks, Florence.'

Florence raised an eyebrow: perhaps all were not so privileged. 'If I'd known it was you, Sophie, I'd have brought biscuits.'

'Richard always used to keep some in his bottom drawer,' I explained to Dan. 'Expensive chocolate ones. Perhaps it was those that gave him his gallstones.'

'How is he?' Florence asked.

Dan flicked imaginary dust from my file, his patience clearly evaporating.

'Fine, as far as I know. I thought I'd pop in and see him one evening.'

'Send him my love. He was one sweetie, that guy.' And Florence left, not quite scowling at Dan.

'Did you keep in touch with anyone in your group?' I might as well wrong-foot him again.

He ticked them off on his fingers. One had been on the board of Tarmac, but had left to start his own firm of building developers; another was an architect; a third a landscape gardener. No unemployed road-sweepers, I noticed. Though perhaps there hadn't been any in his class.

'You've got a useful range of contacts, then.' I tried not to sound ironic.

'We play squash together. And Harriet – do you remember her? – she does my accounts. She's set up her own practice. You should talk to her, Sophie.'

'I'd be delighted to. But only socially. I'm PAYE, and nothing else to declare.'

'I'm sure you could remedy that if you wanted. Now, about this liaison work. Would you be prepared to continue with what you were doing last year? If we found someone else to help?'

'Not help. Share the burden equally. Provided you can find someone good to take on the classes I shall be dropping.'

'Dropping classes? Sophie, this would be in addition to your present timetable.'

'In that case, Dan, no deal. Not if you want the liaison done properly. Last year I was on seventy-five per cent of my usual teaching hours, and I had to cut a lot of corners. Making contacts takes time. Employers don't like it if they feel you're rushing them.'

He drummed an elegantly manicured hand, then stroked back that wing of hair. His diamond winked at me; I did not wink back.

'These are difficult times, Sophie.'

'All the more important to maintain standards. This coffee's good.'

'I bring in my own. Sophie – I wonder if it might be better for – for morale – if people didn't know of our previous relationship.'

'*Relationship*? Dan, I was your lecturer, not your lover!'

'All the same.' Another flick of that wing. It was similar to but by no means the same as Shahida's touch on her scarf: hers betrayed her anxiety, but I hadn't worked out the significance of his yet. 'Right, then. The mixture as before, Sophie.'

He pushed aside my file, and stood up. I didn't.

'What mixture?'

'Seventy-five per cent of the average timetable, plus the work experience liaison.'

'For A-Level and GCSE students only.'

He havered.

'Don't I have to sign some form or other?' We both knew I did: a form summarising the discussion, and evaluating my staff development needs in the light of my contribution to the college. And agreeing my timetable.

'I'll have to take this back to Fairbairn.'

'Fine. Perhaps we should write something like "negotiations continuing" when we sign.' Little Miss Helpful. And it meant I got my hands on the carbon.

I wrote it in block capitals and signed. He glowered – and signed.

The assignments I had to mark were so bulky I decided to stay late and tackle them in college rather than haul them home. From a selfish point of view it was a mistake: instead of marking I had to deal with a surge of students wanting to enrol for evening classes, something they should have done weeks before. I sorted them all out, directed them to the office to pay their fees then showed them into their classrooms. And suddenly it was after seven, and the canteen was shut. I promised myself a treat. If I finished all my marking, I could take myself to my favourite Italian restaurant for supper. Call it motivation.

By eight-thirty I'd finished. I'd also expanded my plans: a couple of my colleagues on late classes were coming along too, so I had another half-hour or so to kill.

William Murdock was gradually coming round to the idea of computerized records for all its students, but was too poor to attempt to put the backlog of previous years on to computer. So the older paper records were kept by the departments that originally made them. Ours were kept in a huge cubby-hole; this was kept locked, but the key was the standard one. No special security.

Each floor at the college was designed on the same pattern: an outer ring of classrooms and a central core of lifts and stairs. The corridor ran round three sides of a square, with the storeroom door recessed at the end of the corridor. With all those right angles – and the lifts and two sets of stairs as escape routes – in addition to a murder there'd been countless petty bits of vandalism and one or two minor assaults. And the perpetrators had usually managed to escape. What the place had long needed, but never been able to afford, was surveillance cameras at judicious points. Had I been a burglar, I'd have had a clear run, the set-back door protecting me still further.

I let myself in. There was the shelf for the early nineteen-eighties. And there was the cardboard box bulging with files – originally they'd been in filing cabinets, but they'd been needed elsewhere. And there he was: GODFREY, Daniel. Since I'd put everything into alphabetical order myself, I was gratified but not surprised.

I fished it out and was settling down for a good read when I remembered my part of the implicit bargain. If I was found reading his file, albeit one fifteen years old, it would seem dubious at the very least. But I am irretrievably nosy. On impulse, I trotted down to the photocopier; at this stage in the term I had enough copies left on my card to sacrifice a few. I zapped through the little pile, shoved everything back in place, and was sitting serenely at my desk when my colleagues appeared, the photocopies well hidden at the bottom of my bag.

There were enough fellow diners at Ciao Bella to give ambience without noise – although it rapidly transpired that one table seemed determined to change that. Four women, all loud-mouthed to the point of raucousness, and foul-mouthed too. I don't like laddishness at the best of times, but when it's women that are laddish I find it quite repellent. They should know better.

And then I realized I knew one of them. The woman nearest me, facing away from me, was a police officer I'd encountered when my cousin Andy was having difficulties. It wasn't an acquaintance I wanted to renew, present behaviour aside. Obscurely – and unfairly – I blamed her for a deep rift that had developed between me and my lover at the time, DCI Chris Groom. So I continued talking to my colleagues and demolishing a succulent calzone without trying to attract her attention.

It was only when she got up to leave that she saw me.

'If it isn't little Sophie,' she said, leaning over me, knocking my glass of wine over the table.

The owner and his wife emerged from the bar, clearly poised for action. Then six foot six-plus of Abdul the chef came too. I was to be protected.

'Hi, Diane. How are you?' Rule number one: never provoke a drunk.

'You know your boyfriend? Well, he's mine now, of

course. But I'll tell you this – he's fucking useless when it comes to fucking.'

It would have been nice to think of a cutting retort – but I sensed she was too drunk to be damaged by anything as abstract as words. Besides, I couldn't think of an appropriate reply.

'I *said*, he was fucking useless at *fucking*!' Her face was about six inches from mine. It took a lot of effort not to flinch.

One of her colleagues took her arm.

I dabbed at the wine, which was threatening to drip on to my skirt.

'Why didn't you tell me he was—'

'I don't remember your asking. Look, Diane, I'm with some friends now, and so are you. Let's talk another time, eh?'

'*Talk*! I don't want to fucking talk! Not with *you*. *He's* always fucking talking about *you*!'

Her friends had her by either arm now, and started to pull her away. A third turned back as they got her to the door. 'Don't mind her, will you? It's her birthday and we've had a bit of a drink.'

The danger over, Raj and Bella withdrew.

'She's not really one of your friends, is she?' demanded Abdul, filling my glass. 'Here – this is on the house.'

'An acquaintance. I'm sorry.' Though there was nothing I could have done.

'She's bad news, that lady. All that swearing, all that drinking. Bad news.'

'Does she come in here very often?'

'Once or twice with a very tall guy. Tall and thin. Fair hair, not much of it.' That sounded like Chris. 'She drinks too much, and he tries not to notice. Not that I've ever seen her like that before. She holds her booze well, that one.'

'Policewomen do.'

'My God, Sophie, she's a *policewoman*? Tell me, what sort of country is this, if women like that are supposed to take care of the rest of us?'

I was station-hopping on the radio, hoping to find something that wasn't Mahler or Bruckner and wasn't wholesomely educational, when I found a local station: chat and news. Not my usual listening – in fact, my finger was already poised to zap that too when the news bulletin came up. The usual stuff, with a Brummie accent. Threats of road works on Spaghetti Junction. A sewer collapse in the middle of a road in Kings Heath. And news that the police were now involved in a murder hunt because a man who'd been assaulted in a Saturday night brawl in the city centre had died of a brain haemorrhage.

And vital evidence was in my garage. I reached for the phone.

Within minutes I was making decaffeinated coffee for Inspector Cope, a man in his mid-forties. An attendant, taciturn woman constable drank fruit juice.

Cope stared in disbelief at the tissues, smeared with dark brown make-up, that I'd produced from the freezer bag. 'I don't get it,' he said. 'Why are you saying this is evidence?'

'My companion and I saw white youths scarpering away from the Mondiale, but the victim was very positive that he'd been assaulted by Asian youths. If you want to commit a crime and get away with it, you could disguise yourself. It wouldn't have to be too thorough a job – it was dark.'

'What about their accents?' WPC Wright put in.

'White Brummie or Asian Brummie – not much difference.'

Cope thought. 'Funny thing – we've got this lad up from Cardiff. Strong Welsh accent. Hear him on the phone, you'd expect him to be seventeen stone of rugby player. Turns out he's a slight Asian lad. Tajinder Sahota. You know him, Helen?'

She nodded.

'I think the lads we saw were wearing those jackets with hoods,' I said. 'Wouldn't need too much make-up and it wouldn't take long to remove it. Did Maxine manage to ask him anything about the smell, by the way?'

'Smell?'

'The guy apparently mentioned something about the

attackers' smell. Maybe Maxine didn't have time to ask before he died.'

'I'll check,' he said, standing. He was too heavy for his height and his breathing sounded a bit laboured. 'And sorry to hear about you and Chris.'

I must have looked blank. So far as I knew Cope and I had never met.

'He dropped his wallet once and your photo was in it. Ian tells me Chris is going out with Diane Stephenson now.' His voice formed a little question mark over his head.

I ignored it.

Chapter Seven

Here I was again, on a sunny Thursday afternoon, drumming my fingers on the sill of a south-facing controlled window, waiting again – for my repeat GCSE class. It occurred to me that if I had to shed classes in favour of my work experience role I'd love to lose this one; but a tiny little voice kept muttering that it would be unprofessional to pass it on to anyone but a hardened teacher like myself. Perhaps the agency through whom we recruited all our part-time staff would come up with a retired secondary teacher, still tough enough to break them – as I would, if I needed to. Actually, of course, Sarah had been quite right: most of our students did want to be here, though the employment situation fed us more of the reluctant variety each year. Like these, for example. I'd been firm last week and it hadn't really got me anywhere – this time I'd have to be positively brutal.

When they arrived, that is!

I returned to the window. Some nice cars down there. My little Renault lurked out of sight – I parked it in a different spot every day, hoping to avoid the attentions of Glasgow Maestro and anyone else I'd offended. A friend of mine had produced a custom-built car-alarm for me, one capable of telling the world if anyone so much as breathed on my vehicle.

At last! At bloody last! I went out into the corridor and gestured them in.

The girl had abandoned her jeans for a long loose skirt, quite fashionable, with boots; her baggy top was recognisably student gear. Her hair, however, was now completely covered – not just a scarf covering the back of her head, not even a *dupatta* but a complete veil, pinned under her chin. She sat, as before, by the window. Then the men came in, the Sikh last. There was no sign of Sam Jacobson.

I stood behind my desk, my pen at the ready. 'Sit down quickly, I want to take the register,' I said, all brisk efficiency, but with – if anyone cared to listen – a frosty undertone.

Clearly no one did care to listen. No one moved; the bags stayed on the desks. Then, at a signal I must have missed, they sat down as one, with the exception of Zia Yamin, who stepped forward, arms folded. He was one of the tallest in the group; looking at him meant looking up. Bad strategy. So I sat down, leaning my arms on the desk, hands loosely clasped. I wanted him to look like an importunate pupil. It might just work. He glanced round for the first time at the others, perhaps not as brave as he seemed.

'You want to say something, Zia?' My voice was arctic. 'May I remind you that you and your colleagues are ten minutes late for this vital class? Whatever you want to say, please get on with it so we can begin work.'

'That's just it. Miss.' He put more insolence into that syllable than any old-fashioned policeman. 'You're not going to teach us. Not until –' he looked round again '– not until you're properly dressed. OK?'

And before I could say anything, they were all on their feet and streaming out of the door. For a moment the girl lingered, but at a sharp word she scuttled after them. The Sikh – Guljar – looked at me with a welcome glint of irony. 'Sam Jacobson yesterday,' he said; 'you today. And no doubt me tomorrow. You wouldn't know, but there's to be a motion before the Students' Union tonight that in future classes must be segregated.'

'You mean – apartheid?'

'I mean by race and by gender. This isn't what I came to college for.'

'It isn't what I'm here for either, Guljar ... Tell you what, let's look at your homework.'

I owed it to him. Indeed, I owed it to myself. There was no way I would go chasing down the corridor after a bunch of teenagers, and I did not want my colleagues to see me shaking like this. But if Guljar noticed how unsteady my voice was he was too polite to mention it.

When we'd finished and he was ready to go, he suddenly put out his hand. 'I'll say goodbye, Sophie. I like William Murdock, don't get me wrong – you teachers are great. But I'm not going to take what you had to take today. I'll find another college. Perhaps you should too.'

'No problem,' said Dan, when I reported the matter to him. 'You wanted to lose some hours – we take you off that class and give it to someone else. Easy.'

'If you do that the students will think they've won. It'll set a terrible precedent.'

'Let's be pragmatic, Sophie. You want to drop hours. The students don't like the way you dress. They have a different teacher. You're happy; they're happy.'

I stared at him. 'So what if the next teacher is Jewish or black or has a squint—'

'Oh, we'll find someone.'

'You don't want to understand, do you? All you're concerned with is bums on seats!'

'I am adjourning this conversation until you have learned to speak to me with respect.'

'Tosh!' But I lowered my voice and sat down again. 'Look, I can see it's right for people who were oppressed to want to exercise power against people who had oppressed them. But it isn't as simple as that, is it? There's a girl in that class they forced to conform, there's a Jew who never got beyond class one, and a Sikh who's leaving today. I wonder what sort of time the other women on the staff are having? Have we any Jews on the staff, or Hindus or Sikhs?'

'You're over-reacting, Sophie. Can't you just wear longer skirts and give up the class?'

'I think we should adjourn this discussion. I'll go away and talk to NATFHE, and you can go away and chat to Fairbairn. And at the very least I'd like the Equal Opportunities Committee to be involved.'

'The Equal Opps people are there to help ethnic people to – to get equal treatment.'

'*And* to fight ageism and sexism. And we've got a big dollop of sexism here.' I flipped out my diary. 'When shall we talk further?'

'*If* we need to talk further, my secretary will contact you.'

'*Our* secretary, Dan. She's supposed to be there to help everyone.'

He stood up. 'I think you've said enough for one afternoon. Just go home and come in looking respectable tomorrow.'

There was no chance of seeing Frank, the union rep; he was closeted – according to a note pinned to his door – with the Principal, discussing democratic streamlining. And we all knew what that meant. It would have been nice, wouldn't it, to get pissed out of my mind, like Diane Stephenson? But I get hangovers – and there was a nine o'clock class tomorrow. So I'd be rational, and talk the whole thing over with Shahida, whom I trusted enough to give me sensible advice.

But she and Tanvir had presumably been required to go out so a mother-in-law could enjoy herself – not the samosas one, as I discovered when I phoned. In the end, I went for a long run, coming back with fish and chips for me and Aggie. Comfort food.

It occurred to me, as I got dressed on Friday morning, that no one – myself included – had attempted to discover what constituted proper dress in the young bloods' eyes. Compared with most of the women students', my mini-skirts were quite long: OK, they stopped several inches above the knee, but then I've got good legs, thanks to all my running. No tights. Sandals. The recent warm weather had seen me in short-sleeved cotton tops, but I've got a bony chest, so my necklines were always quite high. And I wouldn't go braless in a skimpy vest, not at work – even I have some sense of decorum! But not a lot, it seemed. Even Dan didn't find me 'respectable'! I wouldn't wear trousers – the only summer-weight ones were jeans, and I didn't see them improving the shining hour. A talk with the union was vital. I would get to work very early.

When, of course, I'd got dressed. At last I settled for a reasonably modest top and a pallid floral skirt that I should have despatched to Oxfam ages ago. Oh dear. And it was a bad hair day, too . . .

A bunch of my friends from yesterday, all dressed ethnically, were already outside the main doors with collecting tins when I arrived. For Taliban, apparently. I had a hazy idea I'd heard something about it on the news the previous night, but I'd been too angry to take anything in. On the principle that I bore them no specific ill will, I was prepared to fork out a couple of pounds. As I fumbled with my purse, however, the first wave of students from the number 8 bus arrived, and swept round me, to be stopped by the collectors. Some sort of discussion ensued in a dialect I couldn't place. Mirpuri? I'd rather give the money to Oxfam than penetrate a mêlée like that, so I walked on.

The problem with teaching is that, whatever else is happening, your prime duty is to be in front of your class, teaching it. You might want to rush round sorting the world's problems – but there you are, stuck. Of course, it works both ways: no matter how hard someone wants to talk to you, it's an unwritten rule that they wait until you've finished. So from nine till ten-thirty I was incommunicado. Then I remembered that, in the midst of yesterday's stress, I'd forgotten to phone Sam Jacobson – with Dan Godfrey in his present mood he might choose to discipline me for failing to chase a truant student. There happened to be one phone not in use in our beargarden of a staffroom so I stuck a finger in the ear not jammed against the handset.

Sam answered the phone himself.

'Hi! It's Sophie Rivers here – your English teacher at William Murdock. How are you? I noticed you weren't in class yesterday.'

There was a long silence.

'Sam?'

'Would you have been in class if someone had just pushed you in the fountain in Chamberlain Square?'

'My God! Who?'

'A big gang. I couldn't identify anyone,' he said, too quickly for me to believe him. 'They were holding me under the water when the fuzz came.'

'That's appalling, Sam. I'm so sorry. You don't know why – I mean, could it be anything to do with the whole Arab-Israeli situation? Someone thinking they'd bring the conflict closer to home? Or could it be more personal – have you annoyed anyone recently?'

'Is there a Jew who doesn't annoy someone by his very existence? Hell, Sophie, I may be orthodox in my beliefs, but that doesn't make me a red-hot Zionist. And a friend of mine, the most secular Jew I know, had dog shit put in his college bag the other day. He's left William Murdock too.'

'*Too*? Does that mean—'

'I've got an interview at King Edward's on Monday. I didn't want to go to an elitist sort of place. And in many ways William Murdock was wonderful. But – when it came down to it – I had to go. Sorry.'

'Sam – were you telling the truth when you said you couldn't recognize the people who assaulted you?'

'That's what I told the police.'

'But?'

'Sophie – I just want to put it all behind me. Right?'

'Right. But there may be others in – in your situation. Is there anyone – anyone I should keep an eye open for as a potential bully?'

'An actual one, more like. And I don't reckon he'd like it if a woman tried to stop him doing anything he wanted to do.'

'Could you tell me his name?'

'Let's just say, don't get stroppy with any unexpected Muslims. 'Bye, Sophie.'

''Bye, Sam. And good luck.' But I spoke to a humming phone: he'd rung off.

What the hell did he mean by 'unexpected Muslims'? I'd think about it while I made some tea. The kettle was just ready to boil when Janet called me: there were loads of students to see me and she'd arranged them in an orderly row in the corridor. By the time I'd sorted out timetable clashes and bus passes and whether someone should have free books, break was over, my tea-bag was still dry and I was no nearer talking to Shahida – or anyone else for that matter – about yesterday's class.

I was due for a lunchtime meeting with all the A-Level tutors – I didn't want to miss that. So I gave my second class some written work and scribbled a quick note to Frank, giving the union an outline of yesterday's problems. Then we got stuck into *Hamlet*.

This lunchtime's meeting was supposed to discuss Dan's diktat about chasing absentees, but naturally other problems got aired.

Perhaps I should have waited until I'd talked to Shahida and the union and had another meeting with Dan – but I found myself blurting out my problem with that GCSE group.

'Sod this bums on seats business. Get rid of the whole fucking lot of them,' Bill said. 'And wear a really short skirt. Get one of those tops that shows your tummy button. Come on now, Sophie – you can't give in to that sort of blackmail.'

Liz, who habitually dressed in clothes as black and unrevealing as any orthodox Muslim's, but who also sported black spiked hair and black nail varnish, shook her head. 'Maybe it's like the choice of texts we were discussing on Wednesday. Maybe Sophie should simply choose the longest, most decent clothes she's got.'

'I think there's a more serious issue,' Malcolm began. 'Maybe if she'd been asked, she would have considered that as a possibility. But you can't have a class telling you to do anything – it undermines the structures we depend on. Shahida, you must have a view on this.'

Clearly she did. I've never seen her look so troubled, and I was angry with myself for being so tactless. She deserved better of me than this.

Before she could speak, the fire bell started.

59

'Meeting closed, I think. Come on, I suppose we have to set a good example,' Malcolm said, getting to his feet.

We each had our role. Between us we had to check each room and each set of lavatories and make sure the block was completely emptied. With fifteen floors it was natural for some students to want to stay put and essential that they learned how to get out quickly and safely. I was sure that her role as floor warden on the fifteenth would give efficient Janet no trouble; I was less certain about Sarah's confidence to tackle the fourteenth.

The ninth at least was clear, though I'd had to point out to a couple of girls that standing on the lavatory pan in the hope I wouldn't see them when I checked the cubicles was not going to keep them from asphyxiation in the case of a fire. They giggled, quintessential silly blondes, and wandered slowly down the stairs, ostentatiously putting their fingers in their ears to muffle the noise of the fire bell. I followed, a cross sheepdog.

'All these stairs won't do your bad knee any good, will it?' Bill, in private, was a concerned human being.

'The knee's fine. I had an operation at the start of the summer holidays. Keyhole surgery. A real miracle.'

'Oh, you single people and your BUPA!'

'National Health, please. A cancellation – I went in at twelve hours' notice. Out the same day!'

I reported to the safety officer that my floor was clear and went outside.

The car park was chaotic. If the alarm went at a time when lessons were in progress, then the lecturer herded his or her class together for checking; at a break like this, there was no such system. Staff tended to clump together to continue their conversations or meetings and the students milled round, refused to clear a way for the fire appliances and tried to head unobtrusively but inexorably for the pub – or home. I was making for Shahida and Janet when the safety officer called me back: had I any news of the fourteenth floor? Since you weren't allowed to move up the building during a drill, and I'd already told him about the ninth, I wasn't impressed. I sent Janet over, however – she'd had to pass the fourteenth on her way down after all. I could see

60

her shrugging and shaking her head. I did a quick check of all the groups. No sign of Sarah anywhere.

They wouldn't let me back in, of course. But I made such a fuss that one of the fire-fighters came over.

'I'll get someone to go and check.' He spoke into his walkie-talkie.

'Is there a genuine fire?' I asked: we'd had hoaxes in the past when students wanted to dodge tests.

'Sniff,' the safety officer said. 'Didn't you smell it on the way down?'

I shook my head. 'Nothing on the blue stairs.'

'Plenty on the green, Miss,' the fire-fighter said. 'Someone's set fire to some cubby-hole. Stock room or something.'

His radio crackled, and he backed sharply away from us to listen and reply. The only word I could pick out was 'ambulance', and then I was moved swiftly back into the car park. It took me some moments to realize that the still figure they eventually stretchered away, her washed-out skirt drifting in the breeze, was Sarah.

Chapter Eight

'I am sorry to tell you, ladies and gentlemen,' the loud-hailer squeaked, 'that someone set fire to some papers in the stock room on the fourteenth floor. When the miscreant is discovered, he or she will be punished severely. Meanwhile, a member of staff attempting to fight the fire has been overcome by smoke and has been taken to hospital. Could I ask the floor wardens to ensure an orderly return to the building?'

Again the efficient machine moved into operation – our last principal, Mr Worrall, an ex-Navy man, was very keen on good procedures. We stepped round fire-fighters drinking canteen tea and thus putting themselves at greater risk than they'd faced earlier from the conflagration. The smell of smoke permeated the whole building. One staff member operated each lift, so that the building filled up from the top; others made sure that no one went pilfering from the empty rooms. Worrall would have been proud of us. Fairbairn vouchsafed no opinion, largely because she was nowhere to be seen.

My afternoon class started late but we got down to work cheerfully enough. Soon it was four-thirty and time to head for home. I popped my head round Florence's door on the way down the building. She was looking askance at a new sign for her door: MR GODFREY'S SECRETARY.

'The best I can say is that at least they've got the apostrophe in the right place,' she said. 'Departmental Secretary was what I was appointed as. And Richard was happy sharing me with you lot.'

'We aren't sharing you any more?'

'I've just typed a memo about it. Wait till I photocopy it – it's got all the details.'

'Thanks for nothing. Any news of young Sarah, by the way?'

She peered round to see if anyone was in earshot, and leaned forward confidentially. 'Tell me, Sophie—' And stopped. Her ears must have been a good deal sharper than mine; it was a second before I picked up footsteps.

'Florence, could you just – oh, Sophie! What are you doing here?'

Florence looked at me beseechingly for a second.

'Just came down to check my pigeon-hole, Dan.'

'But staff pigeon-holes are outside the office, now.' He dodged back through the door and pointed.

'Thanks,' I said, raising an eyebrow at Florence, who shrugged minutely. I stepped out to check mine: a couple of circulars and what looked like a request for a reference. Nothing that couldn't wait till Monday. I shoved them back in, then, having second thoughts about security, fished them out again and consigned them to my bag. Perhaps it wasn't a good idea to have pigeon-holes to which students had unsupervised access; after all, you could take stuff out as easily as putting it in. But perhaps now was not the best time to tell Dan I thought another of his innovations was a failure.

On the other hand, since there was no notice on Florence's door forbidding access, I popped back in again.

'Tell me, Dan,' I said, 'any news of young Sarah? She's a nice kid and I thought I might pop round with some chocs, or something.'

Dan's face tightened. 'She's not very well. I shouldn't think she'd want any visitors.'

'She's not local, is she? Has she any family up here?' My eyes slipped to Florence, who was watching intently.

'Family? I shouldn't think so. In any case, the hospital will be in touch with them. There's nothing for us to worry about. I'll put a collection envelope round on Monday – organize that, will you, Florence? She's probably entitled to some compensation, come to think of it. Remind me to speak to Personnel, Florence.' He smiled. 'Come on, Sophie – it's time you were going home. You've had a bit of a week yourself, haven't you? Anything interesting on this weekend – apart from marking?'

'Only my choir practice tonight. There's a Midshires Symphony Orchestra concert in a couple of weeks and we'll be singing with them. A nice all-Beethoven concert – the Choral Fantasia and the Choral Symphony.'

'I wouldn't mind a couple of tickets for that.'

'Sold out, I'm afraid. It's Peter Rollinson conducting, you see.'

'Oh. It's professional, then?'

I could see the little grey computer between his ears searching for an exclusivity clause in my contract.

'The orchestra is, of course. After all, it is the best in the country. But the choir is purely amateur. Just people like me. Cheerio, then!' And I let him herd me to the door.

After rehearsals we always repaired to a tiny pub called the Duke of Clarence. If I was driving – or cycling – I always stayed well within the limit, so if I wanted to be convivial, I'd take a taxi home though my conscience was never quite sure about that. Somewhere, deep down, my non-conformist background told me I ought to cycle and be abstemious. But the self-indulgent side of me usually won the day.

At least now I knew Arun was saving for university – he'd just started a part-time Access course – I could justify using his services. When he'd let me into the car he could hardly wait to show me pictures of his new daughter.

'She's bright, man! Could be a doctor.' He put the car into gear, and we set off into some of the less desirable of Birmingham's streets.

'Perfect!' I said. 'You'll make a good team.' Arun was planning to take Psychology.

'Yeah ... Hang on, Sophie – what's up there, d'you reckon?'

Arun slowed from his Damon Hill speed and slewed the car so the headlights picked out the activities on the pavement. A man was hitting a woman about the face.

Arun was running towards them before I knew the car had stopped.

His eruption on to the scene changed the man's mind very rapidly. It would certainly have changed mine. The flashing eyes set deep, the long nose and high cheek-bones – Arun looked every inch the Afghan warrior. He'd grabbed the man by the collar by the time I arrived; any bluster the attacker had left had drained to his knees, which were sagging. The woman was bleeding from her lip and right eyebrow; I passed her tissues from my bag.

'You're shit, man,' Arun told him. 'And I'd like to wipe you off the pavement. But I reckon you wouldn't like that. So you'd better leg it – fast!' One more shake of the collar and Arun let him go. He sank to the ground on all fours, pushed himself up and scuttled off, crablike.

'Christ,' said the woman.

Arun peered at her. 'Stitches, d'you reckon, Sophie?'

'I wouldn't be surprised.'

'Right, love – we'll get you to casualty. OK?'

She could scarcely argue – he was propelling her firmly by the elbow. She peered over her shoulder at me as I followed; I'd rate her sniff as triumphant. From the brevity of her skirt, the height of her heels and the tightness of her top, I suspected that though Arun had helped a damsel in distress she was no maiden.

She settled in the front seat, crossing her legs ostentatiously. 'This is ever so kind of you, sweetheart. And brave. I mean, he's me fucking pimp, isn't he? Got a load of fucking heavies. Tell you what, sweetheart, when they've stitched me up, I'll say thank you properly, eh?'

He removed her hand from his thigh.

'Oh, come on, you been good to me. Can't believe you'd turn down a freebie.'

Arun said, in standard English the Queen herself would have envied, 'When I have conveyed you to the hospital, I shall take my fare on to her destination.'

'Fare? Pull the other one. I know how much you Asian guys like white tarts. Why don't you take on the pair of us?'

I would have loved to intervene in the conversation, but I was intrigued to know how Arun would proceed.

'She is my *fare*, madam.'

Personally, I'd have stopped there, seeing the curl of Arun's lip, but she chose otherwise. 'Go on – we could have a bit of fun.'

Arun stopped the car abruptly. 'The entrance to Casualty is just there. I'm sure my company will provide a cab when the doctors have finished with you.' He passed her his card. Then he got out, walked round and opened her door.

She too flourished a piece of card in reply. 'There's me number, sweetheart! Just give me a tinkle, eh?'

He took it, holding it by the extreme edge. 'I have a wife and daughter,' he said sternly.

He watched her teeter into Casualty before coming round to my door. 'I would ask you back to the front, man, but I want to clean the seat, right?'

I stayed where I was, though it would make conversation tricky. And Arun believed in looking at the person he was talking to. I thought at first I'd wait for him to say something, as we headed briskly back through the city to Harborne. But it seemed churlish not to praise his courage at least. I waited for the traffic to clear a little and then said, 'You know – that man might have had a gun.'

'Shooters! Only cowards carry shooters! A *real* man would have a knife.'

'Either would have been dangerous, Arun. And I hope his nasty little friends don't come after you.'

'I've got friends too, Sophie.' He gave his attention to the road for a moment. 'But tell me, Sophie, why do women do that?'

'Maybe men force them.'

'You wouldn't let them force you. Nor would my Zahida. Tits and bums all over the place! Half-naked whores. A disgrace to the name of women.'

It took me a moment to realize that he was talking, not about the prostitute he'd rescued, but the young women walking along Broad Street, dressed as always for a warm day on the beach. I suppose in real terms there wasn't much difference between their appearance and the woman Arun had helped.

'Asking for it! Asking to be raped. Now you can see why people want to see women veiled.'

'I'd be happy enough if they were dressed for the climate.'

'The veil makes men respect them. Look at that!' He swivelled round to point; the back of a bus approached quickly.

I squeaked. But had to agree. I didn't find public groping on the scale of that in the bus shelters at all attractive.

'You sound as if you should be in Kabul, Arun. With Taliban!' I added, to provoke him a little.

He plunged under the Five Ways underpass, slewing in his seat to look at me. 'Sure I should be in Kabul. But I'd be fighting Taliban. God, Sophie – where you been recently?'

'What d'you mean? I thought they were supposed to be saving Afghanistan. There were kids at college collecting for Taliban this morning.'

'They're bad news. You go and do your homework, man – and then we'll talk about Taliban.'

Chapter Nine

'You were lucky he didn't throw you out there and then in the middle of Hagley Road,' Afzal said. 'I might well have done, had you implied I'd support Taliban.'

He was half-laughing, as the occasion demanded, but his eyes were serious.

'But I thought – Arun's always going on about religion being diluted—'

'What religion are you, Sophie? If you don't mind my asking.'

I poured the excellent tea and passed him his cup. 'I was brought up a Baptist, but never, I promise, a primitive one! I suppose I'm still vaguely Christian. But God preserve us from the Deep South of America variety.'

'I hope he will indeed.'

We were eating a sandwich lunch in Hudson's in the City Plaza – sandwiches as a culinary art-form, no less. He'd been even earlier than I.

'Why would you object to an American Baptist takeover, Sophie? Because it would affect what you see as your civil rights. Religion impinging on the functions of the state. How would you feel if it was decided that not only should women be required to recognize men as the head of the house, but also that women should not be allowed to work, should not be permitted even to go shopping without a male relative in attendance? And that they should no longer have any education, should be denied abortions and access to doctors? Quite! An outrage!'

This time it was I who was half-laughing. 'And are Taliban really trying to impose such – such despotism?'

'That is precisely what Taliban are trying to do. They wish to confine women absolutely to the home. They are not allowed to work, to have any education: they've already sent women home from where they work, from schools and universities. Because no male doctor is permitted to touch a woman, they will be denied health care – for women, of course, cannot be doctors. Because women may not be seen in the street, children also will not be taken to the doctor.'

'My God.'

'Do you not listen to Radio Four? The "Today" programme?'

'Usually I'm an addict. But I tend to shower when it's on – I miss bits. And, come to think of it, I haven't had time to settle down with a paper all week. I'm not usually this ignorant, Afzal.'

He smiled.

'Will people put up with this? I mean, men get fond of their wives – they might object to them dying in childbirth or whatever.'

'After all that struggle, some people welcome the apparent stability. But I tell you, Sophie, if they accept it, in the long run the country will descend into the dark ages. You see, during all the fighting, the only people to qualify as teachers, administrators, civil engineers, were women.'

'*Women*! But I thought—' I dwindled to a halt. 'I mean, in Afghanistan—'

'That all Muslims were fundamentalists? That Islam is the religion of the uneducated? Tell me – what do you think of the Muslims you actually know? People like Shahida?'

At last I was able to smile. 'Almost all of the women and girls I know are lovely – charming, intelligent. Tanvir's delightful. And Arun – I was really impressed. He just sailed in and dealt with an unpleasant situation, and then evaded the young – er – lady's advances with dignity. But some of the lads I teach—'

'Are yobs. Yes, Shahida's told me about them. But there are all sorts of reasons for that, not just religious ones. But now is surely not the moment to discuss them. How's your chicken?' He nodded at my laden sandwich.

'Excellent, thank you. And your salmon?' I nodded at his.

We didn't have an extended lunch: Afzal said something urgent had cropped up at work, and he wanted to sort it out.

'On a Saturday afternoon? It must be serious!'

He helped me on with my jacket. 'Some people do work at weekends, Sophie. Shahida's always complaining about the awful conditions you people at William Murdock are enduring, and I agree – it doesn't sound a little grove of Academe. But there are worse places. The case I'm looking at this afternoon concerns a woman who's lost the tips of her fingers because her employers thought she could work more quickly without a guard on her machine. And, I have to tell you, it was an English employer. Probably one who calls himself a Christian.'

'You're right. It isn't actively dangerous. Except – oh, Afzal! That's Sarah! My colleague.' I gripped his arm and pointed at a newspaper seller's headline: CITY COLLEGE FIRE VICTIM LATEST.

I bought the paper. But there were very few details. Sarah had been fighting the fire when she received head injuries ... smoke inhalation ... life support ... parents at bedside ... suspected arson. There was a large photograph of the college building, taken from a very low angle so the perspective was distorted.

'How on earth do you get injuries fighting a fire in a stock cupboard?' I demanded.

'What sort of cupboard?'

'Walk-in. A cubby-hole, full of old exam scripts. The sort of stuff they keep for a couple of years in case there are any queries.'

'Maybe if a lintel fell on you. Or shelving – Sophie, you look very pale. Are you all right?'

'Fine. Well, a bit shocked. She's a nice kid.'

'Why don't we call Arun to take you home?'

'No – I owe him an apology, and I'm not sure I could handle him right now if he were being gracious. I'm truly all right, and the 103 bus will be fine.'

'If you're sure? Well, until I see you at the Rep, Sophie.'

Another chaste cheek-to-cheek kiss and he was gone.

Engaged. All engaged. The colleagues I tried to reach must have been doing the same thing I was – trying to find information and comfort from each other. I gave up. I had to go out: I'd promised Aggie to do a big shop next time I went to a supermarket, and I realized I'd not stocked up my freezer after my German interlude. This would be a job for a car, not a bike.

Preferably a car with a windscreen.

My shiny red car! Desecrated! Some obliging soul had smashed the windscreen – with, I discovered when I examined the mess on the driver's seat, an edging stone from my front path. Hell and damnation!

Fortunately my insurance covered vandalism and broken windscreens, and I had an emergency number stuck to the inside of the screen. I'd cleared the glass from the inside of the car by the time the repair van arrived, though no one could have asked for a swifter service. The young man worked quickly: all sorted in ten minutes.

'I'm surprised the damage wasn't greater,' I said.

'Laminated,' he said.

I nodded, sagely and uncomprehendingly.

A car was parked outside my house when I got back from Safeway: Ian Dale. His face lit up as I waved.

'Cup of tea, Ian?'

'Please. And one of those chocolate biscuits I can see on top of that bag. You shopping for an army?'

'My freezer's empty. And Aggie's off colour. Septic big toe.'

'I'll pop round before I leave. Must be lonely, stuck in her house all day. Here, leave that lot to me and you go and get that kettle on.'

He brought in the last of the carrier bags. 'Which ones are for Aggie?'

'Those two bags there. Oh, and those kitchen towels.' I stashed frozen goods in the freezer, refilled cupboards.

'I'll take them round while the kettle boils.'

'Now,' he said when he got back and sat heavily at the table, 'how's young Sophie?'

'Upset.' I poured the tea, straw-weak, passed his mug and a saucer of wafer-thin lemon slices. 'Sarah. That's why you're here, isn't it, Ian? I'm grateful.'

'That's what friends are for. And what the police are for. I'm here sort of official, too.'

'Official?'

'The police do tend to get involved when people are injured like that. I'm gathering up evidence – I thought you might want to talk and I might – listen. Nice tea. But I'd better not have a chocolate biscuit after all – my cholesterol's a touch on the high side. All that rich French food.'

'But I thought red wine's supposed to reduce it! How about a plain one?'

'That'd be great.'

The chocolate ones had originally been destined for Richard, so I had a plain one too.

'Sarah's a nice kid. Idealistic. The sort of person to try to fight a fire because she'd see it as her duty. The rest of us might try to fan the flames! We've got a lot of new managers, and we preferred the old ones.'

Ian managed a dour smile. 'Fire's no laughing matter, Sophie.'

'Is it arson?'

His mouth tightened; he hated my habit of asking such direct questions. 'That's for the fire service to say. I'm talking about young Sarah.'

'The two seem to be connected. How badly was she hurt?'

'Fractured skull. Bruising on her face. The hospital staff – they can't see how any fire-fighting she did would have caused them.'

'Who the hell would want to beat Sarah up? I told you,

Ian – she was *new*, too new to have made any enemies amongst either the staff or the students. Now if it was an old stager like me – there must be dozens of people who want me out of the way.'

Ian grinned. 'I can imagine.' He waved the biscuit packet away. 'Haven't you got a proper tin to put those in? They'll go soggy.'

Doing as I was bidden, I pursued the idea of the fire, refusing to be deterred. 'The college said it was arson. The papers are saying it's arson. Why are you so bloody cagey?'

'Habit, I suppose ... The fire seems to have started at several places – mind you, with so much paper around it wouldn't have taken much starting. You're a messy lot, you teachers! Your staffroom'd go up like tinder if anyone put a fag down carelessly. I'm surprised the place gets a fire certificate.'

'One of the problems is lack of storage. We're all rationed to either a bookshelf or a filing cabinet – most of the new staff have just one filing cabinet drawer, or one bookshelf. And teaching's paper-based – all those handouts. Any idea who started the fire?'

'Not a clue. Which is why I'm talking to you. Anyone with a grudge? Staff or student? And no more jokes about fanning the flames. Any people who've had a row with the boss—'

'Apart from me, you mean? I'm in dispute with him over the number of hours I'm supposed to teach, and when I had a little local difficulty with a class he didn't seem inclined to back me. But I'm in the clear, unless you've located a timing mechanism on whatever incendiary device started the fire. I was in a meeting. A lot of the staff would have been in meetings – there's time set aside for them on Fridays so we don't miss any classes. It doesn't matter if we miss our lunch, of course.'

'Why wasn't Sarah at a meeting? Why was she wandering round upstairs?'

'She may have been – I've an idea the language staff were planning the students' trip to Paris. I expect she went straight to the floor she was warden of, when the alarm rang, like I did.'

73

'You're a warden too?'

'It's all to do with timetabling and which floor you're on at what time. Very complex – Worrall took it extremely seriously.'

'Hmm. That's what you lot need, if you ask me: a bit of discipline. And, before you say it, I agree – it's got to come from the top. A good boss is worth his weight in gold.' He sighed.

I felt guilty but I asked nonetheless. 'You're still not getting on any better with Diane Stephenson?'

'She's – erratic. That's the word for her. Most of the time she's fine – a good officer. Thorough. She really grafts. Then there's times she skimps. Well, we all cut corners, no denying that, but this is something else.'

'Any special pattern?'

'Not so you'd notice.'

'Not PMS? Her time of the month?'

'I might have known you'd come up with something like that! No, there's no particular pattern, or not that I'm aware of. The trouble is, of course, the effect it has on Chris.' He looked at me closely, watching for a reaction. I tried to look cool.

'It just didn't work out, Ian. It wasn't meant. But that doesn't mean I don't wish him well with any other relationship.'

'What about you? Have you got over – things?' Ian looked at me hard, then lowered his gaze. 'None of my business, but you were pretty keen on that other man, weren't you? Your cousin?'

I nodded.

'Chris know?'

'He guessed. Anyway,' I said, intending to sound bracing, 'let's hope he makes a go of it with Diane. What'll happen about his promotion – and hers? She was only Acting Inspector, wasn't she?'

'Still acting. Not a nice position to be in. Right.' He got to his feet. 'Thanks for the tea, Sophie, and for the chat. By the way, there's a wine-tasting coming up in November – All right if I put your name down to partner me?'

'Absolutely. Just give me the time and date.'

He grinned. 'You're a good kid, Sophie.'

Which would have been a delightful exit line, had I not called him back.

'I've got involved in fund-raising for a mother and child hostel, Ian. The one in Moseley that caught fire last week. Any news about that?'

'News? Why should there be?'

'It's just – I've a nasty suspicious mind. And – ' I grinned 'I'm sure the Fire Service have to investigate any blaze involving property and people.'

'This isn't one of your hunches, is it?'

'Far from it. Come on, Ian, you must know some fire-fighters. Do me a favour, eh? And Shahida.'

'Is she involved? Then I'll do my best. How's that kiddie of hers? Perhaps she'd like to come along to the station Christmas Party. They've asked me to be Santa this year . . .'

I walked with him to his car, showing him mine en route and telling him about my smashed windscreen.

'That's William Murdock for you,' I said. 'I knew I should have stuck to my bike.'

'William Murdock? But you said it was parked here.'

'Poetic licence. Just someone's mindless vandalism. Booze and bravado.' I kicked a couple of cans lying in the gutter. 'Never heard of this brand of lager.'

'Cheap and potent. Don't let me see you trying it, Sophie. Bugger your palate in no time, that would.' He laughed, but his face set suddenly.

'Ian? What's wrong?'

'See you. Clear out that garage of yours so you don't have to clutter up the public highway!' And he was in his car and away.

Chapter Ten

I was spared the general nastiness of going to work first thing on Monday morning by going to see someone else's work. This was part of the work experience role I'd agreed to take on; it involved being charming to a solicitor in the hopes she'd take on one of our students for a week of rope-learning. Miraculously it took only ten minutes to persuade her, and I set off back to college in ample time for my first class, which started after break. It occurred to me I could ask Afzal to take on work experience students; it would provide an excuse – if I needed one – to contact him.

I thought about it some more while I sat in a jam caused by a dustcart preferring to bed down in the middle of the road while it was loaded with sacks. I didn't come to any particular conclusion about my emotions with regard to Afzal, but it would be useful for William Murdock anyway. Placements were like gold-dust, particularly for African-Caribbean and Asian kids from unfashionable colleges.

When I at last pulled into the college car park, it was to find the whole student body of William Murdock shambling aimlessly around, threatening to overwhelm the little knots of staff who, abandoning all attempts to keep order, were keen only to ensure that if any car was vandalized it was not theirs.

A couple of fire appliances were thundering up the road. Fire. Again. This was becoming an unpleasant habit.

I nosed my car round, looking for a space; there seemed to be a gap in the fourth rank and I trundled over, only to find a familiar beat-up Maestro slewed across two slots at such an angle that not even the most determined and ruthless driver could have squeezed in. Not even me. At last I spotted a very narrow space; and, although it took a bit of manoeuvring, I eventually parked with sufficient space left on the driver's side to allow me to ease myself out. I was quite pleased when I inspected my handiwork – just three inches between my near-side and the next car. I'd just have to trust he was as meticulous pulling out as I had been squeezing in. Another latecomer arrived; exasperated by the Maestro, he parked at right angles to it, leaving a curt note on his own windscreen.

'You're brave, Mike,' I said, as we walked towards the entrance, where Dan was waving a non-functioning loud-hailer with visible frustration.

'I said in the note that the security staff would contact me if he wanted to move first. No problem, surely?'

I shrugged. 'If it's the student I think it is, I wouldn't have risked it.'

'*Student*! Right!' He turned on his heel and strode back towards his car. By the time I'd caught up with him – delayed by the smart skirt and shoes I'd worn for the work placement interview – he was scrawling another, much ruder note.

'Mike, the owner of this car is *trouble*. I've seen him in action. Tell the security guards – it's their job to sort out parking violations! Not yours!'

'I've been teaching nearly thirty years, Sophie, and I've never hesitated to bollock a student who needed bollocking. This one does. He shouldn't be here at all, and he's parked with a total disregard for anyone else.' Mike strode round to the windscreen. 'Hang on, Sophie – you're mistaken. He's one of us. Look, he's got a sticker.'

'If that's legit, I'm Father Christmas.'

'You and your nasty cynical mind! You probably confused the car.'

I smiled. 'Must have done. But I'd still be careful, Mike. Anyone who chooses to park like that – ah! Dan's got his infernal machine to work at last!'

This time there'd been no fire. A hoax. We shared Dan's exasperation with any student who thought it was cool to set off alarms. This one had been smashed on the fifth floor:

the canteen. No staff supervision there, of course; that was the students' territory.

And that was the start of my college day.

Not quite the end, however. After a shortened late-morning class, and a normally hectic lunch, at about two-thirty I popped back into the staffroom to get some chalk – someone had removed the whiteboard from my room, so I had had to resort to an elderly blackboard. The phone was ringing, and obeying the imperative, I snatched up the nearest handset.

'Is that the fifteenth-floor staffroom? This is Personnel here. Mr Godfrey has instructed me to tell you to inform your colleagues that Sarah Robertson died today.'

'But—' I felt as if someone had punched me hard in the stomach. Winded, I began again. 'But—'

'Could you ensure that his wishes are implemented? Stick a message on your notice board or something.' The voice ended abruptly, without sympathy. Well, there were some fifteen people to tell.

Sitting down hard, I tried to make my head work. At first all I could do was stare at my hands, seeing them but not registering them. Poor Sarah. Poor little Sarah. God, it was so unfair!

I brought my hands into focus. Classes were sacrosanct; and I should be with mine. Other people needed to know and I had to tell them. Not because Dan had ordered me to, but because I wanted them to learn more gently than I had. Most would be teaching on the three top floors, apart from those relocated because the police had sealed off the area where Sarah had been attacked.

The first thing to do was make sure my own students were kept busy. Somehow I managed to make the muscles of my face work just long enough for me to threaten them with slow death if the assignment I set wasn't finished by the time I got back. Outside in the corridor I stood wondering what on earth to do next. Brisk footsteps made me look up: Janet. Slowly I told her what had happened and what I had to do.

'Poor kid,' she said. 'Look, don't worry – I'll tell everyone on the fourteenth, and I'll get Shahida to do the thirteenth.

And I suggest we all take an early break, so we can get a bit of privacy for ourselves. I'm sure the kids who knew her will manage without our comfort for a bit.'

I gaped. Division of labour: obvious. Where had the sensible, practical Sophie gone?

'Go on, Sophie – get moving or the rumour mill will beat you to it.' Janet patted my shoulder firmly and set off down the stairs.

I must do as I was told. But the pain I felt was so out of proportion to my loss, it didn't make sense. I pushed away from the wall, and straightened. Then there were more footsteps.

Ian Dale!

'Thank God I've found you. What the hell does that man think he's doing? Sophie, go and get yourself a coffee. One of the kids you lot are so blithely telling may be the one who killed the lass! This is a job for us! We want to see their reactions. When they learn what's happened. My God, bloody amateurs.' And then his voice softened. 'It never gets easier, Sophie, dealing with sudden death – not even for us old pros.'

I swallowed back tears. 'Who'll be on the case?'

'Acting-Inspector Stephenson and the rest of her team. Chris'll be overseeing it, but he spends more and more time at his desk these days.'

'Poor bugger. He's such an up-and-doing man.'

'Right. But at least it means you two won't be running into each other every five minutes.'

'It's all over, Ian. Has been for ages.'

'On paper, if you like. But if you ask me – Ma'am!' Ian came to attention.

The last time I'd seen Diane, no one would have stood to attention for her. Today, however, she was her chic and expensive self, elegant in a trouser suit. I wondered if she even remembered the last time we met. Her smile was cool; but we never had been best buddies, a fact possibly more attributable to my sunny belief that the police wanted nothing more than to share all their professional secrets with me than to her general insecurity. Though the fact that

I'd been Chris's lover before he became hers obviously didn't help.

'What's this about you teachers going round telling all the kids about Sarah Robertson's death?' she demanded.

'On Dan Godfrey's explicit instructions.' There were some people for whom I'd carry passed bucks, but Dan wasn't one of them.

'Hmph. Well, *my* instruction is to go down to the conference room and we'll brief you. Properly. Three-fifteen. And no more blabbing to the students – OK?'

'Provided Mr Godfrey knows you've countermanded his orders,' I said. 'And Diane – there are two other women breaking the news too—'

'Oh, for Christ's sake!' And she wheeled away, tapping at her phone.

'I've been saying for years something like this would happen. Years!' Bill was on his feet, jabbing the air with his index finger. 'We've always said security's too lax, that we should have surveillance cameras on each floor, but oh no, there's never been enough money, not to protect the likes of us. And now – guess what – a decent young woman's been killed. No money for essentials – but Management can go and get themselves new desks, new cars—'

'OK, I think you've made your point, Mr er—' Diane Stephenson said.

I sympathized, briefly: trying to silence Bill was like trying to stop an avalanche.

'Not yet I haven't. I want to know what's being done to find her killer. And what's going to be done to protect the rest of us?' Bill gestured; there was a round of applause. Encouraged, he continued. 'I'd bet Management are on the phone now to security companies! Oh, there'll be enough money for cameras to cover Management rooms, just you wait and see. What about us? What about the students, for God's sake?'

Diane pulled herself to her full five foot ten, but her authority didn't reach her face and the hand she held up looked perilously placatory. If she was going to win our confidence – more important, our confidences – she'd have to do better than that.

But Bill decided to be generous. Folding his arms, he said, 'There are the questions, Inspector. We'd all like some answers.' And he sat down.

There was another round of applause.

Stephenson stepped forward at last. If only she could manage an ironic nod, she'd win over a lot of hearts and minds. Instead she coughed, nervously.

'What I want is your help and co-operation. We need to go over all your statements again, those of you who made them on Friday – if you didn't make one then, we'd like you to now. Just where you were, what you know about the deceased, that sort of thing. Mr Daniels has provided me with copies of your time—'

'You mean Dan Godfrey don't you?' someone corrected her, perhaps to see if she blushed. She did – a dull, ugly red.

'Mr *Godfrey* has given me your timetables so I shall know where to find you. Please let me and my colleagues know if you'll be anywhere different. The sooner we can get this investigation under way, the better.'

'Inspector – ' Bill was on his feet again – 'you've not answered any of my questions about security.'

'I really think that's a matter for you and your employers,' she said. At last! For all my dislike of her I didn't like watching her squirm.

'So where are they?' This was Janet, on her feet. 'I don't see any of them here.'

Poor Diane. She looked almost wildly about her. Her eyes must have found Ian, stolid, big-booted, leaning against the door jamb.

He nodded, and left the room.

'I asked Mr Godfrey to come to speak to you. Sergeant Dale's gone to remind him.'

She did not lie well. But we'd got what we wanted, and we let her off.

Dan said nothing new or sympathetic, just insisted on our co-operating with the police; it was almost enough to drive us to be as bloody-minded as we knew how. Bill stood up: we braced ourselves.

'Mr Godfrey, we all want to find that poor woman's murderer,' he said. 'And I think we should have a minute or two's silence in her memory. That is if it's not inconveniencing you, of course.'

Chapter Eleven

Rivers comes fairly late in the alphabet, so it was no surprise that I was one of the last to be called to make a statement. What did surprise me, however, was that Diane should choose to see me herself, in view of our last one-to-one encounter. I was determined to be as helpful and non-confrontational as possible – the woman had suffered enough at lecturers' hands already today. But I wasn't going to pretend I didn't know her.

I greeted her by her Christian name. As I sat down in a student desk – the police had commandeered more classrooms – I nodded amiably at her attendant constable, a Geordie whose hair was the colour of the flashing part of a Belisha beacon.

'Hi, Tom! How's the Toon going to do this season, d'you think?'

'Hi, Sophie, man! Better than yon Albion, I can tell you.'

I couldn't argue with him there. 'You'll take Europe by storm?'

'So long as we've got Shearer up and running.' Remembering where he was, he looked at Diane apologetically.

'Sorry, Diane,' I said. 'My fault – if you think I'm crazy about soccer you should hear me talk about cricket.'

'No, thanks,' she said, refusing to pick up the conversational bait. But she managed to smile, gusting fumes over me – whisky, at this time of day? And on duty? 'Now, I'd like just to go through the events of the fire evacuation—'

'Which one?' Me and my big mouth.

83

'Friday's, of course.' But her face hardened. I'd been too clever again.

'Sorry. I'd forgotten today's was a false alarm.'

'Today's? I didn't know there'd been one today.' She looked at Tom. 'Go and check it out, will you?'

'Ma'am.' He went out, closing the door behind him.

It opened again. Sighing ostentatiously, Diane got up and slammed it, hard. It opened again.

'We need new locks on most of these doors,' I said. 'You have to lock them to make them stay shut. Here, have my key – I'll get another from Personnel on the way in tomorrow.'

Prising it from the ring broke my thumbnail: she fished in her bag and passed me an emery board. Peace overtures from both of us.

'I wouldn't mind betting there'll be a spate of false alarms over the next few days. Students get the idea it's fun to make people miss classes. It's all right in this weather, but not in winter. And it's no joke when the A-Level and GCSE exams are on in June.'

'It was real enough on Friday. They reckon she'd have died from smoke inhalation if chummie hadn't cracked her skull. Poor kid. Mind you, it wouldn't have taken much of a whack to crack it – the cranium was exceptionally thin, according to the hospital.'

'D'you think chummie meant simply to knock her out? To let her die of smoke? And hope the pathologist would assume she'd bumped her head when she collapsed?'

She looked startled, then scribbled in her note-pad. I couldn't believe she hadn't thought of it before.

'Let's go through your part in the fire drill,' she said, 'nice and slowly. Leaving nothing out. And then you can tell me just how well you knew her.'

It was well after nine when I crawled through my front door. The phone was ringing and I was tempted at first to let the answering machine look after it.

'Sophie? Is that you?'

The voice was so anguished it took me a couple of seconds to place it.

I picked up the receiver. 'Richard!'

'Are you all right? I've been trying to get you ever since it said on the news a young William Murdock lecturer had been killed—'

'I'm fine,' I said. 'Fine.'

'What's going on there?'

'Shall I phone you back? I haven't eaten, you see—'

'Get some fish and chips and bring them round here. There's plenty of wine in the fridge.'

There were very few people who could have persuaded me to go out again that evening, but Richard, my former boss, was one of them. I grabbed the chocolate biscuits I'd bought for him, and shoved them in the carrier bag with my marking.

Richard's house was situated at the heart of a pukka little estate built on a landfill site about a mile from me. It was so meticulously maintained I suspected he combed the grass every morning. But if he'd been caring for his home, he'd plainly neglected himself: his hair needed trimming, he hadn't shaved properly and although he'd shed an admirable amount of weight he'd not bought new clothes to replace those which were now far too big for him.

The covetousness of his glance suggested he'd not had chips for some time; he'd already treated the presentation of the biscuits with obvious glee.

Praying that chips wouldn't irritate his gall-bladder, I sat at his kitchen table and pushed the grease-spotted paper across. Sloshing an elegant Frascati into our glasses as if it were lemonade, he swooped on the chips; I pushed the fish towards him for good measure. He looked doubtful, but dived in. Had he never eaten fish with his fingers before?

'The thing is,' he said, 'the weather's interfering with television reception. The picture keeps drifting, and I'd got the sound down because I was on the phone. So all I could see was this young woman's face wobbling down the screen. It looked as if they'd got hold of an old photograph of you.

Except, come to think of it, you weren't blonde in those days, were you? And your hair's thicker than hers.' For a moment I thought he was going to reach out and stroke it.

When we'd finished our meal, and the wine, we adjourned to the living room on the pretext of coffee. I could hear the percolator chuffing away, but what appeared in my hand was whisky, an expensive-tasting single malt I couldn't identify. Perhaps it had been one of his retirement presents. He'd awarded himself half a tumbler, anyway, and, sinking on to the sofa, sipped steadily as if it were a medicine he'd been prescribed, sighing at the burden of his duty with each swallow. But the sips must have been less genteel than they looked; I was only one finger down my first dram when I realized that another, near-empty, glass of what looked like the same tipple was on the phone table next to the sofa. For an abstemious man, Richard was asking a lot of himself.

Gradually the conversation faltered. Leaning gently towards him I took the glass and his spectacles. Next his shoes. Then I tipped him sideways, and hitched his legs up beside him. There would be blankets upstairs. Halfway up the stairs, my world too started to reel. Clearly my stomach wasn't full enough to cope with the alcohol – he'd had the lion's share of the fish and chips. I made it to his bedroom, though, and dragged his duvet down without encountering too many obstacles. A note. I'd better leave him a note! And it had better be so big he couldn't miss it.

And now to get home. There was no way I would drive, not even a mile. I thought for a moment of phoning Arun, asking him to collect me, but I realized I didn't want him to see me this plastered. I had my standards to maintain. That left a bus, or my feet – on the whole, my feet seemed a better option; the walk might sober me up.

On the other hand, as I soon discovered as I stepped into the chill night air, it might not.

I thought it kinder not to wake Richard when I collected my car at seven-thirty the following morning. Getting into college for eight might have seemed a bit extreme, but I still had to sort out the problem of last Thursday's class. I needed to see my union rep and Dan, and both were early starters. Belatedly, I realized why my marking bag had felt so empty the night before – I'd left all my marking in the staffroom. Still, at least it wouldn't matter now that I'd left the carrier bag at Richard's – I'd phone him later to ask him to look after it for me, and to enquire after the state of his liver.

And then my exceedingly well-laid plans came to a semi-colon, if not a full-stop. I couldn't get into the fifteenth-floor staffroom, could I? My key was on Diane Stephenson's ring. That meant I couldn't get into anyone else's room either – not to mention the classrooms, or even the staff loos. All sorts of profanities leapt to my lips. I toyed with the idea of rousting Diane out and asking for it back, but I dismissed that as petty. Besides, I suspected she might not be at her most congenial this early in the morning. All I could do was go down to Personnel and hope someone else arrived before too long. Certainly Dan and Frank, the union rep, weren't in my league – their offices were still firmly locked and in darkness.

Personnel were housed in the low-rise building next to the high-rise one, though we shared a common entrance hall. As I crossed it, Mike waved and stuck up a thumb.

'Still alive!' he said.

'So I see. Congratulations. Were you expecting not to be?'

'After all your doom and gloom yesterday!'

'Did you find out who the Maestro belonged to?'

'No, but he must be a bloody good driver. He managed to wriggle out without waiting for me. Good job, really – didn't finish till gone eight. Hate Mondays – don't see my grandson at all,' he said. 'I'm thinking about retirement, Sophie. A cottage in the country – further away from the grandchildren, but at least they can come and stay. See you!'

By now I could reasonably hope some of my colleagues in Personnel might have arrived, though they were not always keen to do front-of-house business, as it were. But today I was in luck: you could always rely on Kathryn to help you if you had a problem. She operated across a security counter they'd recently installed; with a grille which could be pulled down overnight.

'You lecturers and your keys! What do you do with them?'

'Mine's in police custody,' I said. 'Don't I have to sign for this?'

She was reaching down for a ledger when the phone rang; she left me to find the page and turned to answer it. I signed, and started to push the book back. And then something caught my eye. A polythene folder full of parking stickers, just within reach. To prove it could be done, I extracted a couple and flourished them at her as she turned back to me.

'Do you have to sign for these, too?'

'Supposed to. Another page in the ledger. Two! Have you won the Lottery or something? No, you wouldn't be coming into this place every day if you had.'

'I was just thinking these were a bit – vulnerable – where they are. If someone wanted to nick one.' I pushed the stickers over to her.

'Who'd want to do that?' she laughed, putting them back in the folder.

Who indeed?

We'd got as far as Apologies in our lunchtime meeting when – we were growing to expect it by now – the fire bell rang. The procedure went like clockwork – practice, no doubt, making perfect – with the students' minds concentrated somewhat this time by the unmistakable smell of smoke. Someone had set fire to a rubbish skip behind the building, in about the most inaccessible position a fire-fighter would wish to find. However, it was a calm, grey day, not at all unpleasant for milling around in the open air missing meetings. What cheered me was the thought of the perpetrator being caught on the anti-vandal video; I hoped he'd waved at the camera.

I had to cut short my sojourn in the car park: a work experience visit called. As I trundled off, it occurred to me that I hadn't phoned Afzal about a placement with him: I'd do it when I got back to teach my twilight GCSE class.

The office I visited was on the far side of Cannon Hill Park. As accountants they might have been very successful – their premises were plush enough – but they hadn't remembered the courtesy of offering a mid-afternoon cup of tea. I'm programmed for liquid intake at three-fifteen, and I found my car pulling as if of its own accord into the Midlands Arts Centre car park. I had my tea in their pleasant café, then wandered out into the park itself. OK, it was noisy with jostling schoolkids, and the geese had been liberal with their droppings all over the paths, but it beat William Murdock any day. The space! The green, now rapidly turning gold – at William Murdock even the blades of grass were rationed. You could see a green patch from the administrative offices, but all the rest of us could aspire to was a view of the car park. Of course, a cynic would point out that the central reservation in the road outside was grass, but that didn't make up for the deliberate drabness that constituted our immediate surroundings. I dawdled back to the car and had to force myself to carry on to Five Ways rather than take a direct route home.

Mike's Escort was still in the car park when I eventually escaped at close to eight o'clock. I picked my way through the litter to my Renault, which sat patiently under a tree. A bird had splatted the roof and the bonnet – and the newly installed windscreen, for good measure. I couldn't blame the bird for the flat tyre, however; why are good suit days always flat tyre days? Swearing, I headed towards the engineering block: someone teaching an evening class might be prepared to lend me a lab coat to serve as an overall. The low-rise block was fifty yards from the main buildings, presumably because of the noise from heavy presses, and it was further screened by some bicycle sheds, never used except by the most naive among us who expected to find their machine intact when they returned. If I cycled in, I removed the saddle and a wheel and padlocked my bike in the caretaker's cubby-hole. But there were no cycles in the shed tonight, just a pile of old rags and a dustbin liner. I found a couple of engineers, both men in their mid-fifties, in their staffroom. Heads down, they were so engrossed with the calculations on an A4 sheet on the desk it took a couple of coughs to rouse them.

'Sorry, Sophie. Just trying to see if we can afford premature retirement.'

All these people retiring! What would the place be like without them? Quality teachers, zapping off en masse like greyhounds in sight of the hare. Where would it leave people like me?

They not only found me a proper overall – designed for a seven-foot Billy Bunter – but insisted on helping with my tyre. This wasn't at all what I'd intended. In fact, we were arguing near the cycle shed when I realized that the pile of old rags didn't consist of old rags at all.

If I'd thought about it beforehand, I couldn't have done it. Instinct took over. And someone had to do it. While one of the men called an ambulance and the other went for blankets, someone had to prise apart those swollen bleeding lips, fish out the broken chunks of teeth, try the kiss of life. Someone had to thump on a chest that might have any number of broken bones.

I didn't even hear the paramedics arrive. All I knew was keeping the rhythm going: all I knew was willing that thread of life not to snap. And then I was being moved gently to one side, and there was a man in green going calmly and efficiently into his routine.

Someone guided me to a loo, and washed my face off after I'd been sick. I don't know who. And then the police arrived, and it was time to stop shaking and start thinking.

On a number of occasions in the past I've regarded making a statement as a matter of boring routine. But this time I made it in good and earnest. The police – in the form of a constable from Ladywood nick, a few hundred yards from the college – were treated chapter and verse to the events leading up to the attack on Mike Appleyard. I told them about my encounter with a Maestro, Mike's encounter with a Maestro, the ease with which one could steal car park stickers. I was so fired up I'd have laid into that Maestro driver with his own baseball bat, if he'd been there. If only I could remember the car's registration number! I found myself giving a full, even lengthy, description of the driver, halitosis included. I blazed with fury. I wouldn't let the poor constable use any of the comfortable euphemisms with which he wanted to conceal my allegations.

In the end he was grateful for the chance to silence me by phoning through to find out how Mike was faring. I couldn't hear what was being said; all I could see was his face, darkening slowly with anger.

He stared at the phone in silence for a while before he looked up. 'Ruptured spleen. Damaged liver and kidney. Broken ribs. Broken cheek-bone. Fractured skull. Oh, and a shattered kneecap. I'll get someone to bring you another coffee, shall I?'

I shook my head. 'What's – what's the prognosis?'

'They reckon one of the blows has paralysed him. If he lives, Ms Rivers, he'll have to learn to walk all over again.'

Chapter Twelve

I'd forgotten all about changing my wheel, of course. The constable who'd taken my statement and then run me back to college took one look at it and another at my face. Before I could burst into tears of despair and exhaustion, he'd whipped off his jersey and rolled up his sleeves.

'But—'

'Where's your spare? You have got a spare?'

'I'll get it out while you get the other one off.' I couldn't argue in the face of such kind efficiency. I couldn't argue about anything.

The whole operation took less than five minutes. We shook rather dirty hands as I bade him goodnight.

'I'm not sure you should be driving at all, Ms Rivers. You're still shaking,' he said.

Somehow, I managed a grin. 'Would you leave a nice little car like this overnight? In this car park?'

He grinned back.

'Look – I'm sorry, I don't even remember your name, I know you told me—'

'Sidhu. Parminder Sidhu.'

'Thanks. I'm not usually this stupid, Parminder—'

'It's OK. Take your time.'

'There's been so much *going on* here. I know I'm teaching my grandmother to suck eggs – but you people at Ladywood will be liaising with Rose Road, won't you?'

'Every serious crime round here gets referred to them, Sophie. You think there's a tie-up with the fires and that?'

'Who knows?' An enormous yawn forced its way out. 'I'd better go while I'm still capable of movement.'

The phone was ringing when I got in, and the answering machine was flashing; news travelled fast.

The caller on the line was Richard. It took me a few moments to calm him down.

'The trouble is I can't *leave* the place, Sophie. I know it's not my responsibility, not any more. But I feel I should be there.'

The words came out more fervently than I'd meant. 'I wish you were, Richard. I really wish you were.'

I gave him the latest news, somewhat edited, and we arranged to meet for a meal in a couple of weeks.

'Sophie – shall I bring this disgusting carrier bag with me then, or do you need it now?'

'Is there much in it?'

'Just some photocopies, by the look of it.'

Photocopies? Dan's records! Still, I could always have a nose-round at work if my curiosity became unbearable. 'Tell you what, just pop them into the bowels of your filing system, will you?' They'd be as safe as if they were in a bank vault.

'And the bag?'

'Bin it – it's no better worth.'

'No, it's not, is it? One of these days you might consider a proper briefcase. It'd look more – suitable, you know.'

Yes, perhaps I was getting too old for such affectations as recycling supermarket carriers till they fell apart.

Time to take the calls on the machine. Shahida; Janet; Afzal.

Afzal?

I briefed Shahida and Janet first – they'd both seen the regional TV news – and declined offers of a bed for the night from both of them. Then there was a live call from Carl, who must be concerned indeed if he was braving the wrath of his wife to phone; or perhaps she'd gone out for the evening and he was giving himself an illicit thrill.

Then one of the engineers who'd been with me when we

found Mike. This had decided it – to hell with the paucity of his pension, he'd just written his letter of resignation.

Time to return Afzal's call.

No reply. I left a message saying things had been bad at William Murdock and were getting worse, but that I was fine.

I was making thick, sweet cocoa, as much for something warm to wrap my hands round as anything else, when the phone rang again. Expecting Afzal's voice, it took me a second to recognize this one.

Chris Groom. Chris Groom, currently DCI but expecting at any moment to become a superintendent. My ex, and Diane Stephenson's current, significant other. I sat down.

'You saved that man's life tonight,' he said, without preamble.

'Good job I've boned up on first aid,' I agreed, lightly. 'Question is, would he want to survive with those brain injuries?'

Chris would ignore that – his Catholic legacy. 'What the hell's going on at that place?'

'There's always been latent violence. It just seems to be coming out all at once.'

'Tom Cole says you picked up something interesting.'

'Does he? He hasn't come back to me yet. I presume it is make-up on those tissues?'

'He won't be coming back to you yet. He's had some bad chest pains – they've put him on sick leave until he's had tests. Poor bugger – only forty-four! But he phoned me. Says to tell you the victim said the smell wasn't curry, it was sweet. "Like a woman." Sounds as if you were right, Sophie. So why should blokes put on brown make-up?'

'Maybe they wanted to look like Michael Jackson in reverse.'

He laughed. 'Look, Sophie, I know we're – I mean, you know about me and Diane. But I wondered – d'you fancy a drink sometime? For old times' sake?'

It would be better to meet him first in private, perhaps; if things hotted up any more at William Murdock he might well be involved officially, and it would be better if we'd made our peace first. 'Fine.'

'How about tomorrow? Say about five? In that wine bar at Five Ways? Hort's, isn't it?'

'Fine.'

By now it was after eleven, my cocoa had an unappealing skin on it and all I wanted to do was dunk my still-trembling body in a hot bath. I'd got as far as putting a hot water bottle in my bed – I didn't think I'd ever be warm again – when, predictably, the phone rang again. Aggie! My God, how could I have forgotten Aggie in the middle of all this? Neglecting not only to feed her, but also to do her the basic courtesy of letting her know I was all right. I could have wept with shame. But she was philosophical: 'I dare say I shall hear soon enough if you're not. Now, you take care of yourself, do you hear? And if you want to bring that duvet of yours round here, you know you'll be welcome in my spare room.'

Coals of fire, indeed.

My bath. And let the answering machine do its job for a bit.

Warm at last, and swathed in my new winter-weight dressing-gown, I checked the machine. Two more calls. Afzal again – and, rather to my surprise, Dan.

Afzal second, on the grounds that I liked him, and I'm a great believer in deferred gratification. And it meant I'd be guaranteed a sympathetic ear when I'd had my brief conversation with Dan.

'Ah. I hoped you'd call back. How are you? This Mark Appleyard business—'

'Mike. His name's Mike.'

'Now, he's not my department – but you are. And I'm telling you this, Sophie, you don't talk to the press. Right?'

'How did you hear about it?' I had to say something, and this was the only polite thing I could think of.

'The police interrupted an evening meeting Fairbairn had called for us Senior Managers. We all know. And that's her instruction, too.'

While I had the man as a captive audience, I might as well ask about my little difficulty. 'What about my Thursday class? How have you Managers decided to solve the problem?'

'Fairbairn's looked at your timetable. She agrees to drop you to seventy-five per cent, so you'll lose that class. We've lined up an ex-school teacher for them. Inner-city. May even have taught some of your little dears before! He'll cope.'

I couldn't pretend I liked it. It ignored issues that should have been addressed, that would *have* to be addressed sooner or later. But in purely pragmatic terms, it made sense. And I was too tired to argue; I was too tired even to be rude. Whatever had happened to Dan the Nice Guy?

At last I could turn my attention to Afzal. He picked up the phone first ring, and sounded so pleased to hear from me I was glad I'd made the effort.

'My poor Sophie, you've had such a bad time! I didn't realize those yobs had so insulted you. It wasn't until I spoke to Shahida—'

I waited for a moment, but he left the sentence hanging. At last he continued. 'And now this terrible business on the news! Did you know the man?'

'As a colleague. We'd been talking earlier in the day. I didn't think that next time I saw him he'd be—' I couldn't go on.

'You saw him? After he'd been beaten up?' he prompted, when I didn't continue.

'I found him. Tried to help. A colleague called an ambulance. The police—' I wouldn't, *mustn't* think about trying to give mouth-to-mouth, hearing the grind of the shattered cheek-bone—

'Sophie? Sophie?'

'I'm—'

'I'm on my way.' And the line went dead.

There was no need to worry about being sick in front of him; there wasn't anything left to vomit. How he'd feel about being entertained by a woman wearing nothing but a dressing-gown I didn't know. However, I could do something about that, by putting on a nightie. And slippers. Shame the make-up had gone wherever it goes when you're sick. But even if I'd had the energy to repair it I wouldn't have done:

it would have given all sorts of signals I wasn't sure I wanted to give. Not tonight, anyway.

I hadn't expected him to turn up with his briefcase; I was too preoccupied by that to make much sense of what he was saying. Eventually I said, 'I'm not in any sort of trouble, you know.'

He stared at me. 'Ah! The case! I thought it more discreet.'

'Discreet?'

He got up, appeared to be measuring the sofa with his hands.

'Afzal—'

'Just checking it for size. You shouldn't be on your own, Sophie. So I'm going to borrow your sofa for the night. The case is so no one'll see I've brought my razor and my contact lens kit. And my pyjamas.'

Rubbing my eyes didn't seem to clear the mists. 'You mean, you're staying?'

'Someone has to.' He didn't smile, didn't attempt suggestive charm.

'OK. I mean, yes, please. But not down here.'

His turn to look wary.

'The spare bed's made up. And – the bathroom's first on the left.'

Next morning Afzal showed no signs of having had a late night. I wished I could say the same for me. Perhaps my appearance would discourage him for good from attempting anything more than friendship.

'Are you sure you should be in college today?' he asked, not altogether tactfully.

'Classes, meetings,' I said. 'What about you?'

'Clients, meetings. But I didn't have such an eventful time yesterday. Why not take a day off?'

'It's our ethos, Afzal: work till you drop. There's no money to pay for staff cover if you're off and all my groups have exams in June, so I can't afford to miss any classes. It's not fair on them.'

'June! But this is September!'

'But there'll be flu and Christmas and Ramadan and Eid and Easter – throw in a bit of snow, while you're at it! Enough factors to stop them getting a full year's tuition. And most of the kids I teach come with the minimum qualifications – they need all the help they can get.'

He nodded gently. 'I feel the same about my clients. But none of us is irreplaceable, Sophie.'

'True. But neither of us wants to be late. What would you like for breakfast? And if you say, "Anything", I could turn into a murderer myself.'

Chapter Thirteen

At this point the phone rang. I was still laughing with Afzal as I picked it up, so I didn't hear the voice of the caller for a couple of seconds.

'Sophie? Is that you, me love? It's Aggie. Sorry to bother you this early – only I seem to have hurt my leg—'

'I'm on my way.'

There wasn't time to explain properly to Afzal: I threw him a word over my shoulder and was off at a run. Aggie's key was on my ring, so I let myself in.

'Aggie?'

There she was, on the kitchen floor, her left leg at a hideous angle. Thank God one of her grandchildren had given her a cordless phone, which, after constant nagging, she now carried with her from room to room. How much pain it had cost her to reach it from the table, where she usually put it, I dreaded to think.

'D'you think the doctor'll be at the surgery yet?' she asked.

'I'm afraid this may be an ambulance job,' I said.

'I didn't like to bother them – all these false alarms,' she tutted. 'Still – if you think I ought.'

'I think you ought,' I said, and tapped the digits.

'I think you ought too,' said Afzal, who'd brought my spare-room duvet with him, and was wrapping it round her shoulders. 'In fact, they're already on their way.'

Her eyes narrowed, then she beamed. 'I like the way your young men get on with things, Sophie!' But laughing made her go grey with pain, and she clasped my hand as if she were afraid to let go. 'I couldn't have a drop of brandy, could I? There's some in that cupboard.'

'Best not to, Aggie – I may call you Aggie, may I? I'm Afzal.' He took her other hand. 'You see, when my auntie hurt herself like this—' He broke off.

Cheery voices and loud footsteps in the hall. The paramedics. I couldn't bear to stay in the room while they moved her, so I occupied myself with packing her night things.

Afzal called me downstairs. 'It's all fixed, Sophie. Aggie's worried about you being late for work, so I'm going to go in the ambulance with her.' He flashed his mobile phone.

'Might as well do something useful while I'm hanging round waiting to be seen,' he said, with the shadow of a smile. 'And you're not to worry. I'll be back as soon as I can to keep an eye on that house of yours.'

While they loaded her into the ambulance, I began to feel guilty. 'Afzal – you don't have to – I mean, you're so busy—'

'I can just work a little later this evening.'

'But your car—'

'There are such things as buses, you know. I'll pick it up this evening.' He looked at me quizzically. 'You might have to feed a starving lawyer, though.'

'With pleasure,' I said. And meant it.

I arrived at college more or less on time, to be intercepted by one of the security guards.

'Morning, Sophie. You're honoured!' He waved an internal mail envelope at me. Usually the sender just tucks the flap in; this one was heavily Sellotaped. What was so important they couldn't risk prying eyes taking a peak? 'Principal's secretary brought it across last night. Seems they wanted you to get it before you trekked all the way up to the fifteenth – perhaps they knew all the lifts would be out this morning.'

I looked sceptical. 'No. Or they'd definitely have waited till I got up. Thanks, Arthur.'

The note invited me to a meeting in the Principal's room at eight-forty-five. Well, I'd have to be a bit late, wouldn't I? I phoned upstairs to ask Janet to let my class into their room and to set them some work, then I presented myself as I was bidden.

Whatever I was expecting the new boss to look like, it wasn't this. She was no taller than I, nor much heavier. Her hair was more naturally blonde then mine, but going grey; she looked a bit like Hannah Gordon, with a wonderful facial bone structure and perfectly made-up blue eyes. I wondered if I detected a hint of a Scots accent – or perhaps Irish. She must have been in her mid-forties. Her suit was elegant, but she certainly hadn't chosen the shoulders for power, and the skirt wasn't much longer than the offending one in my wardrobe.

'Hello, Sophie! It's good to meet you at last.' Her smile reached her eyes. 'Barbara Fairbairn.' Her handshake was warm and firm. 'Tea or coffee?' She gestured at a pair of armchairs and a coffee table; beside the cups was a plate of croissants.

Was this the ogre that Dan had threatened me with?

'You must have had a very stressful time these last few days,' she began. 'The police – and your colleagues in the Engineering Department – tell me you made heroic efforts last night.'

'Is there any news of Mike?'

The compassion in her eyes told me the news wasn't good. 'He's on a life support system, I'm afraid. He's deeply unconscious – his family are with him. I'm organising a collection – but that's such a futile gesture, isn't it? All it does is give the impression you're doing something. I'll let you know as soon as we have any news. In the meantime, Sophie, it's you I can do something for. I think you should take a few days off – paid leave, of course. Go and find some sun.'

Stunned doesn't begin to describe my feelings. I suspect my jaw hit the floor. I had visions of myself in a French *pension*, or that Berlin apartment . . . And then remembered Aggie, now in hospital, needing attention when they let her out.

'I'm fine,' I said.

She shook her head. 'How *can* you be fine? Sophie, you're only human – do have another croissant – you can't endure

101

stress like this forever. We'll find the money from some-where to cover your classes.'

Damn it, she was refuting my arguments before I even had the chance to put them forward!

I produced my diary, fat with appointments with potential work-placement employers. I didn't even need to open my mouth.

'As for that,' she said, 'I'm concerned about the pro-portion of your time this is taking up.'

'*If a job's worth doing, it's worth doing well,*' I quoted, though just at the moment I wasn't sure whom.

She smiled again. 'If you won't take time off – and if I could, I'd order you to! – I'd like you at the very least to talk to the college counsellor. Will you do that?'

I nodded.

'Good. Now, I do want you to do me one more favour. I want you to promise me not to talk to the media.'

'I wasn't proposing to,' I said. First Dan, now her . . .

Flinching at the change in my tone, she widened her eyes. 'I'm sure you weren't. I know how professional you are. But gossiping about college business can only damage the college's reputation—'

'I've not been here for fifteen years without wanting to preserve our reputation at all costs,' I said.

'Fifteen years!' Her eyebrows rose. 'You don't look old enough. You must have been very young when you started. I wonder how many students you've taught?'

'It would be interesting to work it out, wouldn't it?'

'I taught – let me see – that black politician who's always sounding off. And there's that TV weather-girl they sacked for wearing shorts when it was supposed to be a suit.'

I had this terrible feeling she wanted me to reveal that I'd taught Dan; she was willing me to trust her with his secret. I wanted to share it – to establish myself as a friend of this nice woman – but it was not mine to share. I smiled. 'I actually taught–'

She leant forward eagerly.

'–my local councillor. And that guy who wrote the scandalous novel about Westminster.'

She exhaled. Deeply.

So did I. I looked at my watch. 'My class will have run out of work,' I said.

'Work?'

'I phoned up and got a colleague to tell them I'd be late. I set them some reading, with the threat of a test.'

She smiled at me again. 'You really are an old pro, aren't you!'

On my desk was a little heap of peppermint-green telephone message jotters: mostly colleagues, wondering how I was. There was one from PC Parminder Sidhu: I'd return his call before I went into class. The rest must wait.

It took several minutes to get through to him. With each moment that passed I became more and more convinced that he wanted to tell me Mike was dead. At last he came to the phone.

'Ms Rivers? I just wanted to ask how you were feeling this morning. I could only get your answering machine on your home number,' he added, as if apologising for bothering me.

'I'm fine,' I said. Wasn't that what I'd told Barbara Fairbairn too?

'I'm surprised you're at work. Police officers – we get time off after a bad incident, to sort ourselves out.'

'Yes. My boss has offered me a week off.'

'Take it! Before he changes his mind!'

'It's a she.'

'Well, in that case—' He laughed. 'Think about it, anyway. It won't do Mike Appleyard any good, you being a martyr. He's about the same, by the way – I'll call you if I get any news.'

On my eighth attempt to get through to Casualty, it occurred to me that there was more than one way of skinning a cat. Trying not to look self-conscious, I asked Shahida if she knew Afzal's mobile number; trying not to look arch, and then trying even harder not to laugh, she dictated it. Then my phone rang: Afzal.

Aggie was no longer in A&E. Because she'd been considerate enough to fall before breakfast, before she'd had even a cup of tea, Afzal reported that they'd been able to take her into theatre immediately. They were going to pin her hip: she wouldn't be hospitalized too long, that way. Two granddaughters had already arrived at the hospital, but it was me she was relying on to water her plants.

'Now, Sophie,' he continued, 'I am not expecting you to feed me tonight. We'll eat out or get a take-away.'

'We'll see about that,' I said. He was a fishietarian, not a pure veggie, and I could cope.

I spent the rest of the day teaching and phoning and writing to absentee students. How Ms Fairbairn spent hers, I'm not sure, but it certainly included dictating a couple of memos. One was addressed to all staff: to commiserate with us on Sarah's death and inform us that if we wanted to go to the funeral, whenever that was arranged, we had her permission to go, even if it meant closing classes. She had the sense to send a separate note about fires. If we could fight them safely, we might do so, but under no circumstances whatever should we take any risks. Safety was paramount. She gave the impression that she'd rather see the burned-out shell of a building than one singed hand, which was encouraging. And, given her position, surprising.

At four-thirty, deciding I'd had enough, I started off down the building though not with my usual haste. Something was holding me back. Perhaps I should make an appointment with that counsellor: I had made an implicit promise, and she was the boss, after all. I wasn't sure how I felt about the whole thing. On my advice, dozens of students sought help, but our counsellors tended to be teaching staff who counselled as an optional extra. I didn't relish the idea of baring my soul to someone I'd see regularly in meetings or in staffrooms. They'd all been trained, would be totally professional – but I wasn't happy. There was a fairly discreet system of arranging appointments – you filled in a slip of paper with your preferred time, they contacted you – but still I hesitated.

I reached the floor where the counsellors worked, but did

no more than stare at the closed door. At this point one of them opened, to reveal a middle man who was everyone's idea of a counsellor: bearded, middle-aged, comfortable in baggy cords.

'Hello,' he said.

'Hello. Are you one of my new colleagues? I'm Sophie Rivers – I teach English.'

'I'm Sherry. Before you laugh, I'll explain – my surname's Sherringham, and I've always been Sherry. A rich Amontillado, I fancy.'

It was hard not to grin, even though he'd obviously made the same crack dozens of times.

'I've joined the counselling team,' he continued. 'In fact, I'm supposed to be leading it, but they all seem so well organized I don't know that I'm needed. You won't tell anyone, will you?' His expression was deliberately comical.

'Perhaps I need you.' There – it was out. 'I had a bit of a bad experience – you might have heard about it. Maybe it would help to talk.'

'What better time than now?' He flung the door wide, gesturing me to a low chair; then he closed the door, and pulled another chair at right angles to mine. 'Now, is it connected with what happened yesterday? Or is there something else you want to talk about?'

I looked around his room. It was newly decorated, and someone had attempted to make it friendly. But the rib-high radiators that ran along all the outside walls, so that the windows were so high you had to stand to see out of them, were intractably there. We were at William Murdock, all right, trapped in poverty and mean-spirited design.

'What brought you here?' I asked. 'There must be better places than this.'

He blinked. 'In what way?'

'Oh, places with resources. That's one of the things I want to talk about really. Why am I still here?' The loathing, the longing in my voice surprised me. 'Why am I still in this underfunded, unloved place? Every day I see people with infinitely better working conditions than this. Places with canteens and rest rooms and staffrooms for socialising, not work. Why am I *here*?'

Despite my sudden preoccupation with a question that I'd never known I wanted to ask, his response surprised me.

'You must have taught a lot of students over the years?'

'Quite a lot.'

'Anyone in particular stand out?'

I thought. 'There was a blind girl, Alison – we got her into university. She's a professor, now. And an Asian lad who's just got a safe Labour constituency to nurse.'

'And – ?'

'And a legion of people who got into university against all the odds and are doing well in different ways. There's one girl doing VSO in Somalia because of a project we did on the Third World. That's gratifying. What are you getting at? That I'm here because I have a purpose?'

'Hmm. Maybe.' There was something in his tone I couldn't identify. 'How do you feel when you meet ex-students who've done well for themselves?'

It nearly came out – 'Like Dan, for instance?' But I bit it back. 'Funny – you rarely meet them again,' I said. 'Perhaps it's because they're only here a couple of years – they tend not to come back and visit. But I have kept in touch with some. Not the ultra-successful ones, though – there's no chance they'll come back and tell me they've got a wonderful job vacancy in this multi-national they run and I'm the only one who can fill it.'

'Can't say that's ever happened to me either.' He didn't sound as if he particularly wanted it to.

'Where did you work before?'

'Up North.'

Perhaps counsellors weren't supposed to be forthcoming about themselves; though if I'd known what had brought him to William Murdock, maybe I could work out why I stayed.

'You haven't told me about yesterday's incident,' he said. And then, correcting himself, 'About what brought you here.'

I shook my head. 'It wasn't just that. It was very nasty, but a one-off.'

'How nasty? Are you sure it wouldn't help to talk about it?'

'Bad enough. It upset me.'

'Perhaps you should take some time off. Go and find some sun. Everyone's entitled to sick leave if they're – they're really stressed.'

What had he been going to say? Goodness knew what the Management would say if they found he was advising people to take sickies.

Or, in view of what Barbara Fairbairn had said to me, were holidays in the sun in college time now William Murdock policy? 'It's all the other things I need to work out,' I said at last. 'Perhaps I should go and have a think and then come back to you.'

'Are you sure?'

'Sure. Nice to meet you, Sherry. I hope you enjoy it here.'

I stood by my car, listening. Nothing but the roar of traffic. The vague whispering of the sort of trees they use for ground cover and inner-city design. The only smell the stink of petrol and diesel – and some phenol from a nearby factory. Yes, I had questions to answer – but I wasn't sure the answers were those Sherringham wanted to hear.

Chapter Fourteen

Afzal had chosen salmon sandwiches when we'd lunched together, and I knew he drank in moderation, so I hoped that salmon steaks poached in butter and wine with fresh parsley would be acceptable. With new potatoes and fresh carrots and beans – interesting tastes, colours and textures, without being pretentious. I didn't want it to look as if I'd tried too hard. I had some cheese and fruit for afters, not to mention some exotic ice creams in the freezer, some of which were of my own making; I thought he might like the apricot and amaretti.

I'd done no more than lay the table, however, when I was interrupted by the phone: Shahida, obviously upset.

'We've just had the report from the Fire Service,' she said. 'Arson. At the refuge.'

'Arson! How can they tell?'

'The source of the fire. Not just the chip pan, but a couple of other places in the kitchen too – something to do with the intensity of the heat. Anyway, how it happened is irrelevant. The point is that someone tried to burn the place down, Sophie.'

'Any idea why?' Too many questions, Sophie.

'I've just spent an hour with the police, when I was supposed to be in class, telling them I'd no idea why. I don't care why! It doesn't matter! I just want to get hold of the person who did it!'

'Knowing the one can lead to the other,' I said, mildly.

'You sound just like Chris Groom!' And she slammed down the phone.

Yes, I did. He always said getting his head involved kept his heart in check – no bad thing when you were dealing with the sights and sounds that comprised his working day. But I wasn't in the police; I was an ordinary teacher. I was allowed emotions.

I felt I'd let Shahida down. Failed her. She'd wanted sympathy – and I'd treated her like a witness. But shouldn't she have made allowances for me? She must know, surely, about my part in finding Mike? Though not efficient, the Murdock grapevine surely hadn't withered altogether.

Perhaps we should re-establish contact straight away. I went to dial her number, then hesitated. What could I say? That I was so out of my mind with stress I couldn't take any more emotion? That would simply make her feel guilty. Better to forget it and make sure we had a friendly natter before class next day, when we were both calmer.

The phone. Please, God, don't let it be Shahida, apologising!

It was Chris Groom. Apologising. 'I hope they passed the message on to you in the bar.'

Chris! My God! I'd stood up Chris.

'Message?' I asked cautiously.

'About this meeting I got called to. I'm really sorry, Sophie – I had literally two minutes to call Hort's and that was that for two solid hours. Cost analysis; cost centres; nothing about crime. Anyway, I'm sorry. Could we make it another time?'

'No problem.' I could have told him I'd forgotten, but in the circumstances I wasn't sure that that was wise. 'You know Aggie's in hospital?' I explained about the broken hip. Damn, I hadn't phoned Interflora – I hadn't even phoned the hospital yet to check her progress. 'I haven't had a moment to tell Ian the news. Though she prefers you,' I added. 'Tell me, is there any inside info about our goings-on at William Murdock? Any connection between Sarah's death and the attack on Mike?'

'Not that I know of.' Was that his way of reminding me that it was Diane Stephenson's case? 'But the good news – and this is another reason I wanted to talk to you – is that Mike Appleyard is actually a little better. Oh, they don't expect him to come round properly for another forty-eight

109

hours, maybe longer, but there are hopeful signs. Though his injuries are severe, they think he'll live. And – hopefully – walk.'

'Oh, thank God for that.'

'Amen. And no small thanks to you, Sophie.'

'Forget it. I'd rather.'

'It must have been – very unpleasant.'

'You could say that. Yes.'

There was a pause, which lengthened. He'd never forgiven me for the rift between us, and, to be honest, I couldn't defend myself even if I wanted to. There'd never been a future for us – he'd loved me far more than I cared for him – but in the way of things, now I couldn't have him, I missed him. Not as a lover – we were never at our best together in that relationship – as a friend. I would have given a great deal to be able to pour out my heart about the goings-on at William Murdock. Chris and I had always managed to spark ideas off each other, which sometimes led to Chris haring off at risky tangents. But taking risks often got results.

'When—' We spoke simultaneously; I waited, laughing.

'So when shall we have that drink?'

'Tomorrow lunchtime,' I said positively.

'What, no meeting?'

'Two, probably. But if you promise to talk to me about college – and pick me up with a blue flashing light – I could say I was helping the police with their inquiries, couldn't I?'

I was still only at the potato-scrubbing stage when Afzal arrived, looking harassed.

'Look, this is awful – I have a couple of calls I simply must make. I thought if I made them from the office I'd only be horribly late. May I be very rude?'

'Help yourelf.' I pointed at the phone but he shook his head and burrowed in his briefcase for his mobile.

While he talked, I cooked. Nothing took more than fifteen minutes. He wandered into the kitchen as I was making the sauce for the salmon.

'I meant to bring some wine. I'm a bit of a failure as a dinner guest, aren't I?'

I opened the fridge door – plenty of wine. I passed him a bottle of Gewurztraminer and a corkscrew.

Over dinner, I found myself telling him about Shahida. We'd never had the mildest of cross words before, and though I felt guilty for not responding to her revelation with more passion, I really couldn't face phoning her.

'You can't anyway. It would be impolite to abandon your guest, in the middle of such a delectable meal.' Afzal smiled. 'Seriously, let it rest, Sophie. Isn't Wednesday the day she teaches all those hours? It's just possible she doesn't know what you've been going through.'

'Of course! Oh, shit! Afzal, I seem to be losing my grip at the moment. I even—' No, it wouldn't be tactful to tell him I'd forgotten my date with Chris. 'I even forgot to order flowers for Aggie.'

'Her grandchildren came with armfuls – I doubt if she has room for more. But seriously, Sophie, forgetting is a sign of stress. Are you sure you were right to go into work today?'

'I didn't want to sit round here on my own, moping. I'm better at work.' Was it my imagination – or did my voice carry less conviction than usual?

We lingered over our ice cream – there is no way to deal with apricot and amaretti ice cream other than to linger. Although we were by no means at the Häagen-Dasz stage in our relationship, we were relaxed with each other. I was wondering what the next stage might be: coffee on the sofa, perhaps. Or perhaps not; it depended on how the conversation went. At the moment it was turning to washing-up, so much of an anathema to me that I'd actually bought a dishwasher. At the mention of the word, I could have sworn he flinched.

I said nothing, but waited, mystified.

'Funny,' he said at last, 'how you think you're over something, and then a really trivial incident – even a word – brings it all back.' His eyes were full of pain.

'Something – bad?'

'Something very bad.' He took a deep breath that turned

111

into a sigh. 'Has Shahida told you anything about my family?'

I shook my head.

'Good. Sophie, I liked you as soon as we met, and I hoped you liked me. But I could tell from your body language that you weren't interested in – attracting me. And I was happy with that. I asked Shahida not to tell you about my past because I was afraid it would turn me into a martyr in your eyes. I didn't want you to like me just because you felt sorry for me. Now I think we're friends. Whatever happens, we are friends.'

The silence deepened. I could hear my heart thumping; I was hoping he might want to be more than friends. But I wasn't sure. I waited.

'The very nature of my work attracts enemies. Sometimes I have to take on powerful organisations who oppose me in court and that's fine. I trust to justice. But sometimes they seek vengeance. I had an arranged marriage, Sophie, though I don't suppose you approve of that. But I was the happiest man on earth. I fell in love with my Nusheen, and she with me, and I thanked Allah for his overwhelming kindness. And then we had a child. When my daughter was born, I knew I couldn't ever be happier; when Nusheen was pregnant again – Sophie, there aren't words to describe how I felt. I was working down in London, then, and I crossed swords with a clothing concern in the East End. Machines without guards, inadequate light, no regard for health and safety provision . . . They wanted me to keep my nose out of their affairs. So they tried persuasion. Verbal warnings. When I carried on, they gave me another warning. They tried the oldest trick in the book – tampering with my brakes. But it was Nusheen who drove the car. Going to choose a dishwasher.' His voice didn't change; but tears were running down his face. 'They hit a petrol tanker. Dear God, they hit a petrol tanker. And she was pregnant. And my daughter was in the back—'

All I could do was kneel beside him and pull his head on to my shoulder. He wept for some time, sobbing so painfully I wondered if he'd ever wept for them before. At last it was time to soothe him, to stroke his hair, pass table napkins to wipe away his tears.

He was motionless, his head on my shoulder, his arms around me. Then, suddenly, he pushed away.

Touching his hand gently, I padded to the kitchen. And found the brandy.

His face was still puffy, and his whole body shook from time to time in a little paroxysm, but he drank his brandy and seemed ready to try for some semblance of normality. I was icy cold. It was nothing to do with the temperature of the room – in late September I turned on the central heating – but I lit the gas fire anyway, as much for something to do as anything else. Where did a romantic evening go, after such naked agony? Bed? It might offer him comfort – me too – but I had a feeling that if I suggested it I'd never see him again. I returned to my end of the sofa, maintaining a sensible distance between us. I'd just have to leave the initiative to him, hope I could make an appropriate response. I didn't like feeling so inadequate; I didn't like knowing just how inadequate I was.

At last, he leant over and touched my wrist. 'Thank you, Sophie. I – I wanted you to know, but I didn't want to—' He broke off, shaking his head.

'I did the same thing once,' I said. 'A good friend died, and I coped well. Everyone said so. Then something made me realize he'd gone forever, and I lost it, far more publicly than you did. But it was cleansing. There he is – there's George.' I pointed to the photo on my mantelpiece. 'He wasn't my lover. A friend. But I loved him more than I'd ever loved anyone. And he died. Left me. They say, don't they, that anyone's death is a loss? Well, George's death was certainly a loss.' I managed to look at Afzal. 'But now – most of the time – when I think of him it's to remember the good parts of our time together. And to thank him for having been with me for even that short time.'

His hand closed over mine. The fingers were long and bony, well-manicured; it was tempting to turn my hand to clasp his. But even such a slight movement would disturb

113

the total stillness of the room, would push the relationship one way or another. It seemed right therefore to reach with my left hand to touch the hand on my wrist.

The stillness returned. How long we sat like that I didn't know.

And then the doorbell rang.

Whoever it was didn't give me long; after only a matter of seconds the door knocker pounded. And even as I reached the door, the letterbox opened and a loud, Australian voice boomed, 'Are you there, Soph? Are you all right?'

Chapter Fifteen

Greg tumbled through the door, propelled by his backpack and a large handgrip. Relinquishing one to me, and released from the other by Azfal, he straightened and treated me to an extravagant kiss, patting my bottom as he let me go. 'You in some sort of trouble, Soph? Kept hearing these things on the news – thought I'd better come over and keep an eye on things. But,' he said, taking in Afzal for the first time, 'you seem to have someone else doing just that.'

Before I could speak, Afzal stuck out a hand. 'Afzal Mohammed. And you're—'

'Greg. Greg Silverdale.' He surged into my living room. 'Nice place, Soph! It wouldn't run to a beer, would it? I don't want to interrupt anything,' he added, as he took in the dinner table and the pair of brandy glasses on the coffee table by the sofa. But he sat down anyway.

'Chilled?' I asked, unable quite to keep the irony from my voice.

'Is there any other way? She's a great girl, Soph, isn't she?' he continued, while I banged about in the kitchen. 'Did Berlin together. Great time. When I heard about all this college stuff on the radio – yeah, your college has made it into Europe, Soph! – I thought I'd come and stick my nose in. Took some leave owing me, and here I am.'

'Greg's an engineer,' I called, 'working on the rebuilding of Potsdammer Platz. Responsible for all the concrete. We met when someone tried to—'

'From Oz, originally. Though maybe you can tell. What part of India are you from?'

'Bradford.'

I returned in time to see Greg open his mouth, close it and then laugh. 'Sorry, mate. Always jump to conclusions. Took me some time to work out that the guy Sophie went to Berlin with wasn't her bloke. Queer as a coot, he turned out to be.'

'Gay, Greg. The word you're looking for is gay. Here.'

'Cheers! So what d'you do, Afzal? How d'you earn your crust?'

'I'm a solicitor—'

'Christ, you're not in any trouble, Soph?'

Afzal shook his head. 'I'm a friend. In fact, Sophie was helping *me* with a problem, not the other way round.' He smiled, holding my eye for a second longer than socially necessary; I smiled back. Yes, whatever happened, we'd be friends. But I wanted to establish a few facts, for everyone's benefit. That Greg and I weren't and never had been lovers; that wherever Greg was to sleep tonight it was not in my bed; that Afzal's presence in the spare bed was as welcome as it had been the night before.

'Where are you staying, Greg?' I asked: full marks for directness, if not tact.

'Well, I thought – here. I thought you might need some protection.'

'Afzal's—'

'Hell, I've come all the way from Berlin to see you! I'm sure Azfal won't mind if I muscle in for a couple of days.'

'It depends,' said Afzal, earning my eternal gratitude, 'on what you mean by "muscling in". And whether Sophie minds if I'm elbowed out.'

'Greg, Afzal is a friend. Afzal, Greg is a friend. So there is to be no muscling in or elbowing out. I have a spare bed and a sofa-bed – sort yourselves out. One upstairs, one down. OK?'

I bustled back into the kitchen, acutely aware that I was playing my familiar role of bossy teacher, and that it jangled in discord with my earlier self. I just hoped Afzal could work out which was the real me. I stacked the dishwasher, crashing plates in irritation. Suddenly there came a chirruping from the corner of the kitchen: from Afzal's brief-case, to be precise. Perhaps he hadn't heard. I carried the case out at arm's length and handed it to him.

The call was short but clearly, significant, ending with the ominous words, 'I'm on my way.' He turned, collapsing the aerial. 'I'm sorry, Sophie – that was a client. He's in a cell in Digbeth nick.' He turned to go. 'Remember, Greg; he who fights and walks away, lives to fight another day.'

Greg grinned. 'Right. But my old Granddad, he used to have another saying: "Faint heart never fucked a pig."'

I walked with Afzal to his car.

'Are you sure you'll be all right? I mean, I could come back, but goodness knows what time I'll get away.'

'I think he's more mouth than trousers, to use yet another colloquialism. He might be insensitive, but I don't think he'd try and rape me. I think he's genuinely come to look after me. My knight in shining armour.'

'I'd rather you'd called the RAC.' He kissed me lightly on the lips. 'Thank you for this evening.' And then he kissed me again; and I kissed him back. 'I'll phone tomorrow.'

I watched his tail-lights out of sight.

Greg had found another can of lager, and was investigating the remaining contents of my fridge. He settled for bread and cheese – there was plenty, since Afzal and I had preferred the ice cream.

'I reckon I'm a bit tall for this,' he said, bouncing on the sofa.

'It opens into a full-length bed. But you might as well have the spare bed – Azfal won't be back.'

'He sleeps in the spare, does he?'

I nodded firmly. 'Same as you.'

'But he fancies you, Soph. You mark my words.'

'Well,' I said, confirming what I already suspected, 'I quite fancy him too.'

It was well after one in the morning when I persuaded Greg that I really had to stop nattering and head for bed, on account of my nine o'clock class. He followed me to the spare room; Afzal hadn't stripped the bed, but had made it to hotel specification. I lifted clean sheets and pillow cases from the chest.

'Hang on – that looks clean.'

'Only been slept in one night.'

'Well then.' And then his face clouded. 'Look, Soph, this sounds really daft – but it was Afzal who slept in this, right?'

I nodded.

'Well, I've – don't get me wrong – never slept – you know, him being Asian and all – I'm—'

I stripped the bed and remade it with ruthless speed. But the corners weren't up to Afzal's.

'So I thought what I'd do was be an extra pair of eyes and ears, Soph,' Greg said, expansive over a bowl of porridge. 'I'll come and enrol for some course or other. Bunk off the classes.'

'That's really kind of you.' I didn't tell him, that under the new Godfrey regime, bunking off was strictly forbidden.

'What it was, see, I liked you, Soph. And then you walked out on me – I went to your apartment that evening and you weren't there – and I was a bit cut up about it. Worked every hour of overtime going to get you out of my mind. Holiday romance, that's all it was for you, wasn't it, and I thought it was for me. But I'm not sure. Mind you, you're different from when you were in Berlin. Your clothes and all. You look like you could stand up for yourself. But I still like you, and I don't like the thought of you sitting there with this arsonist trying to get you.'

'Why me? Lots of other people teach at William Murdock!'

'But you're the sort of woman who sticks her nose in, aren't you? Like looking at that bike shed and realising it was a bloke lying there – Afzal told me. So what I'm going to do is come into college and get myself a place on some course. German, maybe I could do with learning some proper German, as opposed to the stuff we use on the sites.'

'You must see some of the tourist spots while you're here.'

'As long as I can see them with you, that's fine.'

I pondered. 'Would you like to come on my work experience visits with me? You'd get a sense of Brum, and we could do other things in the evenings. How long are you here for?'

'Until we sort this bastard. If you'll have me,' he added.

'Friends?'

'Friends. But – never say die, Sophie!'

Unbidden, another smidgen of homely wisdom crept to my mind. Men are like buses: nothing for ages, then you get two together.

So it was that William Murdock took another student on to its roll, though clearly we'd miss out on the dollop of money that marked a student's completion of his course; I rather wondered how the college would like my making phone calls to Berlin to discuss why Greg was no longer attending. Age-wise he'd be at home in the place – we had plenty of mature students, some of whom constituted my favourite classes. There might be other difficulties, but I'd wait for him to raise them. Meanwhile, I got on with my daily round.

I'd just made my breaktime cup of tea when the fire bell rang and it would be hard to say whether the gasps of 'Shit!' outnumbered the yells of 'Bugger!' These fifteen minutes of the morning were ours: fifteen minutes when the students were their own responsibility. Except of course for those waiting to see one or other of us, standing by our desks and clogging up the narrow corridors.

Bill came bursting in. 'It's real! It's on this floor. Shift your arses. Get those kids out!'

We bundled the students out. Sean grabbed the staffroom's extinguisher and hurtled round the corridor; I followed, with an extinguisher I collected en route. It was too heavy for me to be able to manoeuvre easily, but it might help Sean or Bill.

'Get those from the fourteenth, too! We might just be winning!'

They were. Just about. But the smoke wasn't going to let me help. My asthma decided it was time for me to call it a day. And soon the men started choking too, blundering, streaming-eyed, away.

'Shut the door on it,' I wheezed, 'stop it spreading.'

Bill crawled back.

'Well done! Now let's get out!'

I had to stop between the fourteenth and the thirteenth for a couple of drags at my salbutamol spray. Then I caught up with the others, the bell still driving into our ears. All the way down. At least we should get a hero's welcome.

But, 'Where the hell have you lot been? What kind of example is this to set the students?'

'Hang on, Dan,' Bill said. 'We've been trying to fight the fire.'

'The Principal said you weren't to attempt it. Leave it to the Fire Service, she said. Don't take any risks. We don't want another dead teacher on our hands.'

A fire-fighter rushed over. 'Which floor?'

'Fifteenth! Room 1501. It's a stock room!' Then Sean turned to Dan, deliberately conciliatory. 'With all due respect, Mr Godfrey, we didn't take risks and we may have prevented a lot of damage. Think of all the computers on that floor! And all the staff desks and cabinets – years of work, there!'

Dan looked wholly unconvinced. 'You were given orders. Now, get out to the car park. You know this building has to be completely evacuated.'

'After you,' Bill gestured gravely.

But Dan stayed put, risking his all to inconvenience the Fire Service.

Ms Fairbairn treated us all to coffee and exceptional cakes.

'My passion, baking,' she said. 'Try some of this shortbread.'

It was an order we were happy to obey.

Now it was all over, now the adrenalin had dispersed, I felt drained. Bill and Sean looked dirty – and drained. Heroism had its price.

'I'm very proud of you all,' Fairbairn said. 'You did very well.'

'Not quite well enough,' Dan said. 'According to the officer in charge, everything in the room was destroyed.

There's smoke damage to the staffroom and water damage in the classrooms below.'

'What was in the room, Dan?'

He shook his head. 'I'm sorry, Ms Fairbairn – these lecturers are a law unto themselves. Goodness knows what they keep in those cubby-holes! They're going to have to clean their act up now – we won't get a fire certificate if they keep leaving piles of paper everywhere.'

'Try giving us enough filing cabinets and bookshelves,' Bill suggested. 'There are no books in the library, so we have to prepare handouts. The blackboards and whiteboards don't work, so we have to prepare still more handouts. And handouts mean paper.'

'We have no resources for—'

A gentle wave of Fairbairn's hand silenced him. 'If there's a problem, we must try to solve it.'

'One of the problems has been solved.' I said. 'There were stacks and cardboard boxes full of files in 1501 – we'd had to take them out of the filing cabinets so they could be used for something else.'

'What was in the files?' Fairbairn asked, smiling as she passed the plate of scones round; I wondered how she had time to keep her hands so perfectly manicured.

'Student records for the last twenty-five years. Up to about five years ago, when they started to computerize them. And the computer doesn't keep copies of references and so on – so they were in 1501, too.'

'And can nothing be retrieved?' Fairbairn looked at Dan. He shook his head. 'Nothing.'

'Absolutely nothing?' The plate of scones had paused.

'Absolutely nothing.'

Chapter Sixteen

Greg was waiting for me outside the staffroom when I got back – I'd taken an hour off to go home for a shower and a change of clothes to get rid of the smoke. It seemed a waste of time, considering the lingering smell of charred paper that permeated the whole college.

'Hi,' he said. 'You Sophie Rivers?' He didn't even wink.

'Yes.' Neither did I. 'How can I help you?'

'I'm Greg Silverdale. Just joined. Seems you're to be my review tutor,' he said. 'Or so the German teacher said.'

'Welcome to William Murdock, Greg. As your tutor, I'm responsible for your moral and physical welfare while you're on the course. I must also make sure you attend every single class, do your homework and don't set fire to the college. I see you at the end of every term to review your progress and write any references you need – for university entrance and so on. And, oh,' I continued, lowering my voice, 'I'm on a visit to West Midlands Airport this afternoon.'

'Where's that? Anywhere interesting?'

'Out by the main city sewage works!'

'Ah. 'Cause the German teacher - what's her name, Shirley? – offered to help me catch up with some of the work I've missed and she's a little sweetie.'

I grinned. 'It'd suit me fine. The guy at the airport and I—' I paused, suggestively. 'Well, you never know. And the good news is that – unlike Shirley – he's single!'

Mark Winfield, the airport training officer, greeted me like an old friend. He promised without preamble to take on a succession of suitable students and treated me to tea in his office; he also produced some biscuits, speculating – correctly – that I wouldn't have had time for lunch. He knew my needs by now.

'You're looking tired,' he stated. 'In fact, you're looking knackered. Problems?'

I shrugged, but it was an affirmative shrug. 'Work's getting me down – you've heard about our fires? And about the lecturer being beaten up?'

'And about the woman dying. I was afraid for a second – put it this way, it gave me a nasty moment. I've tried to phone several times, but I'll swear it takes ten minutes to penetrate the college switchboard. And your line seems to be constantly busy, or if it isn't, you don't answer.'

'I'm teaching a lot. And doing this. And then there are those meetings we all know and love—'

'Give it up. Get something better. A job like mine – you could do it standing on your head. How's your stomach, by the way? Was it an ulcer?'

'Gastritis. All those missed meals, rushed meals ... And the stuff with Andy.' The worst of it was, I had a suspicion the symptoms were returning.

'And the problems with me and Gurjit. How's she getting on this term?'

'Gurjit's fine. On line for top grades in all her A-Levels. She should walk into university.' Alas, she loved her family and culture even more than she loved Mark, and she was fiercely ambitious; if success meant eliminating Mark from her life, so be it.

'And her parents?'

'Will back her all the way.' I smiled; I'd hurt him enough. 'Are you still an eligible bachelor?'

Mark was in his early thirties, good-looking in a quiet sort of way. He had a slight limp, but this only served to make him more attractive.

'I loved Gurjit, you know. Still compare other women to her.'

'And find them wanting.'

He nodded. 'Most of the time. But I've decided to pull myself together. If all else fails, I'll advertise in the *Guardian*! Now, how about lunch next week?'

I flipped through my diary. 'Meetings every day. And for the week after.'

'Then come over one evening to check up on one of your students – it'll still have to be evenings that they work, I'm afraid – and we'll have dinner. It's my turn to pay, and I've found a lovely Thai restaurant. Bring your toothbrush so you don't have to worry about drinking and driving.'

Oh dear. This couldn't be a third bus, could it?

There was only one thought on my mind as I parked outside my house: a long, cold beer. I'm usually a wine drinker, but for some reason I was salivating for beer. A lager. And when I'd sunk that I'd pour another and take it up to the bath. And then – and only then – would I return to the human race. But first I'd better phone the hospital to see how Aggie was getting on. How could I keep forgetting? Best do that first. No, best go and pay a visit: with or without flowers she'd want to see me. A quick supper, and I'd be off.

Except I'd got Greg to consider.

Hell, Greg could come too! Aggie would like Greg. Another young man for her to charm. And perhaps I'd treat him to a balti – it's a Birmingham speciality, after all, and he was a tourist. But I was hungry *now*. All I'd eaten all day was Mark's biscuits and Ms Fairbairn's shortbread.

No lunch . . . No Chris. Hell! And I hadn't even remembered to phone!

There were three messages flashing on my answering machine, but I tapped Chris's number before I even thought of listening to them.

No reply at his home, so I tried his direct line at Rose Road Police Station. And got Diane Stephenson.

We greeted each other amicably enough, and skirted cautiously round the morning's events. She'd heard of my part in fighting the fire; I asked her, politely, if she'd made any progress on finding the arsonist.

'The problem is,' she said, 'we can't be sure it *is* just one. There are often copy-cat incidents, especially in big institutions.'

'What about the fire in the skip? There should be something on the security video.'

There was a pause.

'Someone,' she said at last, 'had forgotten to put a tape in the video recorder.'

'You're joking! No, you're not, are you? Don't tell me – the caretaker says there isn't any money to buy tapes.'

'Got it in one. God, it's worse than in the Force! Though you may have heard about the Devon police and their speed cameras – took so many photos of speeding motorists that they ran out of film! And other forces are leaving the cameras empty because they don't have the money to make the prosecutions!'

It was the first time she'd relaxed enough with me to make what could be described as conversation. Pity I was going to have to remind her of my former relationship with Chris . . .

The temperature changed as soon as I mentioned him.

'He's not available at the moment.'

'You couldn't leave him a message, could you?'

'He's very busy.'

Would I ever be so possessive if I had a man? *When*, Sophie – think positive!

'I know he is. But I do need to speak to him.' I nearly added a cringing 'please' but stopped myself in time.

'OK. I don't know when he'll be in, though.'

'If he left his answering machine on at home it'd be sensible. Tell him that from me, with my compliments! Now, how's Mike Appleyard?'

'Still unconscious, still in intensive care.'

'Any change?'

'None that I know about. Now. Sophie. I really do have things to do.'

'That,' I said, truthfully but not tactfully, 'makes two of us.'

Before ringing off I extracted a promise to ask Ian to phone me if she couldn't raise Chris. And regretted it at once; made me sound as if I were going behind her back on police business, which wasn't at all what I intended. Fearing that the more I explained, the messier it could get, I resisted the urge to tell her I needed to speak to Ian about the wine-tasting; she'd find out about that soon enough, if she was planning to partner Chris again.

The first phone message was from Chris, apologising for leaving me standing on William Murdock's front step and hoping I'd realized there must be a very good reason for it. Saved again. The second was from Greg; he'd found an Australian bar and was hoping to meet 'a mate'. The third was from Chris again, his voice full of suppressed excitement, telling me to expect him at about ten, when he'd bring in food for both of us.

Congratulating myself on my prescience, I headed for the fridge for bread and cheese to keep the grubs from biting in the particularly vicious way they'd recently started all over again. But Greg had finished the bread, and I didn't fancy the goat's cheese, which smelt for some inexplicable reason of billy goat. I'd have to pick up some bread from Sainsbury's when I headed to the Selly Oak outpost of the newly renamed University Hospital to see Aggie. Meanwhile, I'd made some chocolate muffins in a burst of domesticity during the summer holiday, and concealed them in my freezer for just such a moment. They wouldn't go with lager – I'd better stock up with that, too – but then, neither would a drive to Selly Oak on a virtually empty stomach. So the lager stayed where it was, and I settled for coffee milky enough to turn a purist's hair grey.

Aggie looked every one of her nearly eighty years. She seemed happy to lie with her eyes closed, resting her hand loosely on mine. There were sufficient flowers for an outpost of Interflora, but she'd insisted I put my roses, picked from the autumn beds in my garden, where she could smell them.

'Better than those shop ones,' she said suddenly, opening

126

her eyes and sniffing. 'That stuff I got sorted out those greenfly, me love.'

'I'll give them another dose this weekend – there's one or two of the little dears getting above themselves. I'll squirt yours, while I'm at it. And I'll feed your indoor plants, when I've a chance – this fine weather's confusing everything.'

'It'll be that global warming. I'm glad I got a new freezer. CFC free, they reckon. But I bet it's got something else in it just as nasty.' Her eyes closed again; when she opened them it seemed to be with an effort of will. 'They say I can only stay here a couple of weeks. They'll send me to some convalescent place if I'm not up to going home.'

'What about your granddaughters?' They were the only members of the family Aggie had any time for. 'Wouldn't they be offended if you didn't go to one of them?'

'Sophie, me love, that'd be lovely. But what about getting there? I wouldn't want them to take time off work to come and fetch me and I couldn't manage the bus, you know.'

'Not this week, maybe. Or even next. But there's always ambulances.'

'But they live out the back of beyond, both of them.'

'I'm sure we can sort it. Don't you worry,' I said, with more confidence than I felt. After all, I could always hire a private ambulance if necessary; I owed Aggie that much.

Greg wasn't in when I got home, but another message flashed on my machine. Afzal this time. I grabbed another muffin and ate it, still frozen, before I dialled. There was no doubt about it: my stomach was beginning its tantrums again. At least I still had some of the medicine left over from last time, and if I got desperate there was a little cache of the magic tablets that had settled it when it got bad enough for me to take to the doctor. The trouble with going to Dr Burrows was that she had the unpleasant habit of pointing out the obvious: I looked after my heart and legs by running; I conditioned my hair; I treated my skin to expensive cosmetics. Why therefore didn't I give my stomach a modicum of a chance by eating regularly and sensibly? I'd argued about the second adverb – I was proud of my diet and all the fruit and vegetables I managed to cram into a largely carnivorous regime. But the concept of regular meals and dedicated meal-breaks had long disappeared from William Murdock; even Worrall had believed that lunch was for wimps.

Afzal sounded as weary as I was beginning to feel.

'The arson at William Murdock seems to be catching,' he said. 'Several small businesses in Moseley have had similar attacks. A couple near to that refuge that Shahida's helping to fund.'

'Very small businesses then.' Perhaps I sounded dismissive.

'Yes. Family businesses. It's bad enough to lose your business, Sophie – tragic when your home goes as well.'

'Have the police got any leads?'

'They just want to dismiss them as the result of rivalries in the Asian community. They let people get away with murder, some of these policemen – literally murder! All someone has to do is play the ethnic minority card and the police back right off. One of my friends was in his favourite chip shop when a guy came in and blasted another to eternity, right in front of everyone's eyes. And he got away with it because the police wanted to believe it was an argument about different sorts of Islam and therefore something for "our people" to deal with.'

'That's a very serious allegation,' I said. Damn, there I was sounding like pompous Chris again! I tried to retreat. 'Didn't anyone try the police complaints people? Or talk to someone a bit more enlightened, like Chris Groom?'

'You know Chris, do you?'

'I went out with him for a bit. How do you two—'

'Oh, a lot of solicitors with Asian clients have discovered Chris. He's one of the good guys. It'd be nice to see him again.'

I toyed with the idea of inviting Afzal round to share our supper, but quickly abandoned it. 'He's in overall charge of the William Murdock investigations,' I said, conscious that I was being disingenuous. 'If I see him, can I pass on a message?'

'Just that I'd welcome the chance to speak to him. Er, Sophie – how's Greg getting on?'

'Getting plastered, I should think. He's on the beer tonight. I went to see Aggie.' I passed on the news. The conversation dwindled; a huge yawn gathered and burst. 'I'm sorry. I seem to be almost asleep.'

'I'm very tired, too. See you soon.'

As I ate another frozen muffin, I rewound the conversation. I'd made two comments that could be interpreted as racist, hadn't I? The worst sort of racism, perhaps – the unconscious sort. I sat and stared at the crumbs I'd left on the kitchen table and wished I could unsay them. Better still, unthink them.

Chapter Seventeen

I must have fallen asleep at the table, because it took me several moments to surface to the sound of my bell and door knocker being attacked simultaneously. Chris, with a polythene carrier bag full of assorted curries gently leaking from foil containers.

'Are you all right, Sophie?' he asked, peering at me as if we'd never been unhappy lovers, never broken up with unkind words.

'My usual state of William Murdock knackeredness,' I said, gesturing him in. 'So bad I forgot to put any plates to warm. Come on through – I'll microwave them. Are those poppadoms? Just what I need.'

Chris sat in his usual chair at the kitchen table. It was almost as if he'd never been away. 'William Murdock seems to be more than usually exciting. Any theories?' He tipped back on his chair so he could reach into the fridge for a couple of cans.

'Wish I had. Except – we're so desperate to recruit students nowadays we no longer ask for references. Attila the Hun could turn up to enrol, and we wouldn't even complain about the blood under his fingernails. We've taken in a lot of low-level students, kids who've failed in school or dropped out altogether. As you know, we've no playing fields for them to work off their spare energy, not even a yard for them to kick a ball around. So it could be them just having a lark. Aiming to miss classes they didn't like. Though come to think of it, all the fires have been at break or lunchtimes when they wouldn't be in class anyway.'

'So you wouldn't be able to trace absentees from class?'

'Exactly.' I fished the plates out and opened the carrier. 'Are these warm enough?'

'Pretty hot, probably! I know you prefer the spicier ones.' He applied a judicious finger to the topmost foil container. 'Just right.'

Fortunately he'd also bought a light, creamy korma and plenty of naan, though he raised an eyebrow when I pushed the rogan josh back at him. For explanation, helping myself to what I hoped was a mild dhal curry, I patted my stomach.

'Still bad?'

'Bad again, to be accurate. Fine during the holiday – now it's back. So it's pretty clear what causes it.'

'You must be more sensible about mealtimes.'

'Do as I say, not do as I do! How are your migraines?'

He pulled a face. 'I've got some medication which stops them laying me out cold. I can keep going through most of them.'

'Did you ever pursue the idea of Alexander Technique lessons? Of course you didn't! Come on, Chris – how about a bargain? You start lessons, and I'll eat properly.'

'Done! Any other ideas about the fires? What about the targets?'

'I've been wondering about those. Two stock rooms, a skip—'

'And a waste bin in the library tonight – just before the evening classes started. Damn it, Sophie, the place is swarming with officers, and it's *still* happening.'

Swarming? I wouldn't have used that word. Perhaps they'd been concentrated on other floors than the ones I used. 'The building's design asks to have crimes committed,' I said. 'You can't see from one end of the library to the other, for instance, because of the lift shafts and stairs running right down the centre.'

He nodded. 'Makes it difficult to site cameras: We insisted that Ms Fairbairn finds some money, by the way, although she said there wasn't any to spare. The first one went up this afternoon – vandalized within half an hour. Good job we've got a few tricks up our sleeves.'

'Hidden cameras, you mean? I'm surprised you haven't brought them in long before this.'

He fiddled with his naan before looking up. 'Some people think that ostentatious security is more successful.'

For 'people' read Diane.

'Clearly not, in this case. And what about Mike? What are you lot doing about finding Mike's attackers?'

He produced an enigmatic smile. And then transformed it into a proper one. 'He's conscious, Sophie! Still can't talk, and still partially paralysed, but we've managed to rustle up a computer he can operate with his breath. So tomorrow, as soon as the medics give the word, we can start asking him questions, get moving before the trail goes completely cold. Any questions you might like us to ask?'

I speared a prawn. 'Yes. Ask him if he smelt anything.'

'*Smelt*? What sort of smell? You mean alcohol, or solvents, or – hey, you're thinking about those lads you told Cole about! The ones who killed that bloke in the city centre.'

'Not just them. There's also a thoroughly nasty guy I told young PC Sidhu about, with a severe case of halitosis. And ego. And possibly a propensity for nicking official parking stickers.'

'I'll make sure Mike's asked.'

'You couldn't do it yourself?'

'It's Diane's case, Sophie. I'm not going to undercut her authority. It's bad enough her being on this wretched temporary up-grading. Why they won't consolidate the promotion, God knows.'

Was it that someone suspected she was drinking too much? I could scarcely ask Chris that, however, not if I wanted the mood to stay mellow.

I was spared by Greg's arrival: at least being drunk didn't stop *him* being affable. Chris looked from Greg to me and back again, a quizzical gleam in his eyes.

'Chris, I've not had a chance to tell you about Greg.' I paused while they shook hands, naughtily savouring the moment. 'Greg, this is Chris. An old friend.'

He beamed at Chris, pumping his arm up and down as if he were a long-lost brother. It turned out that he found me that rare sheila, one you can be cobbers with. Was that relief I saw on Chris's face?

'Great sheilas here in Brum. Hold their drink with the best of them. Met one tonight almost drank me under the table. But she hit the deck first, as it happens. Hey, is that going begging? I'm starving.' He grabbed some naan and mopped. 'So you're Chris. Sophie's told me about you. You're in the fuzz? Well, well. You're sure you don't want this?'

He found a plate, tipped the rice in a neat heap in the middle, and distributed the rogan josh, korma and dhal around the edges. Looking in vain for a fork, he tore off a scoop-sized piece of naan and weighed in.

'Where did you two meet?' Chris asked.

'Berlin. We – well, someone had picked Courtney's pocket—'

'Groped him, more like!' Greg suggested.

Chris's grin was cooler. 'Is that the Courtney I think you mean?'

'Yep! They've bought the film rights, and he's a minor media sensation. And still extremely gay.'

'Does Tina know?' Chris valued her highly as an officer and as a human being.

'About Courtney's being gay? Yes. About our trip to Berlin? No. I haven't seen her to tell her myself, and I'd be happier if she didn't hear it on the grapevine.' I liked Tina myself, even though we irritated each other if kept in close proximity.

'Not much chance. She's off very soon to do liaison work with some Third World force – a year's secondment. There's talk of a booze-up to send her on her way. Interested?'

I was sure he'd only asked me to be courteous, but the salient words caught Greg's ear.

'Sure we'll go!' he said, waving more naan. 'Any excuse, eh? Just tell us when.'

I looked daggers at Chris.

'Sure. Soon as I know the details,' he said. 'Sophie, I must be going.' He stood, burping gently and looking as if he'd embarrassed the vicar. 'See you around, Greg.' Greg flapped a hand. 'If you have any brainwaves, you'll give me – give *Diane* a call, won't you?'

'I'll pop down and see her, provided I ever get another one.' I followed him to the front door. 'You won't forget our bargain, will you? Your shoulders need a helping Alexander hand.'

'I'll phone for an appointment first thing.'

'Good. And I'll go and pack a nice, healthy lunch for tomorrow. Make sure I've no excuse.'

He stood on the step, saying nothing, not leaving.

'Give Ian my love,' I said. And closed the door.

I'd already started my car the following morning when I remembered my healthy lunch, sitting in the fridge. I galloped back, breaking a nail as I opened the front door, and hurtled to the kitchen.

The fridge was as bare as Mother Hubbard's would have been. I exaggerate; various odds and sods always lurked, of course. The brandy butter from last Christmas, some redcurrant jelly ditto. Things like that a-plenty. No sandwiches. The box they'd been in stood forlornly on the draining board, not draining because it hadn't been washed.

Antipodean mice, no doubt.

Greg hadn't responded to my morning yell; he'd no classes till this afternoon, so I could scarcely complain about that. But I'd have liked to complain about other things – the effect he was having on my love life, for instance, not to mention my digestion. Presumably enraged at the fate of its rightful filling, my stomach was in killer mode all of a sudden. I swigged from the antacid bottle, grabbed another tube of tablets – more portable than the liquid – and returned to the car. Oh, I hadn't locked my keys in, or anything. But somewhere down at the bottom of the road, someone had evidently hit someone else. A brand-new queue was congealing nicely.

I was due to make two softening-up visits today: one before, one after, my morning class. I'd picked out my only trouser suit; it had been an expensive impulse buy. Every time I wore it I swore its next journey would be to the

Oxfam shop. Despite the excellence of its cut and colour all it could ever say about me was that I was short. To wear a trouser suit successfully you need to be as tall as Diane Stephenson – though I always looked good in jeans. But you can't wear jeans to chat up employers.

Unfortunately the first employer – a director of a medium-sized stationery supplier who'd been supplying William Murdock for years – thought I was there to do precisely that. I knew within ten seconds of his taking my elbow, ostensibly to guide me through an open door but actually to feel my breast, that I couldn't send any of our students to him. Not even the men – I didn't want latent sexism to burgeon under the example of this over-upholstered man with his Jaguar abandoned rather than parked outside. I had to go through the questions for form's sake, however, though I did truncate the list when his foot found my calf to smarm up to. But at least his secretary thought my trouser suit was smart.

After a pleasant interlude doing what I liked best – teaching – I was on the road again. S Mohinder, Solicitors. This time the premises were unpretentious, the car neatly parked was a Fiesta and the young man I spoke to was more than anxious to oblige. He was so swamped with papers I had to stop myself offering to give him a hand there and then. But he simply didn't have the time to train students in anything meaningful – that was obvious. All they would be able to do was make tea and photocopy, and that wasn't the point of work placements.

'I could do with a full-time assistant,' he said.

I nodded. 'There must be a lot of people who'd love the job.'

'No money to pay them, Ms Rivers. I don't attract rich clients. In fact, I may have to give up altogether.'

'How dreadful! But what would you do?'

'I thought I might go into teaching. Not a school – a college like yours. What do you think?'

How fortunate my job trained me to be diplomatic.

Reminded by the vicious jabs in my stomach, I stopped off

in the canteen to buy some sandwiches. Despite the NO
SMOKING notices everywhere – we'd become a smoke-
free college over the summer holiday – people were
smoking, and I had a nasty suspicion I could smell pot. Over
in the corner: the air was fuzzy with it. I had a terse word
with the smokers, getting even terser ones back. This was a
matter for Security. Five foot one of Sophie was not going
to risk life and limb merely to breathe purer air. Ostentatiously I wrote down what my interlocutors had said, and
where they were sitting, and headed downstairs to find back-
up. Needless to say, there was only one security guard on
duty in the foyer.

'Can't leave here, Sophie. Sorry, but we're really short-
staffed.'

'Short-staffed! With all this arson?'

'We've had people laid off. To pay for the security
cameras.'

Groaning, I headed back upstairs. I'd better talk to
Dan . . .

Florence looked at the clock. 'You might just catch him
– he usually leaves for lunch about now. I'll buzz him.'

He was actually shrugging on his coat when I saw him.
Since the weather was still mild, I presumed it was a display
of status rather than a means of keeping warm. Yves St
Laurent, eh? He produced a comb and tidied that wing of
hair.

I outlined the canteen problem as briefly as I could – no
point antagonising a man by keeping him from his no doubt
splendid lunch.

'So what are you complaining about precisely?' he asked.

'One, they're smoking where they shouldn't. Two, they're
smoking an illegal substance. Three, they were very rude to
a member of staff reminding them of college rules – not
to mention the law. Four, although we're in a crisis, we don't
seem to have any security staff around.'

'Five, we can't afford to lose students. So button your lip.
For goodness' sake, woman, you were sensible about your
skirts. Be sensible about this!'

'Knowingly allowing people to smoke illegal substances

on your premises is a criminal offence. And the police are in the vicinity—'

'Are you threatening to report—'

'Dan, they've got noses. You can smell pot a mile off. All you want is one keen constable to fancy a cup of tea. Imagine the newspaper headlines—'

'OK – you've made your point. Now, can I remind you that this is a confidential matter—'

'No, it isn't! We were talking about it in that staff meeting the other day!'

'You're so bone-headed, woman! Now, if you'll excuse me—' He held open the door. I had no option but to pass through it.

Furious, I couldn't trust myself not to explode to my colleagues if I went straight to the staffroom, so I adjourned to the staff loo, only to find the sole cubicle occupied. At last Diane Stephenson emerged. She seemed to be about to leave without washing her hands – I was shocked how repellent I found this and had a terrible urge to point out rules of elementary hygiene. But she was Diane Stephenson, a woman in a tough job, and I just called her back: 'Could I pop into your room – have a quick word?'

She flashed a look at her watch. 'Five minutes,' she said.

Did that mean I had to wait five minutes, or simply that that was all the time she had to spare? Assuming it was the former, I used the loo and – having discovered the hot water was cold today – I set off after her.

She was wearing the sort of jacket over her well-cut trousers that I'd have given my teeth to be able to wear. She had redefined her make-up, and the way she'd flipped back her hair emphasized her cheek-bones. Yes, she was looking good; I could see in my mind's eye Chris's appreciative smile. OK, I didn't know she was off to meet Chris, but I sensed – perhaps unfairly – that she wouldn't make that sort of effort for a woman.

An ostentatious glance at her watch told me I'd already had more of her time than she could spare.

'Any news about Mike?' I asked. 'Did you ask him about the smell?'

'You sure you wouldn't rather do my job? Look, Sophie, I have seen Mike, but the questions I ask are the ones *I* think are necessary.'

'You *didn't* ask about the smell?' If we were to have a row it might as well be over something vitally important.

'It is none of your business.'

'I rather think it is. One of my colleagues killed, another at death's door – fires all over the place, including out in Moseley—'

'Have you established a connection? Because, try as we might, West Midlands Police can't. When you have hard evidence about anything, Ms Rivers, I'd be grateful. In the meantime, spare me your suggestions.'

Just like that. With an interested audience of coppers, some of whom knew me.

'OK – I presume you don't need me to tell you about the drug abuse in the canteen. Or that Dan's—' My big mouth! There was no reason why the police shouldn't know about his record – whatever it was – but I didn't want to throw the information around simply because I was angry.

'Dan's – what?' She was too much of a professional not to have noticed.

Not trusting myself to keep whatever secret he had, I turned on my heel and walked away.

RIVERS OUT! urged a chalk-written scrawl on my staff-room door. Wishing it was a statement of fact, I rubbed it out. So long as they stayed polite, people were welcome to insult me.

Apparently there was a similar one on the board of the classroom I taught in later, but my students were so outraged they had already rubbed it off when I sailed in. Mature students. I was sure I could acquit them of any part in it. More likely the Asians who didn't like my skirts, or the pot-smoking students.

A couple of women wanted help after the class, so the college seemed uncannily empty when I headed down the stairs for the car park. Suddenly, there was a rush of feet behind me. Before I could turn and rebuke the runner, I was pushed down the stairs.

Not hard. But sharply enough to make me fall. My bag bowled in one direction, my marking in another – and me, despite my frantic grabs at the stair-rail, in a third. And whoever had done it disappeared before I could struggle back on my feet. Where should I check? The stairs? The four lifts? I darted back up to the corridor, but there was no one around to question, let alone chase. Then a lift door pinged shut. The only thing I could do was race down all those stairs and hope to—

Hell, I didn't have a chance, did I? It seemed my dignity was hurt far more than my knees and hands, in any case. Shrugging, I gathered my possessions, dusted myself off and continued down the stairs.

Chapter Eighteen

I fell into step with Carl – more of an old glimmer than an old flame – as we left the building. He'd doubtless stayed late to avoid spending the whole of the evening with his wife; if we hadn't had that tiny affair – how many bonks constitutes an affair? – I'd have suggested we have a quiet drink, but he'd never quite believed that what little we'd had was over. As it was, we stood chatting in the empty car park – Birmingham tends to stop work at five or earlier on Fridays.

'I've had enough, you know,' he said. He took my silence for what it was; an invitation to continue. 'Enough of my job, my marriage – everything. I work my socks off teaching, then I spend an hour or more on the phone in the evening chasing recalcitrant students, then there are all these meetings so you haven't a prayer of doing the marking or preparation you need. And I'm supposed to keep up to date with all the new developments in Pharmacy. And it's changing fast, believe me.'

I nodded, sympathetically. Perhaps I should suggest that drink.

'And then there's home ... She doesn't like me working when I'm supposed to be talking to her – not that we ever do talk, we just stare at the TV. So I start work at nine when she's gone to bed—'

'At nine!'

'Needs her rest, she says.' He shrugged. 'She says her back's so bad I'll have to take responsibility for the housework. Funny how none of the tests or X-rays have ever shown anything. And she won't go to an osteopath. And by the way, it's time I learned to cook in case anything happens to her. Sophie, you wouldn't fancy popping across the road for a quick half, would you?'

'Won't it make it worse if she smells booze on your breath?'

'Believe me, nothing could make anything worse.'

Except it could. We did pop across the road for a half, and I suppose we nattered for half an hour, maybe an hour – talking shop, chewing over the William Murdock disasters. I was careful to keep the talk well away from anything more personal. At last, when his arm started creeping round my shoulders, it was time to call it a day. At least I had something to look forward to: choir practice. And I needed to pick up some sandwiches from Tesco, in an attempt to keep my bargain with Chris.

My Renault sat modestly in the furthest corner of the car park; Carl had parked brashly in the middle, the red of his Alfa Romeo bright against the tarmac. We stood by the barrier, Carl prolonging the conversation. As we talked, his eyes strayed over my head. They widened. Before I knew it, he'd flung himself on top of me.

There was an almighty bang.

If he hadn't knocked me down, I'm sure the blast would have done. When he got up, shaking his head, his knuckles were running with blood. He didn't seem to notice – he was too busy rubbing his ears, pulling his fingers in and out as if to make them pop. Mine were ringing too.

Where the red car had been, red and yellow flames danced.

The last thing I'd have expected him to do was laugh. Albeit semi-hysterically.

'Well,' he said, 'the lengths some men go for an excuse to be late home!'

'What did you see?' I asked urgently. 'That moment before you pushed me over – what did you see?'

'She'll never believe me, Sophie.'

141

'What did you see, Carl? Or who? Come on, while it's still fresh in your mind—'

'There was some body rot. D'you think the insurance assessors will be able to tell?'

I could have shaken him. 'Carl. Listen. Your car has just been blown up, and we could have been blown up with it. What did you *see*?' I may have been shaking him. Certainly I was gripping his upper arms so tightly he would have a set of finger-sized bruises to explain.

Funny: neither of us noticed the huge fire appliance thundering down on us. It wasn't until a fire-fighter herded us away from the barrier that I even heard the klaxon. It wasn't until PC Parminder Sidhu ushered us gently into his Panda that I realized I was crying.

Safely and uneventfully at the church hall we used for choir rehearsals, I passed a splendid two hours. Verdi's *Requiem*: I forgot the pain in my stomach, the ache of my feet, the tiredness that felt like a physical weight. All I had to remember was how to sing, and that's as easy as breathing. It was tempting to join the others afterwards in the Duke of Clarence, but as soon as the music was over my stomach started to jab, and I couldn't stop yawning. Time to head for home, and pray for a wonderful oversleep the next day. Except I was on the late enrolment roster. From ten till twelve I'd be extending a welcome to students who'd finally got their acts together and decided to try a bit of education, three weeks late. Home, and bed. And a prayer that Greg had decided to have another night on the beer and would creep in quietly in the small hours. I couldn't cope with jolly conversation. Maybe the answering machine would be call-free. Maybe I could have a nice hot bath . . .

I'd better eat something first. The stomach pain was so bad, I sloshed down a couple of measures of antacid before I even took my jacket off; if this went on much longer I'd have to buy some shares in pharmaceutical companies. Nibbling at dry toast, I slipped off my shoes and padded over to the phone. Bother the messages: I wanted to talk to Chris.

I got him first ring.

'Yes, I know,' he said, before I could say anything. 'Turned their attention to cars now.'

'Carl Yeoman's Alfa. Carl told that Scottish student off a couple of weeks ago.'

'Not exactly a spontaneous riposte. Not like what he did to Mike.'

'What he did – Chris, what have you got?' I must have deafened the poor man.

'The assailant had halitosis, Mike said. I popped round myself and asked. But the college can't find any Scots on its books, Sophie.'

'What do you mean, can't find any Scots? You can't fake an accent like that. Can't the computer system throw up anything?'

'No one thought Scottish was a useful field. If he'd been Chinese or something, yes. A lot of Macs and Mcs on the system, but none with a Scottish home address. Never mind – only about seven thousand students to interview and eliminate. Well, fewer than that – no one's yet suggested this guy's a woman or masquerading as one.'

'No,' I said. 'But he could be masquerading as something else. Remember the make-up I found in the Mondiale car park!'

'Surely you'd notice if a guy in your class was habitually wearing make-up? No, chances are he's got an ordinary, non-Scottish name and lives in Balsall Heath. Sorry.'

I said something I didn't want to say but felt was necessary. 'Chris, I wonder if you'd give Diane a message for me? It's urgent. It's important – I want her to take it seriously. I was in a hell of a temper at lunchtime and said something I shouldn't – about another member of staff. Could you just remind her that our conversation should be regarded as absolutely confidential?'

'When I see her. She's out with friends tonight. Hen party or something.' He sounded more distressed at the thought of her having a night on the tiles than I'd have expected. Not like Chris to be possessive . . .

'Any chance you could leave a message – ' I nearly said, '*on her pillow*', but quickly substituted – 'on her machine?'

'It's important, you say.' It was a statement, not a question. 'OK. No problem.'

There obviously was; he sounded as strained as I'd ever heard him. But I wouldn't probe, not yet, not now we were just getting back to being friends again. Once trust was back in our relationship – that'd be the time.

'So, when are we going to have that drink?' I asked, conveniently forgetting to tell him I'd missed our second appointment too.

'Monday? No, wait – I'm at Tally-Ho! all day being trained. And Tuesday ... look, I'll try and clear Thursday lunchtime, shall I?'

No evenings, I noted: they were presumably Diane's preserve. I took a risk. 'How about we make it official police business? We've always done well, bouncing ideas off each other, and I need to clarify a few things.'

'What you're trying to say is that you've got stuff that might be useful to me. OK, Sophie, you're on. But I can't make it before Thursday. How do I get you out of college? Arrest you?'

'Not until after I've taught my morning class.' I laughed, sourly. 'This is stupid. All my friends are being attacked, Chris – and – Chris, couldn't we have a coffee over the weekend?' Tears were coming faster than I'd have believed; They ran down my nose, into my mouth, over my chin.

There was a silence. 'Diane and I were hoping to get away—'

'Right. Fine. Thursday it is,' I said, putting the phone down quickly. I didn't want him to hear the crack in my voice, or the sob that was forcing its way out.

I'd just finished a second piece of toast when Greg, like Tigger in mid-bounce, made his entrance. He'd clearly been on the beer, but he was as cheerful as ever.

'Met this sheila again. Turns out she knows you. Any Vegemite? Don't worry – Marmite'll do. Just a couple of rounds. Great.' He spread the toast thickly with butter, slathered on Marmite and sank on to one of the kitchen chairs

144

as if he'd been toiling on his building site all day. 'She's a policewoman. Diane something. A friend of yours, is she?'

'Friend of a friend. That's all.' I turned quickly to pop a couple more slices into the toaster; he hadn't noticed my puffy face and red eyes, and I'd no particular desire to draw attention to them.

'Yeah, she said. That Chris. Decent bloke, Chris.'

'Yes. A good man.'

He looked at me sharply; I'd given the phrase more emphasis than I'd intended.

'The sort who'd like an alkie for a girlfriend?'

'As bad as that?' The pain was so bad I grabbed the table. Antacid. Fast.

'Well,' he said, fishing the toast out and spreading it, 'I drink. Quite a lot. But then, I'm a big bloke. I'm not being sexist – it's all to do with body mass, right? And maybe I do have a couple too many, once in a while. Like tonight. But I'm not pissed, Sophie, even if I couldn't drive a car. Not pissed enough not to notice you've been having a good cry. Right? Well, that sheila was pissed. As a newt. And the trouble is, if you get that pissed on a regular basis, you start letting things drift. Why d'you think I stay on the straight and narrow most of the time? Because of my job, see. If I press the wrong button on my calculator – get the decimal point in the wrong place – we're in a mess. But I'd say she's got a responsible job. Bodies, not concrete. OK, she's great when she's had a few – funny and all that. And I bet she's a good lay – no, I haven't found out, but I could have done, easy. If you get my meaning.' He paused.

I groped for something to say. All I could manage was, 'Where have you come across her? To know about her boozing?'

'Well, I saw her in college first. She's a striking woman, Sophie, no doubt about that. Then she was in the Aussie bar last night. I said hello, what's a nice girl like you doing in a place like this – or words to that effect. And she was there again tonight – without the bloke though, this time. So we got talking again.'

'I take it the bloke she was with last night wasn't Chris,' I said.

145

'Well, no. Course not. Or when we met here we might have been a bit more—' He shrugged. 'Nice bloke, Chris, like I said.'

'So tell me about the man she was with.'

He pulled a face. 'Don't expect me to tell you whether he's attractive or whatever. I couldn't judge that, being a bloke myself.'

'Sexist twaddle. I wasn't talking attractive, anyway, I was talking appearance – height, that sort of thing.'

'Well, not quite as tall as Diane. Quite a flash dresser, specially for a place like that. Forty. Dark hair. She seemed to think he was – attractive. I suppose an Aussie bar is a good place for not running into Chris, if you're having a bit on the side.'

'Oh, God.'

'So what are you going to tell Chris?' He bit into his toast and sat back.

'What *can* I tell Chris? I used to go out with him. It'd sound like sour grapes.'

'Come on, Soph. You're a grown woman – he's a grown man. And he's in the police.'

'And he's her senior officer, wondering why they won't consolidate her promotion.'

'Well, they always say love's blind. OK, Soph – take your point. Hey, you OK? You don't look so good.'

'Stomach ache. And I'm very tired. And I've forgotten to water Aggie's plants. And I've got to go to work tomorrow morning.'

He got up and gave me a crumby hug. 'Poor Soph! Come on, kid – you hit the hay. I'll sort things out down here. And I'll do the old lady's plants tomorrow. Any plans for the rest of the day?'

My conscience clicked in. 'It's time you saw some Brum, isn't it? Tell you what, we'll have lunch somewhere nice and I'll show you a few sights.' After all, I needed an afternoon off. I smiled. 'Where shall we meet?'

'Outside the college? Soon as you've finished.'

'Say one, then.' There always seemed to be someone who came in at the last moment with a complicated problem. 'That'll cover all eventualities.'

146

'Good on you. Now, go and take some more of that medicine and get yourself some shut-eye.'

For once I did as I was told.

I'd got as far as the hall when I realized all was not well. It didn't take much realising. A rubber gloves and disinfectant job, this. To get the excrement off my carpet. No, not just a doggie dollop Greg or I had accidentally trodden in. Enough to make me quite sure someone had posted it through my letterbox.

Chapter Nineteen

Saturday morning is not my favourite time to be in college. Not when there seems little point in being there at all. I'd made a silent, totally useless protest by wearing that trouser suit I so disliked, but it went unnoticed. Eventually I recruited a couple of women, neither especially promising, for our Access courses, and drifted over to the A-level table to see if they needed any help. They were underwhelmed too. It occurred to me that I hadn't checked my pigeon-hole for a couple of days; so I told Malcolm and Sean where I was heading and left my colleagues in the hall to fend off the non-existent hordes. There was the usual junk mail; and also a couple of requests from ex-students for references. On the merest off-chance, I poked my nose into the charred mess that had been our records room; as Dan had said, there was nothing anyone could salvage. I stood looking across the police tape, taking in all those ruined hours of work, and found myself nearer to tears than I liked. Nothing for it, then, but to pass the reference requests to the people in the records section, who'd no doubt organized a standard letter, apologising and explaining. If they hadn't, it was certainly not my responsibility.

'Sophie!' It was Dan. 'What are you doing up here? You're supposed to be on duty in the hall.'

'Trying to clear some of my admin backlog,' I said, tapping the requests. 'All the excitement of the last week – I've got behind. Shame about Carl Yeoman's car, by the way.'

'Yeoman?'

'He's not in your department. He teaches Pharmacy. I

148

thought you'd have heard, though. His car went the way of our files last night.'

'What?' For a second his eyes blazed with anger; then he smiled, coolly. 'Why should I have heard?'

'These things get around, don't you find?' I said. 'By the way, Dan, could I talk to you on Monday about my time-table? There seems to be a problem about dropping some of the classes. We agreed I should drop to seventy-five per cent of my timetable—'

'I'm not aware of any problem. We agreed seventy-five per cent of the average timetable. You'll find many new contract people are teaching twenty-eight hours a week. Without that GCSE class you're about right.'

It was a good job he turned on his heel and walked away: for once in my life I was speechless.

On my way back to the hall, still seething at being so neatly out-manoeuvred, I ran into Frank, the union rep. He was beaming – an unusual state of affairs. I asked him if I could see him on Monday too – it was probably too late to retrieve my situation – although I'd signed nothing I might well have a verbal contract around my neck – but I should warn others.

'Nothing doing on Monday, I'm afraid. You'll never guess – you know this bad back of mine?'

I nodded; he'd been plagued with pain for months, even to the point of missing the odd day of college.

'Well, Personnel have fixed for me to see a consultant, with a view to private treatment. They say now the college is freed from the limitations of local authority control it can dispose of its budget according to its needs. And it's cheaper for them to get me treated than for me to take a lot of time off. How's that for imaginative management?'

'The caring Fairbairn. Well, that's excellent news, Frank. I hope they soon sort you out. Just one thing: *Quidquid id est, timeo Danaos et dona ferenti.*'

'I beg your pardon?'

'It's Latin for watch your back, even when you think they're friendly.'

Early in the afternoon, Greg and I joined a small party touring one of my favourite of Birmingham's tourist sites: perhaps *the* favourite. The Jewellery Quarter Discovery Centre. Back in 1981 two brothers and their sister walked out of the factory they ran, never to return. Somehow it never got vandalized or demolished, and eventually it was rediscovered, the fabric rotting around it. A team of industrial archaeologists repaired the building, and then reinstated the contents: from tools and ledgers to tea-cups. Practising jewellers give regular conducted tours, and a rota of other jewellers demonstrate their craft at an authentic bench. To walk in is to walk into a time capsule, sealed almost twenty years ago on practices dating from the last century and beyond.

Greg was open-mouthed with the delight the place always rekindles in me. All the guides I've met there are good – and I've met several, making it, as I do, a point of honour to take any visitors to the city along – but today's was particularly brilliant, an impish man called Dennis. At various points he and Greg talked health and safety – and chemicals, to Greg's increasing horror.

'All I can say, Soph, is that it's a good job *you* weren't employed here! All these poisons!'

'What are you implying, young man?' I demanded.

'Well, you could have used them on your students. No, seriously, anyone with asthma – I mean, if the atmosphere can do that to that extractor fan–' he pointed to an eroded vestige – 'think what it'd do to your lungs!'

There was the inevitable souvenir shop, this one with some very high-class goodies. Which set Greg off: he wanted to buy me a present. We discussed the idea over a cup of tea and cake at the café next door.

I still wasn't at all sure how our relationship should be defined. 'Mates', was probably how he'd describe it. So what did a mate – or indeed a cobber – let her cobber buy her? A nice chain, he suggested, when I discounted the idea of a ring. And there must be four hundred or more shops in the area selling jewellery made in the area, most of which sold chains. At last, in the shop we'd first been to, I found the one I wanted, only about an hour after we'd left the Centre.

'It's your fault,' I said. 'You should have let me have it in the first place.'

'Never make a decision till you've seen what the opposition have on offer,' he said. 'Which reminds me – how's that Afzal guy?'

That was a question I'd been trying not to ask myself. I should have phoned, if only to apologize for the prejudiced flavour of my comments on the phone last time we'd spoken. Or to ask about him taking on a student. Or simply to say hello.

On the other hand, he might have phoned me.

'Well?'

'I thought I'd wait till we got back to phone him. While you have a beer. Then you and I are going to have a balti. Baltis are Brum's national dish – if you see what I mean. We're heading for the Ladypool Road, you and me, Greg. But first we're going to a chamber music concert.'

'We what?'

'I'm a member of the Chamber Music Society. We don't play – we listen. And tonight it's the Australian String Quartet, so you should feel at home.'

'What's the programme?'

'Haydn, Borodin and Brahms.'

'Not the Borodin one that goes—' He broke into song – one of the big tunes they used in *Kismet*. It was nice to know that even with people you thought were mates – or cobbers – there was always something to surprise you.

The ASQ were heading up the M6 for a Sunday gig in Manchester, so Greg couldn't induce any of them to get convivial with him afterwards. The concert had been a great success, though the Society's membership was perhaps unused to men whistling and yipping their approval of a performance. Personally I felt nothing but envy; I'd tried for years to persuade my mouth and fingers to work as one.

I'd taken care not to offend my stomach, feeding it little morsels all day and dosing it from time to time so it would

151

consume a balti without getting stroppy. To reduce the intimacy a bit, I'd also invited Shahida and Tanvir – and dithered about phoning Afzal. When I finally plucked up courage, he'd sounded off-hand, though he'd agreed in principle to accept some work-placement students. I had mentioned the meal in a casual way, but he said he was tied up. He promised to phone during the week, however.

The meal was a success. Tanvir and Greg had a wonderful time reminiscing about airports they had known, and Shahida and I caught up on William Murdock and other gossip. It was the first time we'd had a proper chance to talk since she'd put the phone down on me. Neither of us mentioned that. It was more pleasant to talk about Maria. Women's talk. All right, maybe sexism had triumphed over racism, but so long as everyone was happy, what the hell. And then, just as we were debating whether we could possibly contemplate a sweet designed to extract fillings from your wisdom teeth – and my stomach had decided that it was not prepared to, whatever the rest of me might think – in came Afzal. He'd brought a couple of four-packs – the restaurant was unlicensed – and the waiter promised him the quickest supper he'd ever had. The table had accommodated four, so we had to shuffle and squeeze; I ended up on a corner, since I wasn't going to eat any more, and it was noticeable that Greg and Afzal took up positions on either side of me. Shahida caught my eye and winked. Tanvir made valiant attempts to continue with his tales of the Duty Free, but Greg was having none of it. He started knocking back Afzal's lager, but since I'd only ever known alcohol make him more affable, I wasn't alarmed.

Meanwhile, Afzal was asking about visiting Aggie.

'She'd love to see you,' I said. 'But don't tell her it was Greg, not me, who watered her house plants this morning.'

'Strewth, I only bleeding forgot, didn't I? Sorry, Soph. Looks like a job we'll have to do tomorrow.'

Did I notice a slight emphasis on the pronoun?

'I was hoping you might come with me to the hospital,' Afzal pursued.

'Of course I will. Tomorrow afternoon. Tell you what –

come and have some lunch first. Then perhaps we could show Greg more of Birmingham's tourist attractions.'

'Like Selly Oak Sainsbury's?' asked Shahida.

'Exactly,' I said. 'Or the Lickey Hills – or the odd museum or two. You like art, don't you, Greg? Well, we could go to the Barber Institute.'

'I've always meant to go there,' Afzal said, quickly. 'Do you mind if I come too?'

'I assumed that you would,' I said.

To my surprise, Greg was smiling happily. Or was happily the right word? There were other qualities to his smile – complacent lechery amongst them. And Afzal was smiling too, but in a rather bemused fashion.

I knew Greg ate anything put before him, but I couldn't ask Afzal to lunch without asking him. Could I?

'Afzal,' I said, 'I know you eat fish. But are you a carnivore or a vegetarian for preference?'

'I prefer halal meat, Sophie, I'm afraid.'

'That's where you cut the poor little bugger's throat, isn't it?' Greg observed. 'And let it bleed to death—'

'We'd all be veggies if we had to kill the animals ourselves,' I said firmly. 'So you're OK with fish again, Afzal? I can pop into Safeway tomorrow – get some trout,' I added, thinking aloud.

'No, you've got all that marking to do. I'll go for you, Sophie. Reckon I'm a good judge of fish,' Greg said. 'Then we'll cook it, ready for Afzal.'

This time there was definitely an emphasis on 'we' and his smile was intensifying. On my other side Afzal now looked distinctly puzzled. As did I. At this point, however, my stomach reminded me that it had endured a great deal of wonderful spicy food without the comfort of its antacid brew. At least I could pacify it with some tablets; as unobtrusively as I could I reached under the table for my bag.

There was Greg's leg, stretched over into my space. And there too was Afzal's.

And Greg was rubbing his calf affectionately over Afzal's.

I sat, holding the bag on my lap, wondering what on earth to do. Malice told me to pat both encouragingly on the thigh: common sense told me to cool Greg as quickly as possible, otherwise I might find him abandoning his chaste spare-room bed. And I was keen to develop the relationship with Afzal; a public humiliation for him was not part of my game plan. Greg's bouncy ego would cope.

Eventually, my stomach tying itself into a knot, I pushed away from the table to retreat to the loo and chomp a couple of tablets. My only regret was that I would miss such a wide variety of facial expressions.

Afzal was subdued when I returned: no doubt about it. On the other hand, Greg was not. In fact, the way he laughed and slapped the table made me suspect that he was about to blow the whole thing. Time for action.

'Shahida,' I said, 'I'm sorry to break things up, but my tum's really bad.'

This produced the response I wanted: chaotic concern. Within five minutes we were on the pavement, distributing ourselves into cars. Afzal drifted unhappily. I went up to him.

'About twelve-thirty tomorrow?' I said reassuringly.

'What about – are you sure you're well enough?'

'Trout'll be much milder than curry,' I insisted. 'No problem. Then we can go to see Aggie and educate Greg a bit.'

'Perhaps you'd care to come back to my place for a cup of tea afterwards,' he said. 'If you're up to it.'

'I'll make sure I am,' I said, and kissed him lightly on the lips.

Dismissing Greg with no more than a peck on the cheek, I took the extra precaution of locking my bedroom door. Quietly, not ostentatiously: after all, he'd had every opportunity to be racist, but he'd managed to be pleasant to everyone all evening. That didn't prove a thing, of course, and it wasn't really cause for congratulation. But I very much wanted us to remain friends.

I succumbed to one temptation on Saturday night, which was to take some of the high-powered stomach drugs designed to reduce the production of acid. Since I'd only a few left, this meant I'd have to take time off work for a trip to my GP.

Well, I'd just have to put up with the scolding I knew I'd get from Dr Burrows.

I felt much better on Sunday. Greg was still snoring when I watered Aggie's plants, and though he was up by the time I'd showered and dressed, I took virtuous pleasure in cycling down to Safeway's while he was in the bathroom. Since my raid involved the *Observer* and fresh croissants for breakfast, I suspected he wouldn't see this as a slight.

Lunch went smoothly enough, and Greg seemed happy to stay in my car reading while Afzal and I visited Aggie, who greeted us with enthusiastic kisses.

Taking my hand, she said, 'I reckon I've fixed it to go down and stay with Luce – that's my eldest granddaughter, Azfal.'

Politely, he didn't correct her.

'That's excellent. And you have transport arranged?'

'Private ambulance. Me health insurance covers that.' I'd no idea Aggie was the BUPA sort. 'And someone'll come in every day to help dress me and undress me. And bath me, once a week. Not that I need that – Luce'll help me have a shower. She's a nurse, you see. Got a university degree and all. I shall pay my way, mind – I get all this money from me insurance just for lying here, so she might as well have it. And look – here she is!'

We stayed long enough to be courteous, but two visitors per bed was the rule, so we returned to Greg more quickly than we'd expected. And thence, since the weather was overcast and chilly, to the Barber Institute, a gallery on Birmingham University's campus. It's small, but most of the items are perfect examples of their kind. Every so often they reshuffle everything, so while it's irritating not to find what you want where you expected it to be, sometimes you have the pleasure of meeting an old friend before you imagined you would. I'd left the men to go at their own pace, while I tried once more to make sense of some of the religious Old Masters, for which I never managed to whip up much enthusiasm. Suddenly, Greg and Afzal arrived, one each side of me, and I was frogmarched – gently – to the end of one of the galleries. We stopped before a portrait by Elisabeth Vigee le Brun.

155

'There!' Greg announced. 'Told you! It's Sophie!'

'It's nothing like me!' I said.

'He's right, Sophie. OK, you're blonde, and she's brunette – and your eyes are blue, not brown—'

'And I'm a couple of stone lighter!'

'But you've got that impish expression about your eyes. Turn your head a little, lift your hand – there you are, the Countess Golovin reincarnated.'

They flattered me, of course. I could never be that sensuous, that flirtatious. But it was nice to see them in accord. Greg bought himself a postcard copy of the portrait when we left; so did I. Afzal didn't, merely replying, when Greg pressed him, that he preferred to see the original – he smiled at the ambiguity – and that anyway the colours were wrong for his house.

He was right, of course. He lived in a terraced house in Kings Heath, much more spacious than the rather poky outside suggested, and he'd decorated it in cool, but light colours. Non-representational art was the order of the day here.

'Nice place, this,' Greg observed. 'Like your fireplaces – were they here when you came?'

'Yes. And the ceiling-roses and cornices.'

We talked house restoration for a while; drank tea; ate cakes from Sainsbury's. My stomach allowed itself the odd rumble, but behaved itself in general. Afzal talked about a trip he was making to Bradford the following day; Greg about his German classes. On impulse, when Greg was in the loo, I asked Afzal for his mobile number.

'You never know,' I said, 'I might be so desperate to place a student I can't wait till you're in Brum.'

'I'll do my best even if I'm in John O'Groats!' he declared.

And there it was; a perfect stress-free Sunday. OK, I was way behind with my marking, but I'd thought of a way to deal with that: I'd take a bundle on my next work-experience visit, and simply sit in a park somewhere and get on with it. That way no one – Management or student – could interrupt. And I'd see somewhere green for a change.

Chapter Twenty

'Ms Rivers? Ms Sophie Rivers?'

I stared. Even the security staff knew me by my first name. And it didn't take two of them standing side by bulky side in the foyer to ask me.

'Yes or no?'

I laughed. 'Come on, Cliff – you know who I am.'

'In that case, Ms Rivers, I have to escort you from the premises and ensure that you do not attempt to return.'

This time I didn't laugh.

Joe, the younger, looking at a point three inches from my feet, thrust an envelope at me. Automatically I took it. I looked from Cliff to Joe to the envelope and back again.

'If you'd be so kind, Ms Rivers, to return to your car and exit the car park,' Cliff said, woodenly.

But I didn't move. Hardly knowing what I was doing, I opened the envelope. The words *gross misconduct* leapt from the page.

'But—' I wanted to scream, *You've got this wrong, This isn't for me!* But no sound came out.

'Right, Ms Rivers, if you'll just turn round and come with us. We've no wish to use force.' They were side by side, impregnable, inching me backwards.

It was too early for there to be anyone else around. No friendly faces to appeal to: not even any students to pass on a message. I turned on my heel and strode away.

At least I'd let myself into the car before my legs turned to jelly. But my hand shook so much I couldn't get the key into the ignition. I tried to read the letter, but nothing made sense.

Dear Ms Rivers
Suspension from Duty
I am writing to notify you formally of your suspension from duty following allegations about your behaviour. The accusation may constitute gross misconduct and therefore the suspension is on full pay and is pending the investigation of the allegation.

Not me. What had *I* ever done? I forced myself to read on. There was to be a meeting in Fairbairn's office under the college's disciplinary procedure. But that wasn't for another month!

Someone tapped on my window: Joe, with Cliff behind him.

I opened the door.

'I have to ask you to leave the college premises, Ms Rivers, and make no attempt to return. Now, if you don't mind.'

The keys were somewhere on the floor; I scrabbled. Then they slipped and slid, refusing to fit into the steering-wheel lock. The men must have seen the state I was in, because they made no further attempt to harry me. At last I got the lock off and started the engine. Only then did Joe lean forward to close the driver's door, courteous as a commissionaire.

The journey to Harborne was blessedly easy, against the flow of rush-hour traffic, so I got home without mishap. Blindly I locked the car, and let myself into the house. Greg must already have left. A cup of tea, that was what I needed. Then I must work out what to do next.

Next! When my day was always planned down to the last minute! Nothing made sense.

I looked at the letter again. What had I ever done – *ever* – that could possibly constitute gross misconduct? The letter specified nothing. If it had said that I'd parked in the wrong place, slapped a student's face, I could have proved I did no such thing. But not knowing what I was alleged – *falsely* alleged – to have done put me in an impossible position. Although I had a month to prepare a defence, I couldn't search for witnesses, for supporting evidence, without knowing who or what I should be looking for.

My students. What would they be told? They knew and trusted me. And my colleagues ... At last there was something I could do – I could phone Sean and set my students some work. But that was what you did if you were ill and going to be off for a couple of days – not four weeks. Dan would have to find another agency teacher, wouldn't he?

The union! They'd be able to advise me. But today was the day Frank was going to see the consultant about his back. With Ms Fairbairn's approval. The caring face of William Murdock ...

Surely Fairbairn would at least tell me what I'd done. Surely the letter was Dan's work – though what I'd done to offend him to this extent I had no idea. But sitting at the kitchen table staring at Greg's breakfast washing-up wasn't going to help me find out.

It took me several attempts to dial. When I finally managed it I had to hang on for nearly five minutes before my call was answered. I'd have to have a word with the college marketing committee about that at the next meeting. Except, of course, I wouldn't be at it ...

'William Murdock College.'

'Hi, Jane.' Thank goodness it was her turn on the switchboard. 'Could I—'

'That's Sophie Rivers, isn't it? I'm going to have to cut you off, Sophie. We're under instructions not to let you speak to anyone. I'm ever so sorry.' She dropped her voice. 'What on *earth* have you done?'

'Nothing. *Nothing!*'

'Well, someone seems to think you have. You sure? Well, you wouldn't tell me anyway, I suppose.'

'Jane, I've done absolutely nothing. But – could you do me a favour? As soon as you hear a rumour about what its meant to be, phone me back. Please!'

The phone went dead. Someone within earshot, I told myself.

No Frank. No colleagues.

Right: NATFHE's Birmingham headquarters. I'd been a paid-up union member ever since I'd come into teaching, but this was the first time I'd ever had to appeal for personal help. Seb, the regional official, was out on a case in Staffordshire, his secretary said, and his assistant had just phoned to say her car had been involved in an accident. The woman was tact and sympathy personified, but what I needed was hard advice. I left my number; she promised Seb or Maggie would phone me as soon as they got in.

By this time I could hardly stand, the pain in my stomach was so bad. Well, I thought, straightening my shoulders, that was one thing I *could* still do. I could go to the doctor's.

'Your blood pressure's higher than I expected,' Dr Burrows said, folding her stethoscope. 'Well within the normal range – but high for you. Get back on your bike, Sophie. Exercise. And promise me you'll start eating regularly. Oh, I know you're eating the right things – your weight's spot on – but you can't go on like this without things getting worse.' She looked at me closely. 'You look pale. I'll give you some miracle tablets, even better than those you had last time – but I think you need a rest. Trouble is, if I told you to take a couple of weeks off to sort things out, you'd tell me where to stick my advice, wouldn't you?'

I started to laugh. And then, to my horror, I found myself crying.

I'd never had a sicknote with *Stress* on it before, even if it had to share it with *Gastritis*. But then, I'd never had many sicknotes. Dr Burrows hadn't made it clear why she'd given it to me; as she'd said, she wasn't a legal expert. But I must fill in a self-certification form, and send them both off to Personnel when I'd photocopied them, she said.

' "Gross misconduct", indeed. Sophie, I've known you for fifteen years, on and off, and admittedly you do some crazy things – but I can't believe you'd do anything to justify this sort of treatment. Pity my son's in Brussels. He'd sort things out for you, but he's too busy nowadays drafting European labour legislation to bother with us minnows. Ah! A smile!'

'Peter might not be able to help,' I said. 'But I know a man who can!'

If only he'd been in his Sparkhill office today. If only he wasn't in Bradford. But the knowledge that I might have a life-line after all brought my brain back into some semblance of working order. Where had I written his number? It wasn't in my diary: where could I have put it? The Barber! They provided free information sheets about groups of paintings – I'd scribbled it in the margin of one of those. My bag? My pocket? The car? Not the bin ... Where the hell—? Just as I realized I could always phone his office and *ask* for the damned number I thought of Greg, and his predatory habits. Yes! There they were, a whole collection, beside his bed.

I got through to Afzal third ring, and blurted out a rapid apology for disturbing him.

'Sophie! What is it? What's happened? Calm down and tell me.'

I tried. 'So I need a lawyer,' I concluded.

'I hope it won't come to that,' he said. 'These matters are usually sorted out with proper negotiation. You must talk to your union rep.'

'I have tried. No one's available.'

'There's actually no urgency – except your personal need to find out what's going on. Look, Sophie, I have to go now, but I'll try to cut short this afternoon's meeting. Expect me some time this evening. In the meantime, try to relax.'

Relax! Easier said than done. And it was only eleven-thirty. Now what? I ought to be – I literally slapped my head. A placement visit! Although I always left a schedule of my off-premises movements with Florence – my own innovation, this, just to make sure in these new contract days that my activities were beyond reproach – I always updated it on Mondays so it was reasonably accurate. I checked my diary. The appointment had been arranged last week, so that someone from William Murdock would have phoned to cancel and apologize. Except – and a cold certainty gripped my stomach – they probably wouldn't have done, would they? It had taken me a long time to cultivate this particular firm – recruitment consultants – and I didn't want to get back to work to find them offended.

Except – gross misconduct meant instant dismissal. I might not be going back.

Should I let it ride, let the college take the consequences? A good half of me wanted to. But I checked the contact name and number in my diary, and dialled.

It was easy enough to produce a valid excuse. I'd been delayed at my doctor's because she'd found something more serious than I'd expected and insisted on signing me off sick. It was mostly true, and I got a bit of welcome sympathy. My contact was a man in his thirties, with more than his share of confidence and no doubt a salary to match, but we'd always got on reasonably well and when, his voice sharp with concern, he asked whether anything was seriously wrong, I explained about my stomach.

'Ah,' he said knowledgeably, 'teachers' tum.'

'How do you know about that?' I asked, laughing.

'Where d'you think the best of our recruits come from? They're ex-teachers, of course! Look, Sophie, soon as you're better, you come along and we'll find a slot for you.'

But would that slot accommodate someone fired from their previous job for gross misconduct?

Chapter Twenty-One

Why are houses so quiet in the daytime? When all the neighbours are at work? Perhaps I could put a tape on, or one of the new batch of CDs I hadn't even got out of their Cellophane wrappers yet. That meant getting up and crossing the room – and by now I felt as weary as if I'd finished a long term. Bone weary. So weary I left the post on the mat, the kettle unfilled. No energy to make a cup of tea. No energy even to lift my legs on to the sofa and go to sleep.

I'm not sure how long I sat.

At last it came to me that I had to move. A glass of water to wash down a magic tablet: that shouldn't be too hard.

Not too hard, but hard enough. Hard enough to convince me that I had to think of something other than my misery.

I wouldn't condescend to daytime TV – that really would be admitting defeat. In the end I settled for the one o'clock news on Radio Four and was then spurred into some sort of activity by 'The Archers'. I tidied the garden a bit, nipped round to Aggie's to sort out some of her borders. I had an idea deep in my mind that actually doing things might violate the terms of my sick leave.

But it wasn't really sick leave, was it? So presumably I could do what I liked. Which was – ? My God, how long was it since I'd been able to do as I liked in term-time?

Over a cup of tea, I reviewed the possibilities. More time at the fitness centre and the swimming baths? Cycling? Decorating the bathroom? Staying at my cousin's farm in Devon? Even if Andy and Ruth, his wife, were out of the country – and the chances were they would be – I had a standing invitation to go down. Their housekeeper-cum-caretaker knew me and would let me in.

Lovely. The M5 called.

Except it didn't call loudly enough. No, half a day of comparative idleness had convinced me that what I needed to do was get busy. There was a lot of mess in Birmingham, not least at William Murdock, and if I couldn't help clean it up from the inside, I'd have a very good go from the outside. Bloody hell, they wouldn't get away with this!

Now I began to realize: anger was a great deal better than misery. So why had I caved in in such a supine way when I was first told of my suspension? I suppose I looked on William Murdock as my extended family – after all, I'd worked there for fifteen years. Maybe that explained it. All those people – staff, support staff, students – I'd given them so much of myself. And the college – my family – had kicked me in the teeth. Disowned me. Cast me out—

Come on, Sophie. Back to anger mode.

So when Greg showed up I was sitting at the dining table surrounded by pieces of paper.

'Consequences?' he asked, looking at a list of names.

'In a way. Get yourself a beer and sit down.'

He came back with one for him and one for me, which I sipped, although usually I have a puritanical belief that I should wait until six before I start drinking: perhaps because I like it so much I have to place some limit on my enjoyment.

But today there were no limits.

'What happened to you? You weren't in your office all day,' he said, slumping down on the sofa.

'That's what I want you to find out,' I said. I explained briefly what had been done to me. 'I want to know what my colleagues have been told. Not to mention the students. I can't even speak to them on the phone – I'm supposed to be incommunicado.'

'You poor kid!' He got up and held his arms open. 'Come on. No strings, Soph – but you need a hug.'

I did. And I got a good one. Warm and friendly. At last I pulled away and he set me back on my chair, pulling one up for himself.

'Right, talk me through this lot.'

'Wish I could. I feel as if someone's bashed me on the head. Befuddled.'

'I recognize this list at any rate. That's people at William Murdock.'

'My friends. And he's the union rep. I've written a short note to each of them – on the computer. I know it's not very intimate, but it's quick.'

'And you'd rather I put the notes into their hot little hands, not their pigeon-holes. And not in front of witnesses.'

'Exactly. It just seems like something I have to do – assuring people I've done nothing wrong and asking for their support—' I broke off. Someone's thumb had stuck to the doorbell.

'Hang on – I'll get it. OK! OK! I'm coming!'

He returned from the front door half-hidden – and he was a big man – behind a basket of flowers. 'Strewth, Soph – looks like someone's offering you support already!'

I was ready to cry again. I fished the card from the envelope. *Best wishes for a speedy recovery and welcome to common sense! Damian.*

Damian? Who the hell—? And then I realized. My contact at the recruitment agency. I bit my lip. I'd have to tell him, wouldn't I?

'Sophie? I said, what shall I do with this lot?'

'Oh, shove it on the hearth. There, it blocks out the empty fireplace nicely.'

'Look here, Soph, you've got to get a grip. You're innocent until proved guilty, aren't you?'

Was I? How could I tell Richard, for instance, whose twenty-odd years at William Murdock had been exemplary in every way, that I'd been suspended for 'gross misconduct'? He'd been a real softie, but one hint that someone had stepped out of line brought his instant and profound disapproval. He might want to believe in me, but deep down he'd be shocked even by an allegation against me, whether or not it could be proven. I had blotted my hitherto spotless copybook.

I scrubbed at my nose, and returned to the piles of paper.

'The other thing you've got to do is eat. I recognize that

165

medicine and stuff you've left in the kitchen – my dad had a stomach ulcer—'

'I haven't got an ulcer.'

'Not yet, maybe. Come on, what are we going to have? Something quick and easy if we're going to work through this lot.'

I rustled up some pasta with tuna and parsley sauce – the sauce takes even less time to produce than the pasta does to cook. There was always plenty of salad in the fridge and I defrosted some ciabatta I'd found lurking in the freezer. By mistake – where was my brain these days? – I made enough for four, but knew Greg's appetite would cope with it all in any case.

As it was, he wasn't called upon to make such sacrifices. Another peremptory ring at the doorbell announced Chris, his face grim.

'What the hell's going on?' he asked, stepping into the hall. 'Diane says—'

'We're just going to eat – there's plenty if you'd like some. Come on through.'

He followed me into the kitchen. 'Hello there, Greg. How's things?'

'Never thought I'd end up playing nursemaid.'

'So long as that's all you play. Sophie has this way of inveigling you into doing things—'

'Lager?' Greg asked, flourishing a bottle.

'Thanks. Now—'

'Before I forget, Chris,' I broke in, 'Afzal Mohammed was asking about meeting you again. He's a solicitor—'

'I remember. Little guy – lost his family back in London.'

'That's right. I've no idea what he wanted to talk to you about.'

Chris took his usual chair.

'He mentioned coming round this evening,' I said.

'Need a lawyer, do you? Sophie, what have you been up to?'

'I've been suspended for gross misconduct.' Perhaps saying it would make it easier to swallow. 'I've no idea what constitutes gross misconduct, and since I've done nothing wrong—'

'No, she only saved some guy's life and helped fight a fire—'

'—I can't say I've been up to anything.'

'I was only joking. Come on, you don't believe I'd think – oh, Sophie—' He grasped my arm, just above the wrist: this was the nearest he'd get to a hug, I knew from past experience.

I took a couple of deep breaths. 'You may have been joking, but what about all the others? I haven't noticed the phone getting red-hot with sympathy calls.'

'Perhaps the rumour hasn't broken yet,' Chris said. 'Sophie, you irritate me like nobody's business when you start cutting corners, but I'd rate you as one of the most honest people I know.' And then he flushed; that was a problematic area, these days. He made an effort. 'This pasta sauce is excellent. Can I have the recipe?'

'Sure.' I scribbled it down. 'There, couldn't be easier. Another helping, Greg?'

'No, thanks. Supposed to be eating out tonight. No, forget it: I'll cancel. It's only that boozy sheila, anyway, and I reckon you need me here. To field all the phone calls, for a start! That'll be the first of many, Soph.'

He got up and took the call in the living room.

Chris looked at me. 'It might help if he did stay. If I know you you've made sheaves of notes, and having someone to bounce ideas off might prove useful.'

I nodded. When Greg came back I looked up, too eagerly.

'For me. She's got to work late tonight.'

I didn't want to have to explain to Chris who *she* was. She was certainly taking a risk, phoning him when she knew I might be at home.

The phone again. This time I took it. Silence.

'Hello?'

Silence. Not heavy breathing, or mumbled obscenities. Just silence.

Might as well put the phone down. I wandered back to the kitchen. Chris looked alert when I told him about the mystery caller, but, apart from checking his watch, which made me check mine – eight precisely – did nothing.

It was the doorbell, next time. Greg was on door duty. Voices in the hall: Afzal!

He kissed me lightly as he came in, then turned straight to Chris. They shook hands enthusiastically, and Afzal pulled up a chair; it was clear I wasn't going to have to worry about having too much pasta. I burrowed in the fridge for more salad, and, seeing the last of the ciabatta disappear into Greg, microwaved a frozen baguette. We had a feast on our hands. When the doorbell went again, I was still on my feet so I pressed Greg back into his seat and went to answer it myself.

I suppose that if you'd asked me to name the last ten people I'd have expected to see on my doorstep, Dan might have been one of them. But there he stood, tossing back his wing of hair, sadly disarranged by the evening wind.

I must have gaped. Certainly I didn't step back to let him in, so he gestured past me.

'May I?' Hearing the men talking in the kitchen, he dropped his voice. 'Is there anywhere we can talk? In private?'

Still perplexed, I opened the living-room door. There was also a door at the far end to the kitchen, but I didn't expect him to know this and I certainly didn't point it out. I was trusting that Chris would have his ear pinned to it. He did look around the room, but it was for a particular item: the mirror. Turning to it, he made another careful adjustment to his hair; then he sank gracefully on to the sofa, with his back to the kitchen.

'You must know,' he began, dropping his voice confidentially, 'that I opposed this morning's move. This is strictly off the record, of course, and I shall deny that any meeting has taken place between us. I know from my own experience that you are a very fine classroom teacher, one we can ill-afford to lose.'

'To *lose*?'

'It's a terribly serious allegation, Sophie. Two allegations, coming from separate individuals. The Chair of Governors insisted that suspension was our only option.'

'What exactly are the allegations?'

'The procedure is outlined in your letter – if you want to

know, you have to apply formally in writing. Now, I'm not happy that your suspension is for a month. We need you back in the classroom, Sophie. Your students need you. What I want to ask you is this: could you consider appearing for the hearing sooner, rather than later? This week, even? You'll recall that you are permitted under our Articles of Government to bring a friend to the hearing – I do most earnestly suggest you avail yourself. As to the sort of friend you should bring, I'd say your trades union representative would be suitable.'

'Frank!'

'Frank.' But his face became solemn, and he flicked back his hair. 'You'll recall that Frank hurt his back a few months ago. He phoned me just before I left work this evening – the latest advice he's received is that he should alternate supervised exercise and deep-tissue massage. Now, if William Murdock had the sports facilities I'd like to develop, we'd have a physiotherapist on at least a part-time contract, and Frank would be able to fit in his treatment with his teaching.' He shrugged, grinning ruefully. 'I wish! Another couple of years, Sophie, with the sort of enrolment we can achieve, my dream will be a possibility! A staff common room, even a staff bar.'

As if on cue a roar of male laughter erupted from the kitchen. Dan raised a gentlemanly eyebrow.

Was his enthusiasm anything more than a diversionary tactic? Certainly it had moved us neatly away from my problem. 'I might not be there in two years. What if the hearing goes against me?'

He sneaked a glance at his watch. There was another roar of laughter.

'It won't, I'm sure. OK. In the unlikely case that it does, you'd have the right to appeal to the Governors.'

'And then?' They might not be altogether unbiased.

'I'm sure you don't need to worry about that—'

'I shall worry, all the same.'

'I suppose your only option would be an Industrial Tribunal. But Sophie, I'm a good judge of character. I know it'll be all right.'

'I don't suppose I can quote you?'

He laughed; I'd expected him to. He got up, and took my hand, shaking it earnestly. 'Can I assume you'd agree to come to an earlier hearing?'

Yes, yes, yes! 'Give me till tomorrow to think about it,' I said. It wasn't until I was seeing him out that it occurred to me that an early hearing would mean I had no time to apply in writing for the details of the allegations. 'How will I let you know?' I asked anyway. 'The switchboard's declared me *persona non grata*.'

He flourished a business card. 'This is my direct line.'

It was hard not to gape. He was giving me hard evidence of his visit.

'If you'd care to write down the number.'

Well, I could hardly have expected him to let me keep it ... But if he could be devious about meeting me – or rather, not meeting me – so could I. Taking his card by the edges, I wrote the number down obediently. I would describe our exchanged smiles as politely adversarial.

Afzal was grinning like a cat getting outside a pot of cream, while Greg was suppressing laughter. At last the two of them broke out, Azfal's giggles almost hysterically high-pitched.

'Don't know what's so funny,' I said, poking at my congealed supper. 'You just kept on yelling. You couldn't have shut up and eavesdropped, could you? No, that was too obvious.'

'Exactly, Sophie. Much too obvious.' Chris, at his driest. He hadn't joined in the laughter. But the crow's feet round his eyes were deepening uncontrollably.

'OK. Tell.'

Afzal was almost weeping with mirth now. He was waving what looked like a Walkman at me. 'Taped it all!' he crowed. 'Dictaphone. Switched it on, opened the door slightly, shoved it on the floor, shut the door. Kept talking very loudly. Chris has a fund of extremely vulgar jokes that Greg's been tapping—'

Chris leaned across and picked up my plate; he could reach the microwave without moving his chair. I tried to imagine him telling vulgar jokes. 'You'll eat before we talk,' he said. 'And then we'll get our heads together for a council of war.'

Chapter Twenty-Two

There was one sheet of notes I knew Afzal wouldn't like: the one headed *Muslim Connection???* Not that I'd written much on it. There was Shahida's encounter with her stroppy Brummie Asian; my own problem class; the Chamberlain Square fountain incident with the Jewish student, Sam Jacobson.

Fire!!! Those notes were extensive. William Murdock's occupied half a page, even without Carl's Alfa. Then there was the crop round and including the women's refuge.

Suspects? Well, I was definite about my Scots friend. And there were the funny-smelling (made-up?) white/Asian lads – any news of them? And Sam had said something I'd almost forgotten about not trusting someone. Someone you wouldn't expect to be a Muslim, wasn't it? Then I'd written *Dan's file!!!* I'd never got round to retrieving it from Richard's and, of course, the original was long gone in the stockroom blaze.

Victims. Mike Appleyard. Sam Jacobson. Sarah Robertson. And the chap in the city centre, I supposed – though he wasn't connected with William Murdock.

'I'm very much afraid we ought to add another page,' said Chris, peering at my work over his half-moon glasses. '*Future targets?*'

Greg sat down heavily beside him. I was on his far side, Afzal beside me; between us we occupied two sides of the dining table.

'More attacks on William Murdock, for a start,' I said. 'You see, when we've had fires before – oh, nothing on this

172

scale! – we've always had a crop. Usually they tail off of their own accord when the weather gets nasty – even fire-raisers like their comforts. I don't think we've ever nailed the student, or students, responsible. Hell, we've been demanding security cameras ever since I can remember! I suppose they thought it was cheaper to bring in a few poorly paid security guards – though now they're being sacked to pay for cameras. What a good job they haven't installed them all. It took two guards just to escort me from the premises this morning.' My brightness faded. 'Why didn't I take time off when everyone wanted me to . . .'

'Who's everyone?' Chris asked.

'Me, for a start,' Afzal said.

'And everyone at William Murdock, from the Principal down. There's a new feminine hand at the helm, lads,' I said, in my best Long John Silver voice. 'Be nice to everyone, offer them tea and home-made cakes – and then suspend them.'

Afzal reached under the table and squeezed my hand lightly. It was good to have someone so unequivocally on my side. The phone hadn't exactly been a-buzz with pledges of support, had it?

And then it did ring.

'My job,' said Greg. When he picked up the receiver, he grinned, covered the mouthpiece and half-turned to us. 'For me,' he mouthed.

'It'll be his drinking partner,' I said hurriedly.

'In my experience, when a man wears a silly smile like that the partner is female, and not solely for drinking with,' Afzal said.

Amid the laughter, I thought I heard Greg say, 'Die'. I looked at him. Then he said it again, but this time I heard it as 'Di'. Did he have to be so blatant? But no one else seemed to have heard anything.

'Are they usually so supportive of staff?' Chris asked. 'Or is it just the new regime?'

'Well, it was only the boss and one of the counsellors. I can't for the life of me remember what Dan wanted me to do, apart from not talk to the media and take on an

173

over-full timetable. But in education the usual cure-all is work harder, longer.'

'That's what I thought,' Chris said.

Greg returned, but didn't sit down. 'Got me a date, kids! I'm off now.'

'Thought she was working late,' I said, in spite of myself.

'She was. She's finished what she had to do.' Greg was irritated; I would have been in his shoes.

'Sorry,' I said. 'See you tomorrow, eh?'

'Sure. Leave those notes where I can't miss them.'

'Notes?' asked Chris.

'For some of my colleagues. Telling them I'm innocent, guv. What's the matter? Surely there's no harm in that?'

'Let me think about that one,' Afzal suggested. 'You see, you have a duty of care to your employer – I'm not sure how an industrial tribunal would react to your firing off what could conceivably amount to unprovoked attacks on your employer. Perhaps it might be different if you contacted colleagues at home. I'd certainly be far from amused if someone I'd suspended started lobbying behind my back.'

'*You'd* only suspend someone if they'd done something wrong!'

'No. If there was any evidence to back a serious allegation I might suspend them anyway. We've no idea what the allegations are against you – and remember, it goes without saying that neither Chris nor I could believe anything bad about you.'

Chris's smile was necessarily enigmatic.

Afzal didn't notice. 'In any case, the news obviously hasn't leaked out yet or your friends would already be rallying round. Shahida would be knocking at your door offering to let you help bath Maria, for a start.' His smile was gentle. 'Just wait another day, see what develops. What do you think, Chris?'

'I agree. There's something going on in the Murdock Management team that smells – a little off, put it that way. And what's this about Dan's file?'

'I taught him years ago. He didn't want anyone to know, so I promised not to tell. Except I think I let it out to Diane, the other day—'

'That was what you wanted her to keep quiet about! Well,' he added, beginning to sound huffy, 'I'm sure you can rely absolutely on her discretion.'

'I'm sure I could have done, had she known I was betraying something I should have kept secret.'

'Why the secrecy?'

'Because when Dan joined my class all those years ago I remember his probation officer brought him to enrol. And I was nosy enough to photocopy all the material in his file.'

'And now his file's destroyed. What a pity.'

Afzal looked up sharply; there was menace in Chris's voice.

'Where are the photocopies now? Here?'

'I only went and left them at Richard's! I haven't had time to collect them yet.'

'I think you and I will do that as a matter of some urgency. No one else knows?'

'No one.'

'Someone might suspect?'

'Not that I took them to Richard's! How could they?'

'That you might have peeped at the file, I mean.'

'No one. Not if Diane was discreet. And she'd no reason not to be, of course. Not that I told her the details, in any case.' My smile was particularly winning.

Chris's was less so. After a few moments he glanced at his watch and pushed himself to his feet. 'Look, I promised I'd go and cast my eyes over the stuff we've got so far. The case is ultimately my responsibility anyway,' he added, as if he needed to justify his interference.

'Of course,' I said. 'It was good of you to come tonight.'

'Oh, I'm sure you'll see a lot more of me,' he said. 'I need to talk to you about the arson attacks in Moseley,' he added to Afzal. 'When's a good time?'

'Tomorrow afternoon? I have to be in court in the morning.'

'Fine. I'll pop round to your office about two.'

Was this the Chris who wouldn't have been able to see me until Thursday? I bit my lip and said nothing.

He turned to me. 'Why don't you come along too? You can't sit around all day getting bored. We were going to talk

175

business in any case. And – I don't know, perhaps it's your track record, Sophie – I'd rather no one knew exactly where you were at the moment.' He shook his head, as if to dispel the fancifulness of his fears. But it didn't work. 'Why not phone Richard and tell him we're going round as soon as we can to pick up the file? And tell him to give it to no one except you and me.'

I found his eyes and looked straight into them. 'Unlike you to have intuitions, Chris.'

'That's what worries me ... Afzal, will you be able to stay here until Greg gets back?'

Afzal spread his hands. 'Sophie – I'm most terribly sorry but—'

'No problem,' said Chris. 'Sophie, get your coat. You're coming with me.'

When Chris embarked on a circuitous route to Richard's, I should have suspected something was wrong. When he pulled sharply into a cul-de-sac, emerging briskly to drive slowly past a parked car and dictate its number into his radio, I knew it was.

'Not a very good tail, letting you do that,' I said.

'Not very good at all. Maybe not even a tail, but we'll see what the computer throws up. Meanwhile, we'll do a tour of the suburbs, just to give my colleagues time to intercept him. Don't worry – I shan't lead him to Richard's.'

'He seemed to find my place without being led,' I said.

'Perhaps he already knew where you lived,' he said.

Richard wasn't in. Our knocking attracted the attention of a neighbour, returning from being walked by a monster of a dog; the dog would clearly have preferred the immediate comfort of its fireside, but the man, who introduced himself as a member of the development's Neighbourhood Watch Scheme, was adamant he saw some ID. And having seen it, was then impressed. But the only information he could give was that Richard had gone down to London to see a relative. The neighbour on the other side knew the burglar

176

alarm code and might have a contact telephone number. But then, the neighbour on the other side was out.

Chris produced his card listing Rose Road's details. 'Mr Thompson, I'd be more than grateful,' he began, his tone friendly but nonetheless compelling, 'if you could ask Mr – Deakin, did you say? – to phone me as a matter of utmost urgency. I repeat, Mr Jeffries has done absolutely nothing wrong – he just has some property belonging to my friend here which may prove – ' his voice was quite chilling now in its authority – 'to be a matter of life and death.'

Mr Thompson was almost standing at attention, had to restrain himself from saluting. Chris and I nodded with utmost courtesy, and bade him good night. Chris said nothing till we were back in his car.

'Shit and corruption! Why does the old bastard have to take off now, of all times?'

'He's not an old bastard. Mid-fifties at most. He took premature retirement.'

'Fancy driving?' He must have been feeling sorry for me.

'Another time, Chris. If the offer's still open. With my luck a lamp post will fall on top of us. Or a pedestrian'll decide to commit suicide under our wheels.'

'Another time, then.'

It was only a short drive to Rose Road Police Station. Equipped with a visitor's label, I trailed through familiar corridors to Chris's room. The untidiness was less familiar. If pressed, I might have described Chris as anally retentive, but the chaos of his desk and floor was more in the anal-expulsive style. He looked outraged, but quickly settled for exasperated; perhaps he'd forgotten how much Diane had used his room. At any rate, he flung open a window, threw out the contents of an ashtray, and poked disdainfully at a bowl of what I suspected was smoker's pot pourri. His coffee percolator had boiled dry, and the packet of ground coffee was open to the four winds. The mugs might have been refugees from a William Murdock staffroom, they were so foul. Someone would have to take strong detergent to the lipstick on the rims.

I dumped my jacket and bag, and grabbed a fistful. 'I'm going on a mission. In search of a sink.'

He opened the door without comment.

I'd neither expected nor been invited to look through any of the confidential material. In fact I was deep in *Birdsong* when I heard Chris swear.

'What's up?'

'I don't like to think. Give me two minutes, Sophie.' His face was so thunderous I thought it better to leave him to whatever phone conversation he was about to have.

Taking some more filthy mugs I withdrew to the loo again – I'd never discovered Rose Road's kitchen area. I found Sharon touching up her make-up as I pushed my way in.

'If it isn't Sophie!'

We exchanged an air kiss.

'You and Chris back together, are you? Thank God for that! He's been as moody as hell these last few weeks—'

I was shaking my head so vigorously she finally noticed. 'No. But there's been those doings at William Murdock – and maybe he thought I could fill him in on some of the background. And Diane, of course.'

'Diane? They're holding up her promotion, you know.'

'Any idea why?'

'Glass ceilings. And glass bottles, to be honest. There's some women think they have to be more macho than the blokes – drink harder, swear harder, fuck harder. Diane, now, thinks she has to prove herself by drinking glass for glass with whatever bloke she's with – and some of the blokes are ten-pints-a-night men.'

'Bloody hell. What does she think that's going to achieve?'

'She seems to think it gets their respect. But it doesn't, see – not as much as decent, reliable work does. Take Jill, now – you'd think she was a civil servant she's so quiet. Pretty in a fragile way. Softly-spoken. But she's efficient – my God, she's efficient. Brain like a computer. Going to the Fraud Squad next month. Chief Inspector. At thirty-five!'

'I hope she knows about Dave Clark's wandering hands.'

Sharon cackled. 'She does. And she's dealt with hands just

178

like them before. Amazing, isn't is, how some women have this gift of slapping men down without denting their egos?'

Ian Dale was with Chris when I went back. The silence was so dense I did nothing more than slide the mugs soundlessly back by the kettle and return to my chair – though I'd have loved to peer at whatever it was Chris held with the hand that wasn't occupied by the phone.

'Must be switched off,' he said at last, flinging the handset down so hard it bounced on to the desk.

Ian retrieved it in silence. 'Answering machine?'

'Off too. For fuck's sake,' he exploded, 'aren't we supposed to be dealing with a murder? I've got people here on unpaid overtime, and—' His return to self-control was swift and frightening. 'Sophie, would you do something for me? Imagine I'd never seen Sarah. Describe her to me, would you?'

Putting aside Sebastian Faulks, I considered. 'She'd be about five foot tall. Wispy blonde, with the sort of pale skin that goes with blonde eyebrows and blue eyes. She was slender. A timid demeanour that really irritated some people. Dressed fairly fashionably – skinny tops and T-shirts, though she did have a penchant for those droopy print skirts. Latter-day hippie sort of thing. She looked very – young,' I ended.

'If you had to compare her to anyone, who would she remind you of?'

I shook my head. 'No one in particular.'

'OK – try this one, Ian. If you had to describe Sophie, how would you start?'

Ian looked quizzical, but played along with Chris's whim. 'She's five foot one, not much more than eight stone. Looks on the delicate side, for all she's as tough as old boots.' He grinned. 'Blonde hair. Blue eyes. Casual dresser, but not scruffy. Tight tops, fairly short skirts. Looks as if she runs everywhere.'

'Apart from the last bit, you make me sound a bit like poor Sarah!'

Chris looked me directly in the eye and held up a scrap

of paper in a polythene folder. 'Exactly.' He paused for a moment. Then he came round to my side of the desk, holding the folder where Ian and I could see it.

On the paper – a corner torn from a sheet of lined paper, the sort every student uses – were written the letters *SR*.

He squatted beside me. 'Your Principal's suggestion that you take time off; this suspension – are these more subtle ways of achieving what they didn't manage first time round? What I'm saying, Sophie, is that someone killed a small blonde woman with the initials SR.' He held up a photo. 'The only thing that worries me is the clothes. What were you wearing the day she died?'

I gawped. How on earth would I know? Clothes were just something I put on without much thought.

'Have a look at this.' He passed me the photo. 'These were the clothes she was wearing the day she was killed. One of what you called her latter-day hippie skirts.'

'Yes. I remember it trailing from the stretcher as they carried her away.'

'You're *sure* you can't remember what you were wearing that day?'

'My usual stuff, I suppose – no, hang on. Some Muslim lads were on their high horse about my clothes and Dan had ordered me to wear something longer. So I did. This awful old bunchy skirt with a gathered waist. Cotton floral print. I keep it for messing around in the garden when it's hot.'

Chris looked grave. 'Sophie, I'm most terribly afraid the SR they were after was not Sarah Robertson. It was Sophie Rivers.'

Chapter Twenty-Three

I don't know how long I stared. All sorts of denials popped up, but his steady gaze prepared to demolish them.

'But – I'm – I'm—' I've always thought of myself as bright and confident: surely no one could have mistaken the shy, self-effacing young Sarah for me, could they? If I'd ever imagined a doppelganger, it would be a stronger, stroppier version of myself. But I suspect I was making such objections to give me time to assimilate the logic of what Chris was saying.

'Do you still think Sarah's death was as a result of her having a thin skull? That she may not have been hit specially hard?'

Chris smiled. 'Are you telling me they'd have had a more difficult time with yours? Because you're thicker?'

'Of course.' I knocked on my temple; that should cheer him. 'Or maybe I was thinking that they haven't made any attempts actually to kill me—'

'You know, I thought you were about to split an infinitive there—'

'Actually to kill me since – since they found out their mistake. They've just made life a bit of a pain. Did I tell you someone shoved me down the stairs the other day? Oh, and someone chalked RIVERS OUT all over the staffroom door. And I've had a few odd things happen at home – someone broke my windscreen. Though round here that's not unusual. Then someone put dogshit through my letterbox—'

'Anything else—'

I started to shake my head.

181

'—apart from the car that tailed us tonight? Any news on that yet, Ian?'

'Stolen numberplate. Doesn't match the car.'

'And apart, of course, from your Management's concerted efforts to get rid of you through more official channels.' He slammed his open hands on the desk. 'Perhaps it's in Dan Godfrey's file. The answer to all this. Because someone wants you silenced.'

'You could simply ask him about his past. What he's got to hide. Or check police records.'

Ian coughed delicately; Chris's voice became a couple of degrees colder. 'I believe the straightforward approach might already have been tried. On Friday.'

Damn Diane!

'And you got locked out on Monday—'

'I did go in on Saturday. And Dan found me outside 1501 – where we had the fire. He wasn't pleased. Come to think of it, he didn't exactly mention me and my colleagues in despatches for our heroic fire-fighting efforts, though the Principal was very sweet. Chris, I keep going over and over this. But I don't seem to be getting anywhere.' I stood up, and then sat down again, trying to keep calm.

'Just ponder the words shock and stress. No wonder you're feeling a bit confused.'

'But I don't want to be a wimp like Sarah! I'm Sophie! She who shins up scaffolds, burrows down mines – Sophie, the Indomitable!'

He laughed; we were closer than we'd been for months. 'Sophie, the Pain in the Arse! It's frightening to have to sit in silence and think, isn't it? A bit of action – that's a more tempting option.' His smile broadened, took in Ian. 'Like this, for example. Ian – get someone on to Richard Jeffries' neighbour, will you? Mr Deakin, Hounslow Avenue – number thirty-five. I want Jeffries' phone number *now*. Just in case it's – er – been overlooked, get someone to run a check on Dan or Daniel Godfrey. And I want Gavin to secure Sophie's house. Immediately. For starters we'll board over the letterbox. Keys, Sophie?'

'The place is pretty secure anyway. Gavin's team—'

Gavin had at one point worked for the police, advising

on personal security for likely victims; now he'd gone independent, but Chris still put a lot of work his way that couldn't have been justified on the police budget. We went back a long way, and I owed to him the fact that no one had ever destroyed my home.

'They've made it safer than the average house, but that doesn't mean it's secured against arson attacks. There's a lot of them around at the moment, Sophie.'

'While we're thinking about protecting my house, Chris, what about Aggie's? If they can't get directly into mine they might try to go via hers. And she's too old for that sort of alarum and excursion. She's away at the moment but when she gets back—'

'It would be nice to have a home to go to. OK, you're right. Her place is a lot more vulnerable than yours. We'll have to have a whip-round—'

'Indeed you won't. I shall pick up the tab for that!'

'We'll argue about that later. Now, get someone on to the Royal Mail to intercept all Sophie's post, as from first delivery tomorrow. And get someone to leave a note at Diane's to tell her to be here by eight tomorrow. Why can't people realize that in a job like ours you have to be methodical? One tiny slip and you miss things. Like this.' He held up the polythene folder.

Ian raised an eyebrow at me and slipped out.

Before either of us could speak, someone tapped the door. Tom. And the expression on his face suggested that this was not the time for soccer chat.

'Chris, man – a bit of news for you. All these fires, like. Another one just reported. And seeing it was to do with education I thought I'd better mention.'

Chris's face lit up; he'd been working hard on Tom, he and Ian. 'Yes?'

'Some teachers' union. They've got offices down Bradford Street. Firebomb through a window, man!'

'Sophie?'

For I had started to laugh. Not an amused laugh: a tired, angry laugh, that threatened to end in tears. 'Not a teachers' union, Tom. A lecturers' union. *My* union. The union that's supposed to be supporting me at my hearing.'

183

'Hearing?' Tom repeated.

'They've got her on some trumped-up charge at college,' Chris said brusquely.

I shot a look at him. No, he wasn't giving me the benefit of the doubt; he was convinced. Wasn't he?

'So they get rid of my union rep – give him sick leave to have his back treated, he'd never argue with that – and make sure the regional official has something else on his mind. I wonder,' I added, 'whether his visit to Staffordshire was genuine. And whether his assistant's car is now drivable. You see, it seems to me – this could be paranoia, of course – that they made sure I had no one to turn to this morning.'

Chris looked at me sombrely. 'It may just be coincidence, of course.' But he didn't sound at all sure.

Tom cleared his throat. 'Shall I ask this union official what he was doing up in Staffordshire? Or get one of the lads at Digbeth nick to ask him – he's over now, talking about the fire. And maybe he'll know his assistant's home number, so we could find out about her car.'

'Make it snappy, eh?'

'Gaffer!' He opened the door, to readmit Ian, and left.

'You haven't got any biscuits in that desk of yours?' I gasped, digging frantically for my tablets.

'You'll get something from the canteen, won't you, Ian, if I haven't?' He burrowed. With extreme distaste he dropped on his blotter a battered packet of tampons and a lipstick that had lost its casing. And then – his face whitened to the lips – a bottle of whisky.

'Would some of this help?' he made himself ask at last.

Ian looked at me. My shake of the head was a response to his unanswered question: no, I wouldn't say anything to drop Diane any further into the mire of Chris's displeasure. And I didn't want any whisky, either. And Ian went out, canteen-bound.

What could I usefully say? That Greg had told me on Friday that his girlfriend was an alcoholic, and that she'd been seen with another man? That she was dating Greg tonight? All our past history – and my compassion for Chris – was against it. But he trusted me: if he asked me direct questions, I'd have to give honest answers. Meanwhile I sat trying to press the pain away from my stomach, and prayed the tablets would work soon.

Chris got up, striding across the room to the window, which he flung open. He didn't do anything so melodramatic as throwing out the whisky, bottle and all: though perhaps that would have been better than standing stony-faced pouring it into some convenient guttering. He stared out into the dark streets, the empty bottle in his hand, until Ian returned with a glass of milk and some cream crackers.

'When you've finished, Sophie, we must decide where you're staying tonight. We can't have you being burned alive in your bed.'

I nodded in acquiescence. 'Better find somewhere for Greg to bed down too.' If he didn't stay at Diane's, that is.

'I'll phone Val,' Ian said, 'get her to air the spare bed for Sophie. That Greg'll have to manage on the living-room floor.'

'Thanks.' Chris and I said it together. Chris continued, 'Any idea where Greg is?'

'That Australian bar, I should think. Tell you what, Ian and I could pick him up from there.' I certainly didn't want Chris to go anywhere near the place.

Another tap at the door, and Tom was with us once more. 'Two things, Gaffer. Seb – that man from NATFHE—'

'My union.'

'Well, he says he was on a funny little case today. Someone threatened with the sack – and then, suddenly, everything's sweetness and light. These things happen, he says. He couldn't swear he was set up. And his assistant says the driver that hit her was terribly apologetic, took her off there and then to have a new tail-light fitted. Paid cash, at a garage Lichfield way. She never learned his name. Fishy, wouldn't you say?'

Chris shrugged.

'The other thing, Gaffer, is this Richard Jeffries' number. Mr Deakin's tried to phone him, but there's no reply yet. And without Jeffries' permission, he won't let even you know the burglar alarm code.'

'Win some, lose some.' Chris was on his feet. 'We'll take an unmarked car – not mine, just in case. Afterwards I'll drop her round at your place, Ian – it's only five minutes away.'

Ian nodded. I shook my head. 'It'd make more sense for Ian and me to pick Greg up.' That way Chris wouldn't see Diane.

He ignored me. 'Why don't you knock off? God knows what time we all started this morning, and it's nearly ten now. You too, Tom. And Tom—'

'Sir?'

'You've done well, lad.'

Mr Deakin, a spry seventy-year-old with a full head of hair, was far from happy about letting me into Richard's house, though he responded with alacrity to Chris's ID. He'd still not been able to reach Richard on the number he'd left; I tried it yet again while the two men exchanged pleasantries. It would make life a whole lot easier if Richard could tell us where we could lay hands on those photocopies. . . . But there was no response.

Chris straightened. 'OK, let's have a quick check. Where does he keep all his paperwork?'

'In his office upstairs,' I said, leading the way and hating every step. 'He was one of the most systematic men William Murdock has ever known. Here you are.'

Switching the light on exposed a perfect office. Four four-drawer cabinets, teak-faced. One wall of bookshelves. A desk arranged for writing one end, using the computer at the other: he'd be able to look across at Chadbrook Walkway and the allotments if he wanted a rest. The only incongruity – one I'd have laid bets on, knowing Richard – was the collection of railway prints on the walls.

Each cabinet drawer was crammed with neatly annotated files. Teaching notes. Going through every file in every drawer would take hours.

'And he might have slipped them inside a book, or under the bed,' Chris completed my thoughts for me. 'If there's no reply from this number first thing in the morning, we'll find out the address it's attached to and get someone from the local force to bang on the door. Maybe the phone's on the blink.' He turned, ready to leave the room. 'Thanks, Mr Deakin. Now, some of my officers will have to come back tomorrow, and I can't expect you to hang around all day waiting for them. I suggest I – and I alone! – write down that alarm code. Even Ms Rivers here won't see it. Either that or we'd have to leave the burglar alarm turned off.'

Mr Deakin glared at even the possibility of such recklessness. He set off downstairs, at such a pace I was concerned for his safety, spry or not. Chris followed. I turned off the lights, shut the door, and dawdled so even Deakin couldn't suspect I'd had a chance of overhearing him tell Chris the code.

'Right, let's pick up Greg and let him know he's on the move tonight.'

'He may not be intending to come home,' I said, trying to conceal my dread. 'He's got a date.'

'I thought he was after you.' Chris pulled out into Woodbourne Road.

'But I wasn't after him, so he's after someone else.' I spoke lightly.

'Any idea who?'

'Oh, someone he met in this bar ... He'll be going back to Berlin soon. He said he only came to look after me, and now the West Midlands Force is doing that he may feel a bit surplus to requirements.'

Chris slowed to let a bus pull out. 'He didn't strike me as the sort of man who'd leave a job half-finished. I bet he won't get on that plane until the last drink's been downed at the booze-up to celebrate the end of the case.'

'But he knows—'

'I told you, I don't reckon he's the giving-up type.' And he put his foot down to overtake the bus.

The Aussie bar was in a pedestrianised area bordering on Chinatown. I desperately wanted to get there first. I had assembled all the sensible arguments about the impossibility of Chris finding somewhere to park, how it would be better for him to drop me and cruise round until he could pick Greg and I up from a pre-arranged spot, and—

'But I'm on official police business,' he said, his tone final. 'I think you might be safer coming with me.'

Chucking-out time. We swam against the tide of couples pushing their way out.

'Where the fuck d'you think you're going, mate?' Eighteen stone of bouncer.

'Where the fuck I like,' said Chris, flashing his ID an inch from the man's nose. This was Chris? The cool, non-swearing Chris? But I was glad of the slight interruption. It gave me the chance to see the expression in Diane's eyes as she spotted Chris. Diane's – and Greg's. And I saw them push apart – though who abandoned whom I couldn't say. Certainly it was Greg who sailed towards us, alone, an arm round both sets of shoulders as he turned us till we were facing firmly towards the car.

'You left it too late, mate! Have to have some of Sophie's lager at home. And you'll need to get some more, kid – you're running low.'

So the crisis was averted. Postponed, at least. And with a bit of luck it would be sorted out somewhere less public. I tucked myself into the back of the car, so Chris and Greg could talk men's talk – whatever that might be.

My house was still standing when Chris pulled up, and so was Aggie's. Not surprising since Gavin was still there, his feet up in my front room watching TV. I thrust a few things into an overnight bag, and Greg, grumbling that this was all a waste of time since he'd come over from Germany specially to guard me, did the same.

Gavin looked him up and down. 'Fireproof, are you? Well, you can guard Sophie all you like when I've made the place secure. As for your car, love, don't even *think* about starting it until it's had a little spring-clean down Rose Road. OK?'

I set the burglar alarm and we all trooped out.

'Uniform'll keep an extra eye on the place anyway,' Gavin said, 'but a fast car and a well-aimed incendiary device don't take long to do a lot of harm. OK, most things'd bounce off your windows – I'd like to get your neighbour's up to the same standard. But we'd need permission. We can't do it till later this week – I'm committed up to here! And it'd cost her.'

'No, it won't. I'll pick up the bill.'

No one argued with me.

Ian's wife Val made us creamy cocoa, and Ian produced a malt whisky chaser. He greeted with disdain Greg's suggestion that he should share my bed.

'Come on, mate,' Greg said, 'you know what drink does. Shakespeare. Tell us, Soph.'

'It provokes the desire but takes away the performance,' I said dutifully. 'But you'll be up and down all night emptying that beer-filled bladder of yours, and the only thing I have on my mind is sleep.'

It might have been on my mind, but it wouldn't come. Blurs of action kept flashing by, as if I were on a long, rapid car journey. Despite the biscuits that had arrived with the cocoa, I began to feel hungry; despite Dr Burrows' miracle tablets, that brought back the pain. My usual cure for insomnia is to go and clean out a cupboard, but I could scarcely do anything like that here, in someone else's house. And just to go downstairs would risk disturbing the rest of the household.

At last, in such pain that even a couple of swigs of antacid didn't help, I padded down in search of bread.

There! Even a single slice eased the situation. Sitting with elbows on the table, I risked another. And another.

'Soph! What's up, kid?'

Greg. In T-shirt and boxer shorts. He squatted beside me, putting an arm around me. And I turned to him. 'Come on, you have a good cry. Then you'll feel better.'

I don't know at what point he gathered me up, and put me back to bed. But it was so good, waking up, to feel myself wrapped against a solid warm body, to listen to the slow, sure rhythm of his breathing.

Chapter Twenty-Four

The bed was empty when I surfaced for the last time to the smell of bacon being cooked. What puzzled me was that I was still in my dressing-gown. And then I remembered Greg's kindness the night before.

'Well,' he said, blushing, when I kissed him on the cheek to greet him, 'that's what mates are for. Don't tell Chris, though, for God's sake! Two rashers or three? Go on – Val says it's organic. Poor old Chris – I nearly spend the night with his present girlfriend and end up in bed with his ex! Wouldn't do the poor bastard's ego much good, would it?'

'Not one scrap.'

'Mind you, things aren't as hundred per cent crook as they might have seemed. Apparently that bloke Diane was with the other evening wasn't another bloke, if you see what I mean. She was trying to get information out of him. A nice, friendly bit of interrogation. Trouble is,' he continued, cutting white bread and jamming slices into the toaster, 'you're asking for trouble if you date someone you're working for. No space, see. I really fancied one of the surveyors back in Kansas when I was on a job there, but we had to have rows anyway because it was our job, and shoving sex into the equation – well!' He shrugged expressively. 'Toast for you, chick?'

'Just dry bread, thanks. I fancy a bacon sandwich.'

'How well done d'you like it?'

'Crispier than that, please. So what are your plans for the day?'

'Got to go in for a class,' he said, exuding virtue. 'Wouldn't want to skive – it might upset Shirley. But don't worry – I shall be sniffing round, Soph. Hey, what about those notes for your mates?'

I explained why I'd decided against them.

'Hmph. Isn't this supposed to be a free country? Can't a bloke write to his mates?'

'Not if I want to be lily-white pure,' I said.

Greg flipped two beautifully-grilled rashers on to my bread. 'Eat and enjoy,' he said. 'And what about you? What are your plans, this rotten rainy morning?'

'Try to phone Richard, my old boss. If at first I don't succeed, I shall leave it to the police. And I shall nip over to Four Oaks to try to talk to my old boss's old boss, Worrall. The principal who retired all of a hurry this summer. I always respected him, and he may have some low-down on this new regime.'

'You *what?*'

'I said I was going to talk to my ex-boss.'

'You off your head or something, woman?'

Perhaps I was. But I didn't feel safe at home, I didn't feel at home here, so I might as well be brave on wheels. I'd fob Greg off with some levity. 'It'd be greener to go by public transport, I know, but I can imagine Chris's reaction to the news that I've been swanning round the West Midlands conurbation with no more protection than my wits.' I didn't think about my own reaction: that way panic, if not madness, lay. 'In fact, I might be doing a lot of swanning before the day's out. So I thought I'd let my fingers do the walking – Yellow Pages!' By now I was very jolly. Whether I was fooling either of us I wouldn't care to bet.

'I don't like it.'

Do you think I do? Do you think I like being harried and chased? 'Greg, if you want to come you can – but what you could do I don't know. You'd truly be more useful as my eyes and ears at college. Truly.'

And what sort of word was that? *Truly*?

So now I was the proud temporary owner of a bright red Fiesta, delivered to Ian's front door: not exactly inconspicuous, but perhaps the very fact that there were so many red Fiestas around would make it less easy to see me.

Halfway down Wolverhampton Road South, I pulled into the kerb for a moment's thought. I set side by side the possibility of white louts pretending to be Asian to get Asians a bad name, with the idea of a foul-breathed Scotsman wanting to lurk incognito at William Murdock. He couldn't have adopted an Asian alias, could he? My Asian students ranged in skin tone from one so delicate they'd pass, should they ever wish to, for home-brewed English, to a quite dark brown, with every shade in between. The whole thing seemed unlikely, but I jotted it down to ask Chris.

Stopping off at my home, I changed into something more suitable for seeing the conservative Mr Worrall. And, listening to Gavin's colleagues' murmur downstairs, I pottered round the first floor. It was a good job I did: I'd left my computer on, and though I always liked watching screensavers, I nonetheless felt guilty about wasting even the smallest amount of electricity. I checked my message-board, but no one wanted me. And I noticed, making my way back downstairs, that Gavin's team had changed my ordinary secondary glazing for polycarbonate sheeting, and had, as instructed, sealed the letterbox.

'Hi, Sophie! You look nice.' Gavin had emerged from the kitchen. 'Look, I had an idea: I've always wanted to get you on a golf course and now you're not at work, you've no excuse. So when shall we make it?'

'When the ball's as big as a cricket ball,' I said, 'and you hit it with a cricket bat. Until then, no chance. I'll come along with you just for the walk, one fine day.'

I headed for the door. On my hall table was a box I hadn't noticed before, neatly wrapped, with a flourish of red ribbon. I picked it up gingerly and popped back into the kitchen.

'No need to look like that, Sophie – they've really got to you this time, haven't they? It's a present. From me and Chris. And Ian chipped in too. Go on – open it.'

I did as I was told. A mobile phone!

'State of the art digital. Here's your SIM card – we've already set it all up for you. First month's line-rental paid, and your connection charge. There's your number. You've only got fifteen minutes' free calls per month, so succinct communication is a good idea. Otherwise you pay forty pence a minute, plus VAT! The other problem is that if you use them too much they microwave your brain. Come on, Sophie – it's a present. People are supposed to look pleased when they get a present.' His thumb and forefinger pushed the corners of my mouth upward.

The tears welled up; I dabbed. 'Sorry. Must be PMS.'

He gave me a friendly hug. 'You'll be OK. Soon as we've finished our coffee, we're off to see what needs doing at your neighbour's – Ian's going round to the hospital to explain. Game old bird, I gather.'

The drive to Four Oaks was uneventful apart from the unnatural use I made of my rear-view mirror and the conviction that gnawed at my stomach that they wouldn't secure Aggie's house quickly enough. I kept on seeing flames billowing from her bedroom; saw the fire-fighters; knew there was nothing I could do and it was all my crazy imagination anyway.

Smart as the Fiesta was, it shrank into oblivion on Mr Worrall's carriage drive, cowering beside a top-of-the-range Ford and a Jaguar so old it must be vintage. Worrall had never used either of these for work, preferring an aged Rover. Although college principals are by no means bottom of the earnings league, it would surely take more than his salary and Naval pension combined to be able to run a pile like this and two fuel-guzzling cars.

His wife opened the door. Tall, slender, she must have been about his age – late fifties. With a classic twinset – and, indeed, pearls – and a skirt that yelled Jaeger, her bone structure told me how she'd speak before she even opened her mouth: in the well-projected but curiously diphthongised vowels of the upper crust. Old furniture; old paintings; old money.

She showed me into Worrall's study. He was working at

193

the sort of desk you generally only see in stately homes, but got up with every appearance of pleasure. We sat opposite each other in a deep bay window, the embrasure almost as large as my kitchen. His wife, Dorothea, brought tea and fine biscuits and withdrew gracefully.

'I'd give my teeth for a garden like this,' I said. It was more like a small park, really, with that fountain and those golden trees.

'Dorothea's preserve. I was at sea for long periods, and this was her haven. Will you pour, my dear? Cream for me.'

Royal Worcester china. A silver coffee-pot.

I poured. And then, not knowing where to start, I plunged in. 'Mr Worrall – you must wonder why I should bother you like this.'

'It cannot be unconnected with the incidents at William Murdock College.'

'I've been suspended. Gross misconduct.'

His eyebrows shifted. 'Indeed. Any action on your part which may have precipitated such a response must have been seriously out of character. Would you care to tell me what this misconduct might be?'

'I wish I could. I wish I *knew*. They haven't told me.'

'I imagine you will deny any charges,' he said, with a forbearing smile. 'Unfortunately the new Instruments and Articles of Government entitle them to make such vague charges, as I'm sure your union representative will confirm. I would point out, however, that during my tenure, the alleged perpetrator was always given details of the alleged offence. In most colleges staff are entitled to ask in writing for details of any allegations, and a written reply must be given well before the hearing. I'm sure your NATFHE colleagues will have told you all this, however.'

I explained about Frank, threw in Seb's fruitless mission, too.

'That case is resolved now, you say?'

'A nine hours' wonder.'

'Indeed. And do you know which college?'

'The police do, but I haven't asked. I don't want them to tell me to mind my own business.'

Worrall laughed. 'Sophie, such circumspection on your

part is a novelty. I don't mean to mock, my dear – I can see this business has upset you. Another biscuit?'

'Does your wife make these? They're very good. Our new principal prides herself on her cooking,' I said. 'As well as tender loving care for union reps. In fact, I can hardly believe she's taken any part in this move against me, she's been so considerate.'

'Allow me to observe, Sophie, that there is merely a disciplinary charge, not "a move against" anyone. Tell me, how do you find your new head of department?'

'He doesn't miss a trick.' I explained about my teaching hours. 'Mr Worrall,' I added, 'why did you retire?'

It was meant to be a rhetorical question, but to my surprise he took it at face value. 'Because the DfEE – Department for Education and Employment, Sophie – will no longer be funding their part of a prematurely retired lecturer's pension. I'm sure there are little groups of staff all over the college busy with their calculators, wondering if and when they can go.' My smile confirmed this. 'Because soon the college itself will have to pick up the bill – which means, in these straitened times, that premature retirement will no longer be an option. I – thought it better to go at the end of an academic year rather than wait any longer.'

Why did he think it necessary to explain all this to me? As if he had to justify himself? I looked him straight in the eyes. 'Was that the only reason?'

He spread a hand as defensive as it was elegant. 'Surely you of all people would understand my motives, Sophie. I went into education because I believed in it – I thought I could do some good. But there are so many financial pressures these days that education itself – the *quality* of education I wanted to develop – is going to the wall. Recruitment, retention, outcomes: not all of them are compatible, Sophie, as you must be aware.'

There was something else, wasn't there? 'What did you think of Dan Godfrey's appointment?' I asked curiously. He didn't seem the sort of man of which the old-fashioned Worrall would approve.

'You can't expect me to comment on specific appointments – after all, I was the chair of the interview panel. But let us say, there were appointments with which I couldn't whole-heartedly concur.'

'Any special reason?'

He waited for a grandmother clock to sound the hour. 'Personality. Background. Experience. Expectations.'

'Might you have objected to Mr Godfrey on any of those grounds?'

'Sophie, my dear! As a matter of fact – and I know I can rely on your absolute discretion – I simply didn't like him. I've worked with men of all sorts for many years, and you develop an instinct, Sophie. He was pleasant, highly qualified. But I didn't like him.'

'He didn't have a criminal record, for example?'

'I can tell from your voice that you want the answer to be yes. But I can assure you that there was no problem with the man's record. And his references – which we checked meticulously – were immaculate.'

All depended on Richard, then. And the Police Central Computer.

Worrall got up and walked to the window. Why did I get the impression he didn't want to look me in the eye? 'If I might presume to offer one word of advice to such a hardy soul as yourself, Sophie, it would be that heroism is not always appropriate. Remember, if you go to an Industrial Tribunal they can't compel the college – I beg your pardon, the corporation – to reinstate you. The best you can hope for is vindication and compensation. That might seem like the end of the world to someone who's invested as much as you in William Murdock, but it won't be. There are other things to do in life, Sophie.' He didn't sound convincing. Perhaps it was not me he was trying to persuade.

Two spaniels bustled up to the window, pawing the glass and barking imperiously.

'Time for their walk. I wish I could believe our talk was of the remotest use, but I fear all you've done is endure an old man's nostalgia for times that might never have been.'

'But—'

'These animals live by routine. Good morning to you.'

I was driving home via Sutton Park, making the best of my unexpected time off, when I pulled into a car park to check my diary. And discovered what I feared: I was missing another work-experience meeting. I said it out aloud, 'Sod William Murdock! Their problem,' and put the car into gear and set off. But I stopped, of course, and, with a sense of adventure, made my first call on my poncy new toy. Pity all I could think of, as I tried to penetrate a labyrinthine phone system, was how much the damn call was costing: at this rate my fifteen minutes would soon be over.

A couple of squirrels danced and leapt through the trees around me. Next time I came this way I'd bring some lunch and share it with them. Next time. When I wasn't spending every other moment wondering whether those who wanted to silence me had traced me here. I shoved the car into gear and started rapidly homeward.

Chapter Twenty-Five

Having no other ideas, I went back to Harborne for lunch.

Aggie's house. There was something wrong with Aggie's house!

Slamming out of the hire car, I sprinted up her drive. Yes, the paint on the front door was definitely blistered. And the door was standing ajar.

'Who's there?' Recklessly, I pushed at the door with my foot.

'That you, Soph? Come along in!'

'What's been going on here?' I sank on to the stairs. Hell, it was a stupid question: anyone could see what had been going on.

'Could have been quite nasty,' one of Gavin's lads offered, coming forward, a flask-top of earthy-looking tea in his hand, 'if they'd gone for someone's face. Funny, there wasn't all that much acid. Could try harder, you might say. Any road, what's a bit of paint? We'll strip that off and repaint it so neat the old dear won't know the difference.'

'Won't she? I wouldn't take any bets!'

'Well, did you notice we'd already tidied yours?' the older man asked.

'*Mine!*'

'There you are, then. And if they try any funny business – well, they've got this lot to contend with.'

Aggie's letterbox was now sealed, and a perspex sheet – twin of the one on my front door – covered the leaded lights of the window. There were other sheets, still with their adhesive paper coating, propped against various walls.

'We'll get them finished this afternoon. We were going to leave it, but the gaffer says prioritize it. And I can't say as how I blame him.' He gestured at the scarred door.

Why on earth were they bothering with lunch? Why not get stuck right into the work? Look how casual they were, leaving the door open so anyone could walk in!

Then I noticed a video camera taped to the picture rail. And blinked.

'Ah. You'm got one an' all,' the bigger man said. 'Just for a trial period. Tell you what, our kid, I could bring me Staffordshire bull and sleep here, only I reckon as they'll have him down as a dangerous dog. Course, he's not dangerous: only if someone he doesn't fancy comes poking 'is nose in. 'Ere, yow all right, me lover? Sit yoursell down again.'

I sat. What on earth was I doing? Seb, Richard, now Aggie – I was sucking them all into danger.

The smaller lad padded off, coming back with something amber-coloured in the bottom of one of Aggie's best tea-cups. And it wasn't tea. 'Medicinal,' he said, swirling it so it gave off heady fumes. 'Found it in the old lady's pantry.'

I shook my head. 'I've got this stomach problem.'

'That won't do her no good at all, Les. Food – that's what she needs! It'll be your blood sugar as is down,' Big Bloke announced. 'Here, you get outside this. *Then* you can have a little nip.'

'This' was a bulky cheese and chutney sandwich.

We chomped in silence. If my face was busy eating, perhaps it would forget how much it wanted to cry.

'Tell you what, Miss. You wouldn't like to try a bit of my special, would you?' This was the big man again: if the other one was Les, he must be Mike.

I nodded, feigning an interest I didn't feel, and he toddled off to the kitchen, returning with three china plates. Then he fished a large plastic box from his snap-bag. The lid sighed open: a thick, fluffy Victoria sponge. He even remembered to wipe his knife on his overalls before slicing it.

'Regular Army,' he said proudly. 'Come on, love – have a taste.' He proffered a slice on his paw.

Angel food!

If my fairy-godmother had chosen to turn up, one of my wishes would have been to stay there all afternoon with these solid, kindly men. But I couldn't, could I? They had work to do. And I was supposed to be trekking across Birmingham. And I ought to pick up any messages from my answerphone . . .

I dithered by the door.

Mike, who was already measuring perspex, looked up. 'Don't you worry, young Soph. We'll be keeping an eye on things here. And at your place. Have a gander in the kitchen.'

And there, displayed on a tiny monitor sitting on Aggie's well-scrubbed table, was my hall. And then my landing.

Only one phone message. From Fairbairn's secretary, confirming that my disciplinary hearing would be on Thursday.

Bloody stomach. All it took was one phone call! I poured some antacid into it, and stood gripping the table grimly while it took effect. Then I called NATFHE, getting, as I suppose I should have expected, seeing that their offices had been firebombed, their answering machine. I left my number and a brief explanation; I also told them the time and date of the hearing. Amongst all their other urgent problems, this needed priority. And it got it. Even as I concluded the message, Seb's voice came through.

'We should talk before the hearing,' he said. 'Too much mess here, though. Tell you what, Sophie, I don't have my diary in front of me – can I call you back?'

Disconcerted, I said I was going out, then remembered my mobile. Wouldn't it take incoming calls too? The miracles of modern technology! The fact that nine-tenths of our students seemed to carry them and use them – sometimes in class – was irrelevant; it gave me as much pleasure as if I'd invented them.

It rang immediately. Seb!

'I take it you're digital?' he asked, without preamble. 'Only there's been odd clicks on the office phone, and maybe I'm paranoid—'

'But that doesn't mean they're not out to get you,' I concluded.

'Exactly. We should meet in an extremely public place, Sophie. But nowhere obvious. How about the Art Gallery? By Lucifer? And we can talk over a cup of tea. Say three tomorrow?'

'Three. By Lucifer.'

And he cut off. No doubt he'd run out of his month's free calls, too.

Afzal's office, just off Golden Hillock Road, boasted its own car park – in reality an ex-back garden – in which his and Chris's cars waited side by side for mine. The young African-Caribbean woman behind a desk, apparently doubling as receptionist and typist, greeted me with enthusiasm and the offer of tea. When I declined, she removed her headset and took me through into what had once been a living room and still looked a bit like one. As premises, they were homely.

Both men stood to greet me, looking at me with concern.

'I thought Ian was bringing you,' Chris grunted.

'I'm all right.'

Apparently convinced by my grin, which aspired to be cheery, they argued about a chair for me. I settled it by taking a hard wooden one, and announcing I had some news.

'Good job someone has,' Chris said, his voice dour even for him. 'Richard's taken off on a walking holiday, bugger him. Needs some space, his auntie says. And there's definitely nothing in our records on Godfrey.'

'According to Mr Worrall, he didn't declare any criminal past on his application form. Applicants for teaching jobs have to declare even "spent" convictions by law, because they're working with young people.'

'That's right,' they said together.

'But the funny thing is,' I added, 'I reckon Worrall's hiding something. About his own precipitate exodus from William Murdock.'

'Not the polysyllabic Worrall? Come off it, Sophie! The man's as straight as a die.'

'You would have thought so, wouldn't you? He's always been such a father figure to the college. Remote, but dependable when you needed advice or support. That's why I went to see him this morning.' I hoped Chris wouldn't ask me to quantify my suspicions about Worrall: my feelings and instincts were all so vague.

'And how did you get there, may I ask?'

I stood up and walked to the window. 'If you look through this window, Chris, you can just see a red Fiesta. Hired. And I shall acquire a blue Rover tomorrow. And a Peugeot for Thursday – don't know what colour yet. It'll cost me an arm and a leg, but as long as mine's being looked at – what did they find?' I sat down harder than I'd intended.

'Don't know yet. All I know is that your Renault's sitting on its own in the far corner of the pound waiting for the attentions of experts in explosive devices. To be honest, I'd like you out of Brum altogether.'

I would *not* let my teeth chatter. 'Not till after the hearing.' My voice came out without a quaver – I was proud of it.

'Which I predict will end in your dismissal,' Afzal said, from behind his desk. 'If they've gone this far, they'll have witnesses ready to testify black's white.'

'What'll be interesting,' I said, 'is who those witnesses are.'

'You've got representation?' Afzal asked.

'Seb, from my union.'

He nodded. 'A very sound man. And when is the hearing?'

'Thursday morning. I'm meeting Seb to talk things through tomorrow afternoon.'

'You know,' Chris said, 'if I were a betting man, I'd put a lot of money on the hearing suddenly being brought forward. To tomorrow morning, perhaps?'

'No takers,' Afzal and I said together. I continued. 'But enough of me. The other fires. The refuge and those buildings nearby. And the pretend Asian thugs – what about them?'

Afzal sighed. 'Some of the local community would be horrified that a refuge for women who claim that their husbands are battering them should even exist, let alone be established in their neighbourhood. You see, some men – and women – cling to the belief that a woman is there for her husband to do what he wants with. Another school of thought is that a man will only treat his wife badly if she provokes him. Some parents ignore their daughters' plights because it would reflect ill on a marriage that they have helped arrange. So we're dealing with a mish-mash of prejudices. My own view, for what it's worth, is that Shahida and her committee were ill-advised to establish it in an area with such a large Asian community. No! Let me finish, please. The police have a very well-established system of safe houses for Asian girls – those I've steered towards the police have never been discovered. Surely, Sophie, you must have had occasion to use such a rescue service?'

'I've passed girls on, yes. And, I admit, security's been so good even I didn't know where they'd gone. But Shahida's group – and I'm part of it, remember – wanted something different. A specifically multi-cultural refuge, to show that wife-battering crosses all ethnic boundaries.'

'Admirable middle-class intellectual theorising. Perhaps an element of NIMBY, too. They don't want fallen women, white or black, in their territory. I've been asking Chris to suggest to his senior officers that these incidents shouldn't necessarily be regarded as mere ethnic community squabbles, but something else.'

'And I shall be doing precisely that. Especially as young Tom happened to drop into the planning office to cast his eyes over proposals for a school extension near his flat and, being young Tom, found planning permission applications involving a huge fitness centre round the area of the refuge. Very lucrative. But they'd need a nice big site, with adequate parking. Do you see what I'm getting at?'

We could hardly not.

'And is there any indication who's behind the application?' Afzal asked.

'Tom's got the details and will be checking them out. But I'd say the evidence so far suggests that we haven't got self-righteous Muslims burning down a house of shame – much as some people might like it to look that way. And I shall tell my superiors that in about an hour's time. So Afzal, if you and Sophie will excuse me, I'll be on my way.' He shook hands with Afzal, who had emerged from behind his desk; and then stood helpless. What could he substitute for a handshake with me?

I settled it by giving him the briefest of hugs, to which he had, perforce, to respond. Then he touched my hair. 'Take care of yourself, Sophie.' He was halfway through the door when he came back. 'Will Afzal be looking after you this evening?'

Afzal patted a heap of folders. 'I can't see me leaving here before midnight.'

If only I could work out whether the man was interested in me or not! A bit of consistency wouldn't come amiss. Still, at the moment personal relationships were the least of my worries.

'So where will you be? Ian's?'

The memory of last night came back in one excruciating blush. 'Chris – Ian will probably have got hold of the wrong end of a particularly thorny stick, and I want to stay on speaking terms with him. Last night, my tum was so bad I couldn't sleep, so I went and made myself toast. And – oh, it was three in the morning and I got sorrier and sorrier for myself ... I must have woken Greg, who was sleeping in the living room. But – he wouldn't have been there when Ian and Val went to work. He was sleeping in my bed. With me.' I was conscious of a deathly silence. 'But I want Ian and Val to know that we were – in the most literal sense, not at all in the euphemistic sense – *sleeping* together. I think Ian'd be really offended if he thought otherwise.'

Chris was clearly relieved; he was trying not to laugh. 'I'm sure he would. You're the daughter he's never had, Sophie – you have to be like Caesar's wife. I'll tell him, don't worry. Whether he'll believe me is another matter.'

The same could be said for Afzal.

'Greg's not really interested in me,' I hastened to add. 'He's got – someone else has the hots for him.'

'A bird in the bed is worth two with the hots?' Afzal suggested.

'Not this bird,' I said.

It was a good job no one *had* taken bets on the rescheduling of my hearing: the answering machine announced it would now be at nine on Wednesday morning. I left a message on the NATFHE machine and there was an immediate callback on my mobile number from Seb.

'OK,' he said. 'This evening.'

'But you must want to go home occasionally.'

'Part of my job. Only problem is where. Not here, not my home, not your home. Like I said, it's got to be somewhere very private or very public.'

My mind wouldn't function. 'Any ideas?'

'I was hoping you'd have some. Not a pub, for preference. Too noisy. Got any friends who might oblige?'

I'd only one friend with any public accommodation. 'What about Afzal Mohammed's office? If he doesn't mind, that is.'

'Who?'

I explained.

'Of course – I know him. OK. If I don't hear from you I'll see you there at six.'

Afzal was only too happy to oblige, provided we didn't mind using the reception area. Since that was what I had had in mind, I was happy to accept.

'I've never dealt with the new William Murdock Management before,' Seb said, whirling round on the receptionist's chair. 'You knew where you were with Worrall and Jeffries: decent men. Not that this woman Fairbairn doesn't sound amazing, from what I've picked up on the grapevine. She was somewhere up North before – really turned an ailing college round. And nice with it. Dan Godfrey – he's never been involved in any strong-arm tactics, either. The awkward buggers get a reputation, see.'

'Well, it's a first for all of us, then.'

'And another first – I've no idea how this hearing will be conducted. Sometimes it's a very formal affair, with witnesses; sometimes it's just written statements. So be prepared for either. I was at one not so long ago where they made the lecturer into a defendant who had to stand throughout, but I shouldn't think your lot would stoop to that. After all, you've got a fine teaching record, and this is your first clash with the powers-that-be. As far as I know.'

'I had the odd run-in with Richard and Worrall when I was younger and stroppier. But I'm proud to number Richard among my friends now. And Worrall and I have been courteous to each other for years.' I wouldn't mention my suspicion that Worrall was hiding something.

'You've never done more than have the odd gripe about your timetable?'

'They didn't like it when a letterbomb came directed to me at the college, but they agreed that was scarcely my fault.'

'Right. And there's been nothing iffy with Dan?'

I told him about my problem with the GCSE class. 'I wanted to make an issue of it, but Frank was involved in downsizing discussions at the time and it got easier just to accept it as a solution, even though I didn't like it. And there was a slight disagreement over the reduction of my teaching hours when I agreed to resume work experience liaison. I assumed seventy-five per cent of my timetable meant just that – not seventy-five per cent of the *average* timetable.'

'Quite a difference?'

'Well, I'm a senior lecturer.'

'So your responsibilities mean you'd be teaching far less than the average New Contract teacher.'

'*Far* less, poor buggers! Nicely conned, I was. But I didn't make a fuss. I should have clarified things properly from the start.'

'You should have got Frank in on the discussions.'

'But I trusted Dan, you see. After all, I'd taught him. Shit, Seb – forget I said that. I promised him no one'd know.'

'Taught him?'

'I was in my first or second year and he was a mature student. Please, Seb—'

'Hang on. Why doesn't he want it known? Seems quite innocuous to me.'

'It's in the hands of the police,' I said. 'Now, what should I—'

'I'll get the grapevine on to this, Sophie. You never know what—'

I held up my hands to stop him. 'Seb, this is a man's career we're talking about.'

'Sophie, this is a woman's life. Sarah Robertson was one of my members. And what about Mike Appleyard? A member for years. And what about you? If they're playing dirty, you may have to try the same tactics.'

'I'd rather play clean.'

'We all would. But there are times when playing clean won't work, not if they're playing dirty. Has it occurred to you that this is a trumped-up charge to get rid of you?'

'Yes. It's occurred to the police, too. Seb, I just want to keep my job!'

'Why?'

'I'm sorry?'

'Why? Oh, you want compensation for unfair dismissal – we'll screw every penny out of the industrial tribunal – but why should you want to work many hours' unpaid overtime – because that's in essence what you're being forced to do – in a miserable old college whose saving grace was once the management? Come on, Sophie – one good reason!'

I stared. 'But – the students, my colleagues—'

'Plenty of students in other colleges. Plenty of colleagues, too. Come on, Sophie: sometimes it's time for a change. For everyone. Even for you.'

Chapter Twenty-Six

Seb had at last gone to his home and family, and I was making coffee for Afzal and me.

'What are your plans for the rest of the evening?' he asked, waving away the sugar.

Keeping every hint of pathos out of my voice, I said, 'I was hoping you might have time to join me for a meal.'

He gestured. 'I'm afraid I shall be here till midnight.'

I waited. There might be a friendly phrase to follow; there wasn't. 'Afzal, has something happened? Sometimes we seem to be getting close to each other – at others you seem to be holding me at arm's length.'

'No, nothing's happened. I just happen to be very busy. You can see that.'

'I can see a mound of files. And I believe that you're busy. But that doesn't explain why sometimes you're warm towards me, and sometimes the temperature drops below zero. Like now.' I looked straight at him, but he made a show of thumbing through a file: time for another tack. 'You did believe me when I said that though Greg and I had ended in the same bed, no sex was involved?'

'What you do in bed is your business.'

Shit! He hadn't. 'Yes. But what my friends think of me is my business too.'

'Oh, your friends care for you very much, I'm sure.'

'And are you my friend?' I sat on my hands so he wouldn't see they were shaking. I was on new ground here, and it felt unsafe.

He forced a smile. 'Of course, Sophie! How on earth

could you doubt that?' At last the smile reached his eyes, softening his face. 'But – but just now, I'm disappearing under my work. I'm sorry.'

'OK.' I spoke as lightly as I could, because while the work was a fair excuse, it was clear it was no more than an excuse. Whatever was troubling him would no doubt emerge sooner or later. And right now I didn't think I had the strength for an emotional showdown. 'I'll – see you around then.' I left the untouched coffee mug where it was, gathered my jacket and bag, and left, without a backward glance.

If I'd been trying to shake off a tail, I couldn't have taken a more convoluted route home. Fighting back tears, I kept mistaking junctions, and heading off into unknown and apparently unloved parts of Birmingham. It was complicated by the fact I didn't really know where I was going. Home? Or straight to Ian's? Then I thought of women friends I could turn to. Aberlene, the violinist – but the Midshires Symphony Orchestra would be starting their Tuesday evening series tonight. Shahida – the obvious answer; I could find out what was happening at college, too. But when I dialled it was a grandmother night. Janet? More of an acquaintance. The trouble with men friends was the complication of their partners. A drink with Carl would have done wonders for my poor bruised ego, and would also have filled me in about college, but my ego wasn't worth the price of his wife's wrath – nor his raised expectations. Chris? But what about his loyalties to Diane? Greg? He might well be *with* Diane. Looked like home or Ian's, then, and on the whole I preferred home. Might even surf the old Internet for a bit, try and catch up with my cousin Andy and his wife.

I got home eventually, via this most devious of routes, armed with chicken and chips. Quite the wrong thing for my stomach, but better than my usual curry or Chinese. A couple of messages on my machine: they'd wait till I'd eaten. A large note from Greg, telling me he'd phone about ten to let me know what was happening. And a very silent house.

The chicken was an undernourished affair, but the chips

209

– a luxury I rarely indulge in – good. I risked a glass of lager – when would I be able to drink wine again? And then I dealt with the calls. Ian: I wasn't to be a silly girl, and I was to get myself round there. Chris: at Ian's, wanting to know where the hell I was.

Before replying, and aware I was being contrary and indeed churlish – how many times had I explained the origin and implications of the word to successions of A-Level students? – I tried Richard's contact number. And got him!

'I've been trying to clear things in my head,' he said. 'You know, you live with someone for years and then find you didn't know them at all. I mean – twenty odd years with Sheila, and no clue she might – prefer other women. I haven't got anywhere. I do seem to have cut down on the whisky, though. Sophie, have you any idea how much I was getting through?'

'More than you used to,' I said.

'Two bottles a week! Getting on to three. And to think I just used to keep an odd bottle in for when one of us got a cold. Well, I can't afford it. So I've stopped.'

'Well done!' And then I thought a little. 'Altogether?'

'For a bit. And then only with people. So it won't stop me asking you out for a drink.'

'So long as you don't go all saintly on me. Now, Richard, I dare say the police have been on to you about that pile of photocopies I left at your place.'

'Indeed they have. And the relevant papers should be in their hands tomorrow. I thought if they were so terribly important they were safer in my bank – what was that?'

The phone was crackling.

Seb, and his not-so-paranoid fears!

'Don't say another word. Don't tell me anything at all. Just contact Chris Groom – that's the guy who's been trying to reach you.'

'Oh, I have done. I shall be meeting him—'

'Richard! Shut up!' But I was sure I hadn't said it in time. As soon as I'd slammed down the phone, I dialled him again, this time on my mobile. He plainly believed I was losing my marbles, but decided to humour me; I'd meet him at Rose Road the following afternoon. He meekly agreed that he wouldn't go home in any circumstances – just straight to the police station.

Exhausted, mentally if not physically, I toiled upstairs. Idly I switched on the computer, and left a message for Andy and Ruth to contact me. And, almost without my knowing it, I was into a game of Solitaire. It wouldn't come out, though. I dealt again, only to be disturbed by the phone; I used the extension in my bedroom, scuttling to beat the answering machine. But it wasn't anyone from William Murdock. The receiver at the other end was replaced as soon as I spoke. And when I tried to 1471-them, they'd withheld their number. What a surprise.

The next call arrived just as I'd started to file my nails: I pounced. Greg, this time, obviously from a bar. He'd decided not to sleep at Ian's tonight, but that didn't mean he'd be sleeping at my place, either. (So where was he sleeping? But I didn't ask.) Oh, and the official line at William Murdock was that I'd got a virus which had made me deaf and given me teachers' throat. Not surprising I'd had no phone calls, really.

Belatedly, I called Ian, who was plainly relieved to have an unaccompanied me in his spare room. Before he could say much, however, Chris took the phone.

'You've heard about Richard?'

'We'll talk about that later,' I said. 'Not on the phone. Not while it's got this fault. I shall have to report it to BT tomorrow. All these funny clicks—'

'Ah. I'll come and collect you.' He put the phone down.

I gathered together odds and ends of clothes: it felt horribly like a good suit day tomorrow. Shoes polished. Spare tights. A note-pad and pencil. Then downstairs for a slurp of antacid.

When the doorbell rang, I looked through my peep-hole to check that it was indeed Chris.

'You look knackered,' I said.

'Feel it. Got your things ready?'

'They're on my bed. And – hell! I haven't switched off my computer!'

He followed me upstairs. 'Hey, you're doing well!'

Grabbing the mouse, he sat down and started to play. 'Red jack on the black queen,' I said.

'And then on to the red king. Have we got a ten ...'

That didn't come out, either. Nor did the next game. But it was so good to be at ease with him again after all this time, I didn't mind. Neither did he. Eventually, of course, we agreed to have one last game: 'The very last, Chris?'

'The very last. Unless we can't get this out!'

We were just arguing about which red four to put on our black five when the front door rattled. He was still seated, so there was no time for him to thrust me heroically behind him, but he followed me on to the landing as fast as I'd ever seen him move.

And I wished to God he hadn't.

His face betrayed him: pain and anger and disappointment.

Who could blame him?

At the bottom of my stairs, her arm round Greg's shoulders, was Diane Stephenson.

A very drunk Diane Stephenson.

Greg was almost sober, and quickly took in the situation. 'Why don't you wait in the car, sweetheart?' He gave her a gentle push. 'Go on – I'll be out as soon as I get my toothbrush.'

Please God, let her do as he says. I raise my hand, so the back of it rests on Chris's chest. I hold Greg's gaze: mine says, 'Get her out of my house.'

He takes her by the elbow and turns her round. She's out of the door; I start to relax.

'Who's that with fucking Sophie?' She's still on the step but has pushed open the door.

My fists are tight bunches of tension.

'Who's that with fucking Sophie? Come on, Greg, I want to see who's with – holy shit! It's bloody Chris. DCI Chris Groom. The big boss man.'

He pushes me to one side, walks slowly down the stairs. 'Yes, it's me, Diane. I—' He falters. 'I'll see you in my office in the morning. Good night to you, Greg. Diane.' And he shuts the front door in their faces.

I wait. I'm glad I can't see his face; the back of his head, the angle of his shoulders are bad enough.

The computer was exited, my bag was packed and beside me on the stairs. I looked at Chris. He hadn't moved; it was time he did.

'Better get you to Ian's,' he said, not looking at me. 'But I think you should drop the hire car off first before anyone gets ideas about that. I'll tail you. I'll take that bag in my car.'

I set the alarm and locked us out. He tailed me first to the nearest filling station, then to the garage, where I handed the keys to the duty security guard. Chris was waiting when I emerged.

He started the engine without a word, driving by the textbook. A glance at his profile was sufficient to keep me quiet.

'You'll come in for a coffee? Please!' For he seemed about to refuse.

'They'll think we've had another row if I don't,' he said. But he didn't laugh.

The house was in silence when we went in. Not surprising, at eleven-fifty. I filled the kettle, and raised my eyebrows in enquiry. Ian's decaffeinated Earl Grey tea? Or camomile and honey?

'Anything.' He sat down heavily at the kitchen table.

Camomile, then.

'How long have you known?'

'That she boozes? A couple of weeks.'

'And – about Greg?'

'Only tonight. Though I did suspect. And you?' Pushing his mug across, I sat at right angles to him.

'About her drinking – rumours.'

I didn't mention the incident in the restaurant. 'She's under tremendous pressure.' She was a woman in a tough job – I felt she deserved some defence.

'We're all under tremendous pressure.'

213

'Only acting in post must put you under worse pressure than most.'

'I tried to sort that out. Not hard enough, obviously.' He dropped his head into his hands.

Ian wouldn't begrudge a drop of one of his malts. I found a glass, and poured him a generous tot. Not tactful, perhaps. But he took it absentmindedly and swallowed the occasional sip.

'What about you and Greg?'

I slopped some of my camomile. 'Me and Greg?'

'How long have you known she and Greg were an item?' His mouth sounded dry, as if he had to work hard to make his lips move.

'Not an item. A flirtation. A fling.'

He sank some more whisky. 'That makes it OK, does it?'

'I'm not the person to answer that.'

He reached for the bottle; this time the amount was more than generous. Shades of Richard! And, since Chris was usually as abstemious as Richard, I was alarmed. There was no way he should drive with that much inside him.

'What about you and Afzal? You seem to like him.'

'I like him a lot. But I've a nasty suspicion he dropped me. At about seven-thirty this evening. And I've no idea why.'

'It was daft of you to mention sleeping with Greg. He didn't like it. Mind you, I wouldn't have liked it either. I don't bloody well like it. Oh, Sophie – what a fucking mess.' He stood up.

I caught him as he swayed.

'Jesus! Can't hold my booze!'

'What time did you get up? And eat? Whisky on an empty stomach? Come on – you'd better have my bed. To please Ian, if nothing else.'

'Just as long,' he said, holding on to me, 'as you're in it too.'

Chapter Twenty-Seven

By the time I'd shaken the creases from my best suit and hung it up, removed my make-up and cleaned my teeth, Chris was fast asleep. I set the alarm for seven – as if I wouldn't wake up anyway – and, wearing my going-visiting nightie, slipped in beside him. He rolled over, presenting me with a long, chaste back, which I fitted myself round. At least Chris wasn't a snorer. Nor, generally, did he wake in the night, so my virtue, such as it was, was unlikely to come under any pressure till the morning – by which time everyone's thoughts would be on other things. Ian would be worrying how much porridge to make; Val would be apologising for the perfectly sound mattress; Chris would be too embarrassed by the audible presence of other people to do anything, and I'd be too anxious about what the coming meeting might hold to be many degrees above frigid. Meanwhile, a warm back was comforting. And should any of my calculations about the morning be awry, I'd got a packet of condoms in my toilet bag, within easy reach.

The trouble was I was too fond of Chris to want a casual bonk with him. For far too long he'd suffered a nasty case of calf-love – if a man of nearly forty can have such a thing. When we'd finally got together, what had been an excellent friendship started to crack, eventually disintegrating when I did something of which he profoundly disapproved to protect someone else I cared for. I knew what being in love was – and it certainly wasn't what I felt for Chris. I was nearer to being in love with Afzal; but when I came to examine my feelings, I discovered more anger at the way

215

he'd treated me than disappointment. And then my head clicked in: a man who'd been bereaved as tragically as Afzal wasn't going to fall in love easily again, not if he could help it. Maybe we could make a joint effort and build something strong; maybe he was too deeply scarred. For several lonely minutes I was afraid that I might be too. Afraid I would never be able to love anyone as deeply as I'd loved Andy. But life wasn't for sitting mooning around, weeping for what you know you can't have. No – life, even at William Murdock, was for making the best of imperfect situations.

Chris rolled over, tangling arms and legs. Silently and neatly I turned too, so that he fitted round my bottom. He hadn't woken. And that was how I fell asleep.

I was awake at six, chasing an errant duvet and trying not to fall off the edge of the bed, where Chris had propelled me. It seemed sensible after all to slip out of bed, and to shower and wash my hair before anyone else wanted the bathroom. OK, I'd have to sit round with wet hair until I could borrow Val's drier, but that wasn't a problem. I smuggled my clothes out of the bedroom as I went.

'Was I very drunk last night?' Chris asked as he unlocked his car.

'Not so much drunk, as exhausted, I'd have said.'

The whole topic had been studiously ignored at breakfast. Ian and Val had a tendency to foolish, benign smiles; but I wasn't in the mood for public dentings of poor Chris's fragile ego.

We knew each other better than to embark on apologies at this time of day; Chris's almost total silence as we set out for William Murdock was the norm for him. And I was too apprehensive to waste effort in idle chat.

'I'd like to pop into Rose Road for a couple of minutes,' he said.

'Fine. No point in arriving too early – they'll keep me incommunicado anyway.'

If I'd been Diane, I'd have been in work by six, clearing out all the stuff I'd parked in Chris's room. Why he'd let

216

her use it at all was beyond me: it was out of character for him to let personal feelings overcome professional and disciplinary considerations. In fact, I was surprised, come to think of it, that he should ever have begun a relationship with someone from his team. I'd have thought he'd have organized her transfer, at the very least. He might have to now. And he'd have the tricky question of her promotion, and his part in it. Foolish, foolish Chris: whatever happened to your integrity?

Tom, at least, was in early, and dashed down to the car park, beaming at Chris as he parked. Before he'd even applied the handbrake, Tom had opened the door and was passing him a folded piece of paper. 'Those Asian attackers, man – we've got some of them. Yes! In action! Halfway down Broad Street. And guess what, they're as Anglo-Saxon as you are!'

Still no handbrake, but Chris was out of the car; I pulled it up, and got out more slowly. Chris had probably meant me to stay in the car while he checked whatever he wanted to check, but this was my case. In a manner of speaking.

'You didn't get one with halitosis?' I asked.

'Not to my knowledge, pet. Two out of three we got. And they're canny buggers. Not talking. Founder members of the "I-know-my-rights brigade".'

'Excellent,' Chris said crisply. 'So they'll know that the courts don't construe silence as golden these days. Anything else, Tom?'

'Only to wish Sophie well, like. And give her this.' He thrust a tiny spray of white heather at me, almost invisible in his large hand, and leaned forward to peck my cheek. 'Come on now, pet – no need for tears. You'll have them on toast.'

'I'm sure she will.' Chris put a brotherly arm round my shoulders.

It didn't feel altogether brotherly, though. I wasn't going to argue with kindness and comfort.

'Will you be wanting to talk to the lads yourself, Gaffer?'

'Who's doing it now?'

'Me and Diane.'

'Don't see any reason to change that. If you don't get

217

anywhere, Ian'll be along later. If you think a change'll be as good as a rest, Karen's very good. I'm off to William Murdock for another sniff round myself. And – when this business of Sophie's is out of the way – I'll talk to Godfrey and Fairbairn. What's up, Sophie?'

'Nothing. Just something ringing a bell. Long way away, though.' I couldn't resist looking at my watch.

'OK. Avanti!'

'Good luck, pet!'

'Have we got time to go back home? Only this shirt is wrong with this suit—'

'Not really.'

'But—'

'I don't think your sartorial elegance is what they'll be worrying about.'

Chris slipped neatly into one of the parking spaces set aside for important visitors to the college. A green Jag which looked familiar occupied another space and a half. In the nearest staff slot was another familiar car – a beat-up Maestro. I looked at the windscreen: yes, an official sticker. My movements attracted the interest of the security guards, however, and two of them started to bear down on me. To my shame, I retreated to the security of Chris's side. With his official note-pad in his hand, he was sufficiently intimidating to keep them at bay.

I could see why they hustled criminals into court with blankets over their heads. No, not criminals. The *accused* – that was all I was. But it was difficult to walk head-high into the foyer and straight to the Principal's room without falling over. I was glad of Chris's company: the very sight of his back kept the security guards at a safe distance. But they were there, nonetheless, watching.

The Principal's secretary, Ann, a woman whose babies I'd sat, barely looked at me. 'You're to wait. Mr Conrad's already over there.' She nodded at a cluster of chairs.

She'd provided Seb with coffee; she didn't offer me any. Chris looked meaningfully at Seb's cup.

'Oh – would you like a cup, Chief Inspector?'

'We both would,' he said. No one could have called his tone aggressive, but no one was in any doubt that he was trying to make a point.

I introduced the two men, who shook hands. 'Chris is here to keep me company until we go in – and to add a little gravitas.'

'And to scare the natives into submission, I hope,' Seb said. 'Now, Sophie, what we're going to have to do is think on our feet. They've had time to orchestrate this: all you and I can do is extemporize. Dan's prosecuting counsel – he may or may not have witnesses. Fairbairn's the judge. Possibly the Chair of Governors will be there as another judge.'

Coffee or no coffee – in my case, *still* no coffee – my nervous bladder was uncomfortable. There was a women's loo just down the corridor, so off I headed.

A voice followed. 'Where do you think you're going?'

'Where do you think I'm going, Ann? The loo, of course.'

'You're not allowed to leave the waiting area without permission.'

'I don't need permission to pee, surely to God!'

But to my intense annoyance and embarrassment, she followed, waiting by the wash-basin while I used the cubicle. She supervised the subsequent hand-washing and checking of lipstick in a chilly, disapproving silence, ostentatiously locking the door behind us. Yes, I'd be required to hand in all my keys, wouldn't I? It would be nice to be able to make a dramatic gesture, slamming the bunch hard into an outstretched palm; but that way they'd get my fob. How about a slow prising-free, one by one? They could watch my nails break as I did it.

My return was greeted with ironic grins and salutes from cups of coffee; still none for me. And nothing would have dragged a request from my lips. But Chris passed me his and, in the frosty voice he used to rebuke idiocy in his colleagues, said, 'I do believe someone offered me a coffee.'

No one ever glared at Chris when he spoke like that – not even Ann. She glared at me instead. When Chris more melodramatically than was necessary took my hand, there was nothing she could do except turn on her heel and walk, fast.

'I gave her children christening presents,' I said bleakly.

'How will you deal with her when you're reinstated?' Chris asked.

'Let me *be* reinstated first.' I started, without much success, to remove the fob from my bunch of official keys; Seb produced a penny, which worked better. Neither man could have missed the significance of what I was doing.

'Admit nothing. Volunteer nothing. If in doubt, ask to confer with me. If possible, leave all the talking to me. Anything else to add, Chris?'

'Nothing – except knock the bastards cold.' He heard the voices and footsteps, and raised his voice a little. 'She's a good woman, Seb. She's done nothing wrong.' Timing it to the second, he stood up, helping me to my feet, and kissed me lightly on the lips. 'See you afterwards, Sophie.' He nodded curtly at Dan, and smiled at Seb. Nothing about good luck, I noticed. And then I rejoiced: the implication was that I didn't *need* luck. And he, the most senior policeman in the college enquiries, was my friend.

Whatever the reason, Dan certainly didn't give the impression that, like Ann, he'd already convicted me. He shook hands with Seb, and ventured a smile in my direction. I didn't return it.

Ms Fairbairn was behind her desk. Dan waved Seb and me to two hard chairs on the far side of the room; Seb asked for a table. While one was produced – a folding exam desk – there was complete silence. Seb unpacked his document case and laid out pencils and ball-points; Dan was, it seemed, to occupy an armchair, though there was another chair to the side of him, near the door. He too had documents to lay out.

I wished I'd been to the loo again.

At last Dan had arranged things to his satisfaction. The trial – for that was what it seemed – was about to begin.

Chapter Twenty-Eight

Dan was on his feet. 'Ms Fairbairn, I have to bring to your notice evidence which will, I'm afraid, show that in recent weeks Ms Rivers has been guilty of gross misconduct. Allegations about her sexual behaviour have come to us from three quite separate sources. Two of the gentlemen involved are able to testify in person. That isn't all, I'm afraid. Since her suspension, Ms Rivers has been trying to subvert your authority by contacting members of staff, despite your prohibition.'

I don't know what colour my face ended: but I could feel the blood ebbing and flowing. Thank goodness Seb was making notes! All these allegations were so far-fetched as to be the stuff of nightmare. I couldn't make sense of them.

'The first complaint comes from one of our students. He made a formal complaint about the standard of Ms Rivers' dress. When I spoke to him about it, pointing out the difference between Eastern and Western notions of correct dress, he made a further, more serious allegation. Unfortunately Mr Yamin is unable through family illness to be here today. Here is his statement, Ms Fairbairn.' He passed her several stapled sheets. 'The gist of what he has to say is this: he remonstrated with Ms Rivers in front of his class, as their representative, and she refused to discuss the matter. Later, when he encountered Ms Rivers alone in a lift, she lifted her skirt, exposing her genitals to him. Ms Rivers, what do you have to say to this?'

I stood. 'Mr Godfrey, you know about the clothing incident. I reported it to you as soon as it occurred. As far as the alleged incident in the lift is concerned, I categorically deny it. To the best of my knowledge I have never seen the student since he left the classroom that day.'

I sat down again.

Seb leaned forward. 'I'd like a copy of the document containing these allegations, please. And you will understand when I say that until Mr – Yamin, is it? – has answered any questions Ms Rivers or I would wish to put to him this allegation must be regarded as what it is – malicious invention.'

'You will let me be the judge of that, Mr Conrad,' Ms Fairbairn said.

'And a copy of his allegation?'

'You will be given a photocopy in due course.'

The next accuser was there in person. Jaguar man: the one from the recruitment agency. He personified sleekness, from his hair to his shoes. He sat on one of the chairs provided, shooting his cuffs and easing his trouser legs to display his silk socks.

'What is the nature of your complaint against Ms Rivers?' Fairbairn asked.

'She made improper advances to me, Ms Fairbairn. She came to my office to ask if I would take any of her students on work placements. I was reluctant, at first, but she was extremely persuasive, and at length I agreed. She then proceeded to ask me about openings for teachers like herself – she said her boss had suggested a change of scene might benefit her career prospects. When I demurred – after all, she had obtained access to my office as one of your employees – she rubbed her legs against me, saying she was sure she could make it worth my while. At this point I cut the interview short and asked her to leave.'

Pat. Beautifully pat. Well-rehearsed, no doubt.

'Would you like to comment, Ms Rivers?' Dan asked.

'I would like to ask Mr Butler one question,' I said, remaining seated this time. 'What was I wearing, Mr Butler?'

'An extremely short skirt. And a tight top.'

'Thank you. I would like to tell you—' I began, forgetting Seb's advice.

Seb raised a hand. 'I think Ms Rivers and I need a moment's conversation.'

'You'll have plenty of time after the hearing.'

I stared. Such ice from the warm and cuddly Fairbairn. I took Seb's pencil from him, and wrote on his pad: *I was wearing trousers. Have witnesses.*

Seb nodded. 'Are you sure she was wearing a short skirt, Mr Butler?'

'Indeed. Asking for trouble.'

I dug my nails into my palms. Now was not the time for a diatribe on the rights of women to dress as they pleased, without fear of molestation.

'As a matter of fact,' Seb said, 'my colleague has witnesses to testify that she was wearing trousers on the day in question.'

'If she chooses to appeal,' Fairbairn said, 'I'm sure the Governors would be interested to hear them.'

Appeal? A foregone conclusion, then. But I'd known all along that it was – had known from the start, even without Afzal's predictions.

Without waiting, Butler stood and walked out. And in swaggered a Muslim youth, broadly built. He wore a Palestinian-style check scarf covering most of his face, as if he were in a desert sandstorm. Beneath his sunglasses, he was quite pale; but then, so were many of our Asian students. I had to pretend to myself he was genuine, to stop myself dashing out of the room to summon Chris.

He sat down, crossing his legs so the ankle of the right lay across the left thigh.

Dan glanced at him, perhaps irritated that he hadn't waited for his cue to enter. 'Mr Riaz. Mohammed Riaz. One of our students. He came to me with a very serious allegation against Ms Rivers, again of a sexual nature. Apparently she—'

'I'd like to hear this in Mr Riaz's own words,' I said, laying a quick hand on Seb's notes. I knew what I was doing, all right.

Riaz and Dan exchanged glances. This wasn't in the script.

'Mr Riaz told me that—'

'I'd like *him* to tell me!' Fifteen years in the classroom

gave my voice an authority I was afraid might have deserted it. 'Well, Mr Riaz?'

He shuffled, and then turned to the Principal. 'Well, it was like this. I was in this lift, see, and she gets in, and grabs my prick.'

'And where was your prick at the time?' Seb asked.

I don't remember the answer. All I remember was a glorious surge of triumph. Oh, there was no way I was going to get through this hearing: I'd have to appeal, go to Industrial Tribunal and beyond. But all that was irrelevant. This was a Muslim with a strong Glasgow accent, and I'd bet my future career that he had a drawer full of make-up at home.

We were invited to leave the room while the Principal considered my fate; but it was clear we wouldn't be out there long. In fact, Seb had already prepared a letter of appeal to the governors for me to sign.

'We should have insisted on seeing the charges beforehand. We should have stuck it out, Sophie. The whole thing's so ludicrous, we could have ridden a coach and horses through their case.'

'And we will do at the appeal,' I said. 'The important thing now is getting hold of Chris.' I fished my phone from my bag and dialled.

He answered second ring. 'There's been a man down here who may have halitosis,' I said.

'I'm on my way!'

'Halitosis?' asked Seb.

'I'll explain when I've been sacked,' I said; the Principal's secretary was taking a call and looking askance at me.

'You're to go back in,' she said.

Fairbairn was back in sympathetic mode. 'Please sit down. Now, Sophie, I've heard these allegations about you, and I must say I find them surprising. On our admittedly brief acquaintance I've found you an admirable member of staff, from your professionalism in the classroom to your heroism in dealing with our injured colleague – and fighting a small fire on our premises. So I'd like to investigate these charges further, and give you plenty of time to find witnesses to support you. I suggest we meet again in a fortnight. Does that suit you? And Mr Conrad?'

'You undertake to supply Ms Rivers and myself with detailed charges and witness statements?'

'Of course. I'll ensure my secretary gets them into the post as soon as possible.'

'*All* the paperwork?' I insisted.

'Of course, Sophie.'

'Copies of *everything*?'

'I've already said that.' Incredibly, she was still smiling. 'And meanwhile, you'll continue to receive your full salary. Any other question?'

Screaming time in the fresh air of the car park.

'Bastards!' I yelled, smashing my fist on to my other palm. 'This means I can't appeal yet, doesn't it? Because there's nothing to appeal against!'

Seb nodded. 'But you're on full pay, for doing nothing.'

'Nothing! I shall be working harder than I've ever worked! To get to the bottom of this – conspiracy!'

'Calm down, Sophie.'

'Calm down!' But I tried to. 'Chris!'

He strode towards us. 'What the hell are you doing out here? I've been hanging around outside Fairbairn's office!'

'Didn't Ann tell you? The cow! I'm still suspended, Chris, so I wasn't allowed to pollute William Murdock's buildings for a second longer than necessary. And I should imagine that those gentlemen are here to see me off the premises altogether.'

Chris treated the approaching security guards to one of his colder stares; they backed off quickly.

'Tell me all about it,' he said.

I was glad to. 'Oh, they've invented the most dreadful charges. All of a sexual nature, would you believe? I want to go and shower, to get myself clean. There's some sort of conspiracy, I'm sure of it.'

'Go on.'

'They made another charge, which they failed to follow

225

up at all: that I'd tried to contact my colleagues to subvert Fairbairn's authority! Well, the curious thing is, I did write to a number of them – but Chris, do you remember, you and Afzal persuaded me not to send the letters out? The only way they could have got hold of a copy is to tap my computer.'

'You're sure? Bloody hell. So what was that about halitosis?'

'One of the witnesses against me,' I said, dropping my voice, 'was a young man swathed in a Yasser Arafat scarf. And sunglasses. And a Glasgow accent. And – look, he's getting into that Maestro.'

Chris flicked the switch on his hand-held radio, dictated the registration number, and grinned. 'What are you going to do now, Sophie?'

'Leave you to sort him out. Leave Seb to sort out other NATFHE problems. I'm going into the city to – do some shopping.'

'I don't trust you when you smile like that. When will you tell me what you're really up to?'

'Let's have lunch,' I said. 'In the Art Gallery. I'll meet you under Lucifer at twelve-thirty. And yes, Chris, it will be official.'

Chapter Twenty-Nine

It didn't make sense to feel elated, not after this morning's session. But I felt unbeatable. I knew I could crack this.

Zia Yamin: I guessed he was so full of righteous indignation at what he saw as my indecent attire and unwomanly attitude he'd seen any opportunity to traduce me as being sent by Allah. I couldn't wait to get my hands on what purported to be a transcript of his allegations. I'd get Ian or Chris to check out the family illness story; perhaps he'd had a twinge of conscience and couldn't bear the thought of confronting me face to face with his allegations.

My Glaswegian friend. Surely we'd got him! For the assault on Mike; possibly for the attack on Carl's car. And wouldn't it be wonderful if he turned out to be part of the trio feigning Asian colouring to avoid detection? I was on such a high, I forgot all about the things that Chris would immediately have thought of: making an identification; getting evidence; bringing appropriate charges; convincing the DPP. Convincing a jury.

The man I was really interested in was Butler. How on earth had someone persuaded him to spout such palpable lies? Why, his secretary had remarked on my trouser suit; all the people at college had seen me in a trouser suit; and S Mohinder, Solicitors was as decent a man as you'd wish to meet and he'd seen the betrousered me too. The joy of it was that my appointment with him had been arranged at the last minute: I'd not had time to enter it in the schedule in the office, so no one but me knew I had an impartial witness. I'd have punched the air in jubilation had I not been afraid of being thrown off the bus.

I was so full of myself I did indeed digress to shop in Rackhams. I nearly bought a scarf, a silk square blazing with oranges and reds and purples – but then I put it back. There'd been too many flames already. And then I was off to Companies' House, a grandiose name for a room lurking in the basement of the Central Library. All I knew was that if William Murdock was a corporation it might have to be recorded on some register with all its directors listed. If I'd been in the college building, all I'd have had to do was ask for the minutes of the governors' meetings; they'd made it a bit more difficult for me, but they weren't going to stop me finding what, if any, relationship Butler had with William Murdock.

Confronted by a cluster of microfiche readers and computers, I did the obvious thing: headed for the enquiry desk.

'I want to look up the directors of a company,' I said.

The young woman smiled, took a pound off me for a plastic card, and emerged to swipe it and show me how to work the system. It was user-friendly enough, and I soon found William Murdock Corporation. Surprise, surprise – Butler was a governor. And he had other interests, too, including a property development firm. I charged my card again before printing the information out. OK – proof about Butler's involvement was one thing. What about other governors' interests? And Dan's, and Fairbairn's?

This time I had my card loaded with £5 worth of operations. And then another £5. All those webs of intrigue to unpick! But if I'd been paying hundreds it would have been worth it.

Epstein's Lucifer was smiling ambiguously on a seething mass of schoolchildren, rounding off their educational visit to the Art Gallery with a raiding party on the shop. He wasn't smiling on Chris, however, because Chris was late. Feeling vulnerable, although even William Murdock's governors could have no clue what I had tucked into my bag, I waited.

228

I heard his footsteps, despite all the racket, before I saw him. Light, urgent. I wondered, not for the first time, if he'd have made a good dancer.

'Sorry – I got held up. Shall we go and eat?' He started through the gallery that leads to the Edwardian Tea Rooms.

I followed, my interview shoes slithering on the polished floor. I'd eat first, then gloat over the china and pottery on the way back – but then I stopped dead. 'Richard!'

Chris turned, and walked back to me. 'Sophie?'

'Richard,' I repeated. 'My phone's been making these odd clicks—'

'Why the hell didn't you—'

I waved my mobile at him. 'Used this, when I remembered. But before then Richard was telling me all about his plans for this afternoon. You never know – there may be a reception committee as he approaches Rose Road—'

'Let's just ensure we provide an even bigger one, then.' He spoke into his radio, as I stared unseeing, at flambé Ruskinware.

We were already on the stairs out of the museum when he paused long enough to ask, 'How would they know his car?'

'All the details are on the college's computer – don't suppose they've got round to wiping old staff records yet. A photograph, too – we had to have them done for Security. And Richard's always early.' So much for my news: I certainly wasn't going to yell it at him as we hurtled along Colmore Row. Even if I'd had enough breath.

'Out of condition, Sophie,' he observed, as he waited for me to scuttle across the road after him to the car, which was neat and law-abiding by a meter. 'Now your knee's better, you've no excuse. We should start getting you fit again.'

We? Where was Diane in this personal fitness scheme? Where, for that matter, Afzal? I was aware that Afzal knew where I was staying but he hadn't phoned.

There was nothing about the car to suggest to a casual observer that it was anything but a domestic Rover in an uninspired colour. However, the way Chris flung it into the traffic and expected people to give way, I hoped it was armour-plated.

'Flashing lights on the front,' Chris said.

Then I heard the siren.

'Not supposed to do this with civilian passengers,' he said. 'Shift your bloody arse, man!'

Broad Street was solid with traffic. He took a left, and then a right, so we ran parallel; he'd take a glimpse up the side roads to see if Broad Street was still blocked. It was. But soon he'd have to join it anyway to get on to the Five Ways Island, always a bottle neck. Whether it was the authoritative-looking car or the sheer grimness of his expression, the traffic melted before him. Now down Calthorpe Road; a right past the Botanical Gardens. And then, eschewing the main road for more than a few hundred yards – Harborne High Street at this time of day would be as impassable as Broad Street – he took to suburban roads again.

He was so obviously in control I forgot about bracing myself. I looked at him; there was a brightness about his eyes I'd rarely seen.

Approaching Rose Road from the bottom end, we encountered his reception committee. Large people smothered in yellow Day-Glo with striped cars parked at apparently random angles across narrow streets can look very impressive.

We were waved through like royalty, but I felt for the poor denizens of Harborne, ambling along their usual rat-runs after shopping only to be confronted by this lot. Chris's face fell into grimmer lines again; his fun was over, and goodness knew what the next part of the scenario might be.

Anything would have been an anticlimax after that. Sitting in Chris's room certainly was. Happier on my feet and moving, I joined Chris at the window. 'There he is!' I gripped Chris's arm. 'The red Volvo. They're just letting him through now!'

'We'll keep everyone in place for a few more minutes. Just in case anyone else comes along. It's not a bad day for standing round in the fresh air.'

'A bit breezy for leaving the windows open, though.' I shivered.

'Fresh air's good for you,' he said. 'More coffee?'

Someone had cleaned up the percolator. And the mugs were in tidy, washed rows.

There was a tap at the door. And there was Richard, tanned and healthy and so entirely in one piece I'd run towards him and hugged him before I remembered he'd been my boss and might be expecting a little residual respect. After a moment's startled stillness, however, he hugged me back: very warmly. At last it occurred to me to make introductions.

'What I thought we'd do,' Chris said, no doubt tired of the touching spectacle of reunion, 'was fax your bank a request for them to fax those papers back here. You may want to phone them first, to tell them what to expect.' He gestured Richard to the desk so he could use the phone. 'By the way, Sophie, there's a wad of mail for you. I'm sorry, we should have passed it to you as soon as we'd established it was safe to handle.' He wandered back to the window, poking at his dispirited plants.

I took the mail, sorting it into piles on the far side of the desk from Richard. Bills; junk; personal. A postcard from Andy – the Taj Mahal. One from Crete, dated early September, from Aberlene. A letter in a hand I didn't know. I tried that first – and wished I hadn't. Afzal. He must have driven into the city centre to catch the late evening post.

Sitting, I scanned it. I knew enough from the opening words to work out the gist. *Better if we remain friends . . . past still too close . . . Islam.* At this point I started to read more closely. *I believe that the obstacles presented by the past would not have been insuperable, given time and goodwill on both sides.* Fair enough: my judgement, too. So what was the problem? *Fundamental to my life is my Islamic faith. I could never share my life with someone who did not have the same beliefs as me. There are women who convert to Islam, but – forgive me, Sophie – I could not imagine you as one of them. If you did, no matter how closely you observed the rituals, I still doubt whether you could really believe in all the Prophet's teachings – those about women, for example. So I am asking you not to contact me for a while, not until we can see each other without the sort of emotions we had begun to feel . . .*

231

I folded it and returned it to its envelope. Then I shoved it into my bag. I tried to dredge up hurt and regret, but in my heart I knew he was right.

Try as I might, I couldn't see myself covering my hair, let alone fasting.

Chris, not one to miss much, looked at me. 'You OK?' he mouthed.

'A "dear Sophie" letter,' I mouthed back. 'Win some, lose some.'

'Diane—' the silent conversation continued. But he didn't finish his sentence. Instead he made a swift finger movement across the throat. So he'd ended it. He looked about the room: yes, he'd reclaimed his territory.

Richard put down the phone. 'They want confirmation by fax. If you've got some paper?'

Chris opened his top drawer with a flourish: his drawers were back to normal, too. Not a bottle or a tampon in sight. Richard wrote his note; Chris, who normally approved of fountain pens, flapped the sheet impatiently to dry it, and then darted to the door.

'Chris!'

'Sophie – for Christ's sake! This is really urgent!'

'I know. But – when you've sent it, could you organize some food?' My stomach hadn't dealt with this morning as bravely as all those tablets should have helped it to.

'I'm sorry – I clean forgot.' He laid a kind – or possessive – hand on my shoulder and sped off.

'Gastritis back?' Richard asked, producing peppermints.

Taking one, I nodded. 'But how are you? All this drying-out business!'

'No problem. I just looked at the number of bottles in my trolley, and at the till receipts, and drew some conclusions. I don't think I'd qualified as a proper alcoholic, Sophie, because I haven't had the shakes or any great desire to reach for the bottle again. Maybe the walking helped. The South Downs. Lovely, especially at this time of year. Do you know them?'

I shook my head. Perhaps some walking would clear my head, too. Now the knee didn't lock or give way depending on its whim, even a scurry over Clent hills would be nice.

232

There was, after all, a fortnight to kill before the next hearing. And then there was the appeal to the Governors . . .

Chris returned, flourishing packets of sandwiches. 'They'll give me a buzz as soon as the fax comes through. Coffee for you, Richard?' He started his now pristine percolator.

'Fine,' Richard and I said together.

I resolved to say nothing about my researches till we'd eaten. I owed my stomach that much. However, before we'd done more than crumple the sandwich wrappers before binning them, a tap at the door produced a uniformed WPC with a sheaf of fax paper. Chris passed them straight to me. 'Yours.'

I walked round to lay them in front of Richard – after all, he'd been at William Murdock longer than I had. And Chris came to join us.

Dan's application form. End-of-year report. A copy of the detailed UCCA report – UCCA being the precursor of UCAS, the university clearing system.

'I remember writing this – it was the first I'd done. Do you remember I showed it to you, Richard? Not that you were so exalted in those days!'

He shook his head. 'I've checked so many over the years . . . But you were right in your predictions. *An extremely strong candidate . . . Will succeed at whatever he wants to do . . . destined to go far . . .* He ought to read this: he'd stop persecuting you. Looks like you helped get him where he is today.'

'The question is, why would he want to stop anyone else reading it? There's nothing inflammatory about this.' Chris put it to one side. 'And this end-of-year report's fine: predicted grade, A. *Dan has been an exemplary student in every way, gaining the respect of all who came into contact with him for his hard work and dedication.* Why should he want to hide that? OK, he might be embarrassed by such lavish encomiums – but that's all. What else?'

'Just his application form,' said Richard. 'Why try to burn down a whole college just to get rid of endless praise?'

'Hang on. Do you know something I don't know?' Chris asked.

Richard looked disconcerted at his tone. 'Well, it's

obvious, isn't it? All these fires, and then they stop. I am right, aren't I? Nothing serious since?'

'That could be because of the major police presence, not to mention the security cameras,' Chris said.

'Look,' Richard leaned back, 'we always wanted security cameras, but when we installed them on a trial basis, we had two problems. Siting the things – the design of the building being what it is – and the immediate vandalism. You're not telling me that this batch of students is any less cunning than the last? If they wanted to destroy your cameras, I'd bet my pension they could.' He looked to me for confirmation.

Chris flicked the papers in irritation, and read through the reports again. Nothing. He flipped them down. You could read his thoughts. All the effort and time – not to mention valuable resources – he'd devoted to getting hold of such useless bits of paper!

Richard shrugged, and gathered them up. 'Hello,' he said, spreading them again, 'this isn't like you, Sophie! You've filed the wrong application form with his papers. I mean, it's easy to see why. Dan Godfrey's not all that far from Godfrey Evans—'

'Godfrey Evans was a cricketer, wasn't he?' asked Chris, absently.

'A wicket-keeper,' I said. 'And – Chris! Look, here's a bit in – is it your writing, Richard? – look! *DP seen*. What does that mean?

'Wouldn't be deed poll, would it, Chris?'

He didn't reply. He was too busy telling someone at the end of the phone line to check the name Godfrey Daniel Evans on the Police Computer.

Chapter Thirty

I'd got as far as spreading the crumpled papers from my bag on Chris's desk when Tom burst in. 'Sorry – but I knew you'd want to hear this, man. Fire Service. A 999 call. To Balden Road. Sophie, pet, they've set your garden shed on fire.'

I was on my feet. 'My *shed*?'

'Well, the rest was pretty fireproof,' Chris said dryly. 'Thanks, Tom. Do you really want to see the damage, Sophie?'

I spread my hands. 'Of course I do. Though why anyone should want to burn a bloody shed . . .'

'Perhaps,' Richard put in, 'they thought your car might be in there. Anyone else'd call it a garage.'

'My car's in police custody. So it's just gardening things.'

'But you'd like to see the pyre. Come on. Richard, what are your plans?'

'I'd be in the way if I came with you?' Poor man; he sounded so wistful . . .

'You could take her. There are enough of our vehicles round there to keep off an army. But – do you hear me, Sophie? – you go in that house and *stay there*. You don't do anything until you've cleared it with me.'

I nearly said it. *No, Daddy.* But he didn't deserve that. Instead, I flashed my mobile phone and nodded obediently.

'Richard, your car would be safer locked up in that nice integral garage of yours. Soon as possible, please. I shouldn't think for long. Once the computer comes up with stuff on

235

Dan Godfrey – excuse me, Godfrey Evans – we should be able to pull him in. At least for questioning.'

The shed was nothing more than a smouldering shell when I got there. A fire-fighter was talking to a woman sergeant I knew vaguely.

'If Sophie can't go to William Murdock, William Murdock can come to Sophie,' I said.

The sergeant – what was her name? – shook her head. 'We've checked with the Fire Service. If it is the William Murdock arsonist, then he's changed his MO. But he was very generous. He left a bottle behind.'

'Petrol?'

'Whisky.' She picked up a polythene bag and waved it at me; I recognized the brand. 'You OK? Here, let's get you inside.'

'No. I'm fine. At least—' Chris had emptied a similar bottle out of his window. I'd have to tell him. Wouldn't I?

Richard steered me back towards the house. 'That bottle rang a bell didn't it? Why didn't you tell her?' he asked.

'Because I could be horribly mistaken,' I said. 'In fact, I hope I am.'

He looked at me, his eyes shrewd but kind. 'Maybe a cup of tea,' he said, 'before I go and incarcerate my car?'

'Of course. I'm sorry, I never thought.' I shut the back door behind us and leaned on it. 'Tea or coffee?'

'You sit down – I'll get it. Cups in here?' He slipped off his jacket and made himself at home.

'Biscuits there,' I said. 'Not as nice as those you used to keep, but OK. And there won't be many left soon, so grab some!' I'd already heard the front door, and the only one with a key was Greg. 'Cup of tea?' I called.

'Whose is the motor, Soph?' He put his head round the door. 'Sorry – didn't mean to butt in.'

'Richard's. Richard, this is Greg, a new enrolment at William Murdock. Greg, this is the boss I had before Dan. How's things?'

He fidgeted with a biscuit before eating it hungrily, then took another. 'So-so. Look, Soph – about that business last night. I really didn't mean – you know, not in your house. I'm not that gross. Just came to get my things. How did Chris take it?'

'Like a man. On the chin. How would you expect a decent guy like that to take it? Especially when he's her boss, for goodness' sake! Damn it, all she is to you is a casual bonk. I could have bloody killed you, Greg. Except I think he's better off without her. Sorry, Richard – another biscuit before Hollow Legs here finishes the lot?'

Richard took one, unsmiling.

'Any William Murdock news?' I asked.

'No – hey, I never asked how you got on in your disciplinary! Sorry, kid.'

'Got on?' Richard repeated. 'Disciplinary?'

'Trumped-up charges of sexual misconduct. Oh, and sending defamatory notes to my colleagues.'

'Those you wouldn't let me deliver? You mean they hacked into your system? Jesus!'

Richard was silent: no smoke without fire syndrome. I took a deep breath. 'And they recruited people to bear false witness. But Chris and the Cavalry are galloping to the rescue.'

'Glad to hear it. Ah! Could be for me.' And Greg disappeared into the hall, leaving me with a grim and silent Richard.

It mattered very much to me that he believed me innocent. I didn't want him to judge the evidence and find me not guilty. I wanted him to believe in me, as Chris had done.

'Soph! For you!' Greg called.

I hesitated. 'Richard – I—'

'Soph! It's Afzal!'

What did I think he was going to say? In the few seconds it took me to reach the phone I'd thought of at least four scenarios. In the event, none of them fitted the bill.

'Sophie. Further to my phone call to you last night I need to speak with you. On a matter of extreme urgency. I know you didn't like what I said on the phone, and I can only apologize, but it would be most delightful if you would be prepared to discuss it again.'

What on earth was he talking about? Phone call? And why was he doing a passable imitation of Peter Sellers?

'Sophie, are you there? Could you favour me with a visit, at your earliest convenience? Within the hour, perhaps?'

'What if I said no, I was too upset?'

'I would implore you to reconsider. Sophie, you know I would *die* for you.'

That was all.

I leaned my head against the wall, leaving the phone to purr. That emphasis on 'die'; all that stage Indian.

'Soph, you all right?'

Greg's voice snapped me into action. 'Richard? I need your car, now. Afzal's in trouble.'

'In that case, I'm coming too. Hey, what do you want your bleeding bag for? This is supposed to be an emergency, Soph!'

But I tapped Chris's number as soon as the Volvo was moving.

Richard did his best, but he was no police driver, and he was battling with crossings which clog up at the merest whiff of rush-hour. Chris was on his way, with back-up and, on the off-chance, a fire appliance – as he said, there'd been too many incidents involving fire to ignore the possibility of another. But, of course, he'd be discreet. Nothing within sight of Afzal's office. And he wanted Richard to stop a good fifty yards down the road.

The police were very much in evidence when Richard finally pulled the car to a halt. He was pale and sweating – had obviously pushed himself to the limit, for all I'd thought his pace funereal. The police had cordoned off the area; Chris pushed past the knot of uniformed officers to let me through.

'I've been getting listening devices in. There's definitely at least one other person there, possibly two. I'd bet one of them is our friend with halitosis – he dodged us as he left college this morning and he wasn't in when we called at his bedsit. But his room is full of most interesting material. The most unpleasant, racist rubbish you could imagine . . . Look,

Sophie, would you phone Afzal now? Here? You'll be thinking on your feet, but try and find out everything you can. Go for it.'

I dialled. He brought his head close to mine to listen in.

'Afzal? I'm on my way but the traffic's terrible. Here's my mobile number if you want to call me. I shan't be long, though. I'm dying to see you.'

There was a gasp. 'And me. I'm dying to see you. In fact, I can't wait much longer. The suspense is burning me up, Sophie.' And the line was cut.

Chris took the phone and collapsed the aerial for me; my hands were shaking too much. His eyes were as serious as I'd ever seen them. 'The man's giving you a message.'

'Remember how his wife and children died,' I said.

'You mean some bastard's in there with him, threatening to set him on fire?' Greg yelled.

'Greg, get back behind police lines,' Chris said. 'God knows what's going on in there, but the fewer people at risk, the better. And take Richard, please. Sophie?'

'Tell me exactly what you want me to do and I'll do it.' I looked him straight in the eyes; I wasn't going to go in for histrionics or heroism.

'I only wish I knew. I've sent for trained negotiators. But the traffic's getting worse and they can't fly. A helicopter would be too obvious.'

'If I went in, what do you think would happen?'

'Don't you think I'd thought of that? It's simply too dangerous.'

'What about some protective clothing?'

He shook his head. 'Protective against what? You've no idea what you're going into. Bullets? Knives? What would you expect?'

In my mind's eye I saw a tanker, and a family car. And Afzal in lonely tears. 'Flames,' I said. 'I'm sure of it.'

Chris was pale. 'Let's try another call. Tell him there's a huge jam in Bordesley Green – ah! Derek! Over here! Derek's one of our negotiators – would you mind if he listened in?'

A negotiator? He looked as if he'd be more at home

239

tending an autumn bonfire than defusing an arsonist. But I suppose that was to his advantage. He watched me dial.

'Afzal, there's a most terrible jam – Bordesley Green's solid—'

'Oh, Sophie. *Please*, Sophie—' The line went dead.

'Was that Afzal?'

'Greg! What the hell are you doing here? For God's sake, get behind the cordon,' Chris said quietly. 'Don't make me have to arrest you for obstruction, man.'

Greg dawdled. Then he nodded, and moved off tamely, briskly.

Too tamely. Too briskly. 'Greg!' I called. 'Chris – send someone after him!'

Too late: he'd melted into the chaos. Chris and I ran, dodging and weaving, Chris yelling orders as he went. 'Stop him! For Christ's sake, stop him!'

For Greg was running, hell for leather, towards the tiny terraced house that was Afzal's office.

Chris grabbed me, and flung me backwards. And himself on top of me, covering my head.

Even so, the blast knocked me cold.

Chapter Thirty-One

Cold. That was all I could think of. The cold. Despite the blankets. Despite the hot drink in my hands – Pakistani tea, thick, sweet, milky, gently offered by a middle-aged woman who spoke no English. Someone was cleaning the gravel rash on my knees. Chris was staring at his hands, bound up like a boxer's: something to focus on while the paramedic swabbed his forehead. Already there were screens where the front of Afzal's office had been. The ambulance sirens were getting further away. Afzal and his secretary. And a man dressed as a Muslim.

Not Greg. They'd be photographing what was left of Greg. Certifying him dead, taking him to a morgue—

I pushed away from the shelter of the ambulance, found a gutter grating, and vomited the tea. Couldn't stop vomiting even when there was no more bile. Chris, white-mittened, came and helped me to my feet.

'Instantaneous, Sophie. He wouldn't have felt a thing. Though I know that's not much consolation.' He put his arm round me. 'Hospital for you.'

'What about you?'

'Rose Road. I want to tie this lot up.'

'Then that's where I'm going too. Where's Richard?'

'Hospital. Asthma – he'd run out of his spray. And you don't take chances with a man of his age.'

'He's only fifty-five!' But I hadn't the heart to bicker. 'They'll keep you posted – about Afzal?'

'Of course. Come on. If the paramedics say you can skip casualty, we'll get back to Harborne.'

Ian produced hot chocolate and bread and butter, and sat beside me in Chris's room, Chris himself was down in the mêlée of an incident room. The sheer scale of what could be done so quickly made me reel: the correlation of the incidents, the officers out searching, the loud, hectic exchanges of vital information. Meanwhile, the Glaswegian Muslim was under police guard in hospital: in what must have been poetic justice, even divine justice, he'd been on his feet when Greg had set off the firebomb, and had thrown Azfal backwards, landing on him protectively in much the same way as Chris had landed on me. Afzal had neck injuries, and what Ian described carelessly as a few broken bones. The Fire Service had got to him before the fire, thank God. Again we had the Glaswegian to thank: although he'd soaked Afzal's clothing in petrol, he'd shielded him from any sparks. His secretary was in a far worse state, and faced a series of skin grafts.

And Greg . . .

'Come on, Sophie, love. It's real drinking chocolate – you don't think I'd give you any of that instant stuff out of a machine? And you need the bread and butter for that stomach of yours. Now, what I'd like you to do is talk to one of our victim-support people. They're trained, you see – all I can do is sit and say I'm sorry. They can do a lot more than that. And Chris is going to be tied up for some time.'

I drank to please him. 'This is good.'

'Ah, so you can still manage a smile.' He patted me on the shoulder.

'Ian – don't go. I'll do what you say – talk to victim support. Afterwards. I want to go and see Afzal first. And I want to talk to you. About – vandalism and whisky bottles. There was one by my shed this afternoon. And I know it was her usual brand.'

He sat down heavily. 'What are we going to do, Sophie? He was fond of her.' Besotted, more like.

'He broke rules for her.' I gestured at his office.

'He won't try and cover this up.'

'Does he have to know?'

'He already does.'

'I mean – *everything*?'

'I don't see how he can avoid knowing everything.' Ian sat, the chair creaking. 'You told him about the windscreen. Not to mention the excrement.'

'I know I mentioned my windscreen had been smashed.' I remembered the cans lying in the gutter. 'But I don't think beer cans came into the conversation.'

'And Diane was partial to a beer or two?'

'Well, it doesn't need to be mentioned now, does it? Let him go on thinking it was Muslim students, or pretend-Muslims, or petty vandals. We can't just forget about the shed, I know, not with Sergeant Whatshername reporting it. But if no more incidents occur, surely it'll just get lost in the files of insoluble crimes?' The chocolate finished, I licked stray milk from the corners of my mouth. 'I don't want to ruin the woman's career. And I suspect that Chris kept talking about me, quoting my little pearls of wisdom – no wonder she hated my guts.'

'No excuse. Not in a police officer.' Ian's face was as hard as I'd ever seen it.

'But it was the police who kept her under pressure by not confirming her promotion. Probably that that drove her to drink. She needs professional help, doesn't she?'

'If you ask me, she should resign.'

'That's the last thing she should do! Sick leave, and counselling, and a transfer. Surely Chris could fix that.'

Ian looked at me sideways. 'Depends who suggests it to him.'

Ian ran me to the hospital, dropping me at the door; he'd park, then come and find me, he said. They let me see Afzal, although it was out of visiting hours – he was in a side ward, with a young African-Caribbean PC sitting outside. Very young. But not so young he wasn't armed.

'Afzal! What on earth—'

They'd fixed him a support collar which made him look like an Elizabethan on a tomb. 'Who did this?'

'The soi-disant Mr Riaz, of course,' he said, and tried to smile.

243

I touched the bruise under his right eye with my finger, so lightly I couldn't even feel the skin, but hard enough to make him wince.

What I wanted to do was take Afzal's hand, and tell him I quite understood about what he'd said in his letter. But no one would be holding his hands for a while. They were encased in plaster, with plastic supports for some of the fingers.

'Afzal!' It was hard not to scream. 'How? Why?' When he shook his head, I tried again. 'I'd guess he had to work hard to persuade you to dial my number. And very hard to make you invite me to your office. And I'd guess his efforts involved breaking your fingers, one by one.'

'Wipe your eyes, Sophie. It wasn't just to get hold of you. He's not keen on genuine Muslims. I'd be interested to hear Chris's views on this, but I'd say he was connected to one of those organisations like Combat 18. Only a bit more subtle.'

'I think you're right. They've found a lot of racist filth in his bedsit, Chris said.'

'Getting Asian youths a bad name by attacking people. Fostering extreme – and therefore unacceptable – anti-women views in susceptible, ignorant youths who already hold a grudge against the whites.'

'The Taliban connection?'

'What better way to get British Asians a bad name than by encouraging them to collect money for such a discredited mob? His next plan – oh, he enjoyed telling me this, Sophie – was to try to persuade Sikh women to turn to Islam. Enrage their community against the Muslim one. A nice bit of aggro, and a right-wing press baying for Muslim blood. I'm sure Chris and his colleagues will find plenty of evidence to corroborate his story.'

'And when he wasn't breaking your bones he was threatening you with fire. Afzal, where do I start to thank you? To apologize for involving you with all this?'

He managed a smile. 'What else are friends for?' But then he was sombre. 'In a movie, at this point, the hero would be telling the heroine to tear up his letter. Sophie, I

244

can't do that. I meant what I said. I only hope I haven't hurt you too much.'

'Perhaps I'd have preferred you to do it face to face.'

'Perhaps I wouldn't have been able to do it face to face. Sophie, it wouldn't have worked – not if both of us had wanted to remain true to ourselves. Do you think you'll get it together with Greg after all?'

I sat down. 'They haven't told you?'

'Told me – ? Only that he was injured. Sophie—'

'He died trying to save you,' I said. 'He was so enraged by the softly-softly approach he charged through police lines and—' By now I was crying in earnest. For the end of a flawed but decent man who'd died trying to save an individual he admired from a race he despised. No saint. Not even a specially good man. But not a bad one, either.

Poor Afzal couldn't wipe away his tears for Greg. I blotted his face as gently as I could, my tears dripping on to his cheeks as I did so.

I bade a casual goodnight to the policeman on guard, and waited for a couple of orderlies pushing a trolley to get past me. Almost immediately, however, they pulled into an alcove, so I carried on past. Big mistake.

I was grabbed from behind, my arms pinioned and a hand clamped over my mouth.

I bit. Very hard. I had no time to shout, and this time the hand was more vicious. All this within twenty yards of the constable! Any moment now I'd be on top of that trolley, unconscious, propelled along by two apparently caring porters. A wonderfully efficient charade. If I struggled they'd break my arms, but it might be worth the pain to attract attention. At least I could kick. If only I could kick hard enough . . .

I kicked. With both legs. And both shoes came adrift, and I was careering along the corridor, cannoning against something metallic. And then there was nothing.

Movement. Changes in light and darkness. And vomit. I was

vomiting. The dentist? School labs? A smell of ether. And a car moving very fast. Blue lights on and off. Noise.

Where are they taking me? I must keep thinking or I'll go under again. Mustn't let them see. Don't want . . .

Easier to stay. Not move. Easier to sleep. Easier to let go. And then lights, and a burning nose. Burning eyes.

'Come on. Come on.'

Pain on my cheek. No. Can't be.

'Sophie, come on! Please!'

More tears.

'Good girl. Come on, Sophie.'

The tongue thick, reluctant. My voice. 'Chris? Chris?'

This time the hand on my cheek was gentle, soothing. But fluffy.

Fluffy?

'Thank God. Oh, Sophie.'

'Talk in a bit. Want to sleep.'

'No! Come on – on your feet. Up you get.'

I'd never been so woozy and helpless. Never. But walking with bare feet on a cold, metalled road sobered me up sharply. My gluey eyes took in a car on its roof, a lot of Day-Glo figures, two fire appliances and more police cars than I cared to count.

'All this for me?' I said.

'And for one or two others.'

'Why does your hand feel fluffy?' I remembered to ask.

He held one up for my inspection. Of course; his bandages. But it didn't make sense. This wasn't Afzal's road. There wasn't any fire.

'Tell me what's been going on, Chris. I seem to have lost my bearings.' And then I pushed away from him, and lost a good deal more. Someone passed me tissues to wipe my mouth. 'Sorry.'

'That's OK. Come on,' and he scooped me up and carried me to a waiting ambulance.

Nothing like arriving in style by ambulance for defeating the three-hour wait in Casualty. The poor bastards working the late shift, however, looked seedier than I felt.

They accepted with grace my suggestion that there wasn't much wrong with me that a good night's sleep wouldn't put right, gave me an anti-tetanus jab and changed Chris's dressings for more manageable ones.

I suppose I'd rather expected a half-hearted discussion about which house to sleep in – we had a choice of three, after all. But Chris simply stopped at his, offering, when he'd parked, to carry me again. It was easier to accept. Couldn't even make much of a joke about the extra pounds I'd put on. He took me straight up to his bedroom, and laid me on the bed. And then he lifted me off again, so roughly I staggered, falling against a chair. With pure, concentrated anger, he was stripping the bed.

Chapter Thirty-Two

The other half of the bed was cold. No Chris. The alarm clock said it was three-forty; perhaps he'd just gone to the loo? But when he didn't come back after ten minutes, I decided to go looking. His dressing-gown had gone – and his slippers. The duvet was too big to use as a shawl. So I went as I was, mother-naked.

He was in his study. He'd already made several sheets of notes and had just switched on his computer.

'How are you going to use a keyboard with your hands in that state?' I asked.

'It'll improve my fingertip work. You were always saying I hit the keys too hard. Hey, you'll get cold, wandering around like that. Jesus, look at those bruises!' He touched my forearms, my hips. And turned away.

'I bet they're no worse than yours. Come on, Chris, be sensible – switch that damn thing off. The only ideas anyone gets at this time of the morning are gloomy ones. I'll get some drinking chocolate and biscuits and we'll have a feast in bed.'

First find your chocolate and your biscuits: Chris's self-denying ordinance extended to his kitchen. It had always been me who introduced such sinful items into his cupboards. In his fridge were: half a stale loaf; the dregs of a tub of low-fat margarine; and some erstwhile mozzarella aspiring to be gorgonzola, in colour at least. There were a couple of eggs and a bag of ready-made salad, both ready for the compost bin. The freezer offered more promise. Bagels, smoked salmon: Relics of our time together. The microwave could defrost them. He'd hardly touched the wine I'd imported. I'd risk a bottle of Gewurztraminer, slotting it into the quick chiller sleeve that lurked in his deep-freeze.

He was still tapping at the computer when I went back upstairs. He took in the implications of my tray remarkably slowly, and then smiled.

'Hey! Don't forget to save that lot!'

'Get back to bed then, and I'll join you.'

I obliged.

'You're freezing,' he said, slipping in next to me. 'Why on earth didn't you put a sweater on or something?' He followed my glance to the dirty heap of clothing in the corner. 'Well, you could have borrowed one of mine.'

'Worn it as a mini-dress?'

He sighed. 'You're right, of course. Well, I shall just have to find another way of warming you up . . .'

Chris clearly regarded smoked salmon and bagels as entirely too frivolous for breakfast – but, as I pointed out, as they'd been sitting on the tray for several hours they really needed to be eaten. At least I wouldn't force the wine down him – we'd never got as far as uncorking that.

You could always rely on Chris for good coffee. He also had a hitherto undisclosed gift for suspense. He refused point-blank to tell me about what he'd uncovered on Dan Godfrey, until, as he said, 'the morning's questioning had put everything into context'. He did consent to phone the hospital, however, the casualty wards of which were cluttered by various good and bad men, and we learned that Afzal was well. The neck injury was minimal; once they could solve the problems caused by his hands, he could be released. Richard was very well: he'd been discharged at nine last night. Halitosis was not as well, but would survive to be charged with arson, criminal damage and attempted murder. Chris even enquired about the two heavies who'd removed me from the hospital: they were apparently a picture of health, and were, according to the officer guarding them, already 'singing like canaries'.

'I just wish they'd find better clichés,' Chris sighed, putting down the phone. 'Let's get you a change of clothes. And then we'll start work.'

Bonking – no matter how vigorous and tender and fun it had been – hadn't solved anything, of course. Chris's self-esteem was in ribbons, and my heart ached. For all it had had a note of desperation about it, it had made the night bearable, and that couldn't harm the day. Which promised to be difficult.

Not that it started so badly. Apart from the news about Afzal and Richard, there was another, truly serendipitous bit. Switching the car radio to 'Today', we picked up an interview halfway through: John Humphrys was interrogating students, whose Brummie accents intensified by the minute. And they seemed to be talking about a student strike. They wouldn't return till all disciplinary charges were dropped, they said.

'Come on, these are very serious allegations. You can't want a teacher wandering round doing that sort of thing!'

'Our Sophie wouldn't do that sort of thing!'

'Surely she wouldn't want you to disrupt classes!' Humphrys said in mock outrage.

'It isn't us that's doing that. It's the Principal. Won't talk to us, see. All she's got to do is come and talk to us, innit? She's OK, is our Soph. We need her to pass our exams.'

Chris touched my hand. 'They'll find it hard to talk to Ms Fairbairn today. We'll be talking to Ms Fairbairn. And Mr Godfrey. And one or two of their friends. Quite a little collection of them waiting at Rose Road!'

'Dan told me he'd kept in touch,' I said, switching off an Orangeman in mid-rant, 'with an interesting collection of his classmates. A building developer. An architect. A landscape gardener. And an accountant. Not to mention Butler, who shouldn't be a governor at all because he's got a financial interest in the place. Sounds like a good team. Ideally qualified to develop that area round the women's refuge, in Moseley, turn it into a bloody great fitness centre. It's all in those print-outs I left on your desk: all the interwoven connections. But why try and get rid of me?' I answered my question myself. 'Just so I wouldn't mention his past?'

Chris nodded. 'So what are you going to do now?' Despite the dressings, Chris parked with his usual consummate neatness.

I was walking into the police station beside him when I finally answered. 'They're so keen to shed staff to stay financially afloat, they've been offering everyone premature retirement. No, despite the way my poor old bones feel this morning, I don't qualify for that. So I thought I could make life cheaper for them by taking a sabbatical. I could afford it – just.'

'I should think the Criminal Injuries Board might be expected to make a small contribution after yesterday.'

'Even without that. George's money – the insurance money for the shed – it'll give me space to look around. Ironically, it was Dan who gave me the idea.'

Chris's laugh was short. 'Let's go and see what other ideas he's had. I wish I could let you be a fly on the wall, Sophie. But there it is.'

'I know. So long as you don't mind me making myself at home in your office—' One of those sentences better left unsaid.

He stopped in mid-stride. 'Stephenson's off the case.'

I turned to face him, putting my hand on his sleeve. 'Don't – forgive me for saying this, Chris – don't be vindictive towards her. We all have problems dealing with stress. You get migraines; I get a bad stomach; she gets drunk.'

'Do you have to be so damned magnanimous?' he demanded.

'Proper little Goody Two-Shoes, aren't I?'

'Sophie, that woman nearly cost you your life. She dropped you in it good and proper with Godfrey, hinting that you'd been talking to her about his past. And I can't forgive her for missing the significance of that scrap of paper.'

The one with my and Sarah's initials on it. 'Did you often talk to her about me?' I had to know.

'I told her to listen to what you had to say. That you were wild and sometimes woolly but always worth listening to.'

'Did you tell her so often she was sick of hearing about me?'

He stared; I sighed. Poor Diane.

'Think about it, anyway, Chris. I'd hate you – if it came out about her and Greg – to look petty.'

'There are times, Sophie, when petty is exactly what I want to be. Vengeful, even. Don't you get the urge to seek revenge occasionally?'

'All the time. Especially at the moment. I'd personally love to watch you extracting Dan's toenails one by one but I don't suppose I'll get the chance.'

'The police never – ah!' At last a boyish smile lit his whole face. 'One of your jokes! Tell you what, Sophie, if you can't come down to the Incident Room or the interview rooms – and believe me, you can't – we'll all come to you. Morning, Tom! You're up bright and early.'

'Morning, Gaffer. Hi, Sophie, pet! You all right now?'

'Why shouldn't I be?'

'Three and a half miles of car chase, that's why you shouldn't be. Miracle you survived that crash, pet. Funny they should have put your seat belt on.'

'What's known as humane killers,' I suggested.

Both men groaned as loudly as I could have wished.

'More likely to stop you flopping about all over them,' said Chris. 'And perhaps you were worth more alive than dead. Fairbairn and Godfrey presumably requested a live delivery and they might get quite nasty if disobeyed.'

'Make them work hours of unpaid overtime, you mean – like they did to me!'

'Chris, man, what I came to see you for was, there's this bloke in Reception. Speaks all posh. Didn't get his suit from Oxfam either. Name of Worrall.'

'Not the polysyllabic James Worrall?'

'He uses a lot of long words, man, if that's what you mean.'

Chris leaned very close to him. 'Tom, what's your degree in again?'

Tom flushed a rich burgundy, ill at ease with his ginger hair and white eyelashes. 'English, Gaffer.'

'And your MA?'

'Linguistics, Gaffer.'

'Thought it might be! OK, I know you don't want to flaunt your qualifications, but you'll look a right pillock when it all goes pear-shaped and they find out your little secret.'

'Sir!'

'Same as you look a right pillock when you stand like that. At ease, for Christ's sake! Go and wheel Worrall in. See if you can find another decent room, too, or we'll have to lodge Sophie in the canteen for a bit.'

Which meant, of course, I was still ensconced in Chris's room when Tom ushered Worrall in. My smile was meant to be affable, but I might have looked guilty as I scrambled to the door to follow Tom out.

'My dear Sophie, how very good to see you,' Worrall began. Then he looked at me more closely. 'Have you been the victim of some sort of attack, my dear?'

'A little local difficulty at the hands of some of your colleagues, Mr Worrall,' Chris explained. 'You'll have heard of the explosion yesterday? And possibly of an abduction? Where there's trouble – there's our Sophie.'

'That appalling car chase? My dear Sophie, you were headline news!'

'If only I could remember any of it,' I said.

'Surely there are parts you remember,' Worrall said.

'Only being very sick afterwards.'

'Dear me! Now, Chief Inspector, I wonder if I might prevail on you to spare a few minutes of your time. Sophie, you don't have to leave on my account. Indeed, it's largely because of you that I am here.'

'Me!' I sat down.

Worrall followed suit; Chris retreated behind his desk, and gestured to Tom to sit beside him. Unobtrusively, Tom produced his notebook.

Worrall raised an eyebrow: 'I had hoped this conversation would be *sub rosa*.' He pointed at the ceiling.

'I can guarantee confidentiality,' Chris said. 'Sophie? Tom?'

We nodded.

'Thank you. If, however, you should need to use any of

253

the information I am about to impart, I trust you will feel free to approach me.'

'Indeed. And you have the absolute right of veto.'

Worrall nodded, graciously, as if he believed him; I didn't.

'Sophie came to see me on – let me see – Tuesday morning. I was disingenuous – economical with the truth – however you would prefer to express it. You tried to find out why I'd left William Murdock so precipitately. The reasons I gave were valid, as far as they went. But there was another, more pressing reason. One of the governors – acting, I suspect, as someone else's agent – informed me that he wanted to put forward a candidate for my post; I was to resign, and make sure that this candidate had my support at the interview. He need not,' Worrall continued bitterly, 'have bothered with my support. His candidate was excellent. The panel of governors was united. But it was noticeable that a gentleman – I use the term loosely – by the name of Butler was especially vociferous.'

'Why should a man of your standing obey such orders?'

'Because, Chief Inspector, I was being blackmailed. When I was a young Sub-Lieutenant, like many others before me, I was involved in a homosexual relationship. I was engaged to be married at the time, to the woman who has since done me the honour of being my wife. Such an affair was illegal in those days; it was also short-lived. I never repeated the experience, despite the manifold temptations. In modern terminology I suppose I am bisexual, but I love my wife so much that I decided that chastity outside marriage was my only course. I have never regretted it.'

The house, the garden, the elegant woman: they would compensate for much. Wouldn't they?

'The information fell into the hands of the man who calls himself Dan Godfrey.'

'Information doesn't simply fall, Mr Worrall. It's usually obtained,' Chris said.

'In this case I have used the correct verb. It appears that the man I considered my lover was closely related to our friend Mr Godfrey.' For the first time he looked distressed. 'I may have simply panicked. Nothing was ever mentioned directly. I couldn't – on the evidence I had – have done

254

what a good citizen should have done and contacted your colleagues immediately. Three weeks after Mr Godfrey accepted the post, he returned to College to collect some of the information he would need to perform his new duties – this is normal procedure for such a responsible position. We spent some time discussing the policies and methods he might wish to adopt – not all of his suggestions being to my liking – and then, as he got up to leave, he asked about my former career.'

'You've never kept it secret,' I said. 'There's a little biography of him in our college information pack, Chris. Plus a photo.'

Worrall nodded. 'All Mr Godfrey did was smile, and say his father wished to be remembered to me. "I gather you were very close friends in the Navy," he said. It was simply the nature of his smile, and the intonation of his comment, that alarmed me beyond the reaches of common sense. Maybe I misjudged him. And in any case, my lover wasn't called Godfrey but Evans. Perhaps I was wrong.'

Chris raised an eyebrow. 'I don't think so, Mr Worrall. He's blackmailed before, on a much grander scale. He threatened to contaminate food at a branch of Marks and Sparks if he wasn't paid a huge ransom. *That's* what we got off the PNC, Sophie. Once we'd got his name – for Godfrey wasn't his real name, Mr Worrall – it was easy.'

I shifted in my chair: all the bits of body I usually sat on ached. 'But to go to those lengths just so his record never came out – that's absurd!'

'May I remind you, Sophie, that he'd obtained his post by false pretences? And the salary of a head of department is something no one would want to give up lightly.'

'Hang on,' I said, 'this doesn't make sense. Why didn't he get himself installed as Principal? He got the job with us while you were still in charge. As Head of Department – two departments combined, come to think of it, with, no doubt, a vastly-enhanced salary. One of your stranger decisions – made under duress, presumably? But why didn't he go for gold and become Principal?'

'Because his experience and qualifications weren't

adequate. And there was another candidate in the wings. Ms Fairbairn.'

'Don't tell me,' I said. 'His partner. If only in crime.'

Chris said, 'And I'd go for her being the senior partner. The sister of one of your ex-students. Harriet Glover.'

I ran through the list of contacts Dan had reeled off at my appraisal interview. Harriet, the accountant he'd wanted me to meet . . .

'Quite a sparky group, that class,' I said mildly.

'Quite a sparky group.'

'But why bother running a college when you've got such criminal talents? You'd be better off running your own company, like the property developer.'

Chris ticked off his fingers. 'Principal's salary: £95,000 a year, plus expenses. Head of Department's salary: £56,000, plus expenses. Quite a lot of cash floating round, if you live modestly, or at least make sure what isn't a modest expense can go on your claim form.'

'That sort of salary at William Murdock!' I said, accusingly.

Worrall managed a thin smile. 'Allow me to assure you, Sophie, that such salaries were unknown during my period of tenure. How they can justify them now, with the financial pressures on further education, I will not begin to speculate. However, it does occur to me – as it's doubtless already occurred to you, Mr Groom – that although it sounds an astronomical salary for a college, even their combined income is the merest chicken-feed in the real world. No: there must be another motive.'

'Someone else joined their team too! Have you checked out the new counsellor, Chris? A man called Sherringham. He was cagey when I asked where he'd come from. Adopted a line very like the party one: take some leave. And, by the way, had I ever taught anyone interesting. Like Dan, no doubt!'

Chris cocked an eye at Tom. He'd already written it down. 'I think it's time for some coffee.'

Tom put down his pen with a sigh of relief and waggled his hand. 'I suppose that Dan bloke didn't practise fire-raising, just as a party-piece, like.'

'Anyone could have started most of those fires,' Chris said. 'That college – how it ever got its fire certificate is beyond me. All that paper lying round!'

'A chronic shortage of money, my dear Chief Inspector. What do you buy – new paper or somewhere safe to store the old?'

'On salaries like theirs, Fairbairn and Godfrey could have afforded to buy a few filing cabinets and give them out,' Tom observed quietly.

Nodding, I added, 'Most of us haven't had a pay rise for a couple of years. And in any case further education salaries are way behind those in schools and universities.'

'So who *did* start the fires?' Worrall asked. He'd always been a good chair.

'Anyone looked at Fairbairn's record, Chris?' I asked.

'Why d'you ask?'

'I don't know. Association of ideas. Cakes. Cooking. Burning.'

'Hardly a *woman's* crime, surely!' Worrall expostulated.

'What is? But even if she instigated them, I'd guess she employed our Glaswegian friend to do the dirty work. They've all got more or less the same MO except for the job he did on your shed.'

'That could have been just a passing vandal,' I suggested, failing to sound airy. 'What'll happen now?'

'Charges will be brought.'

'Afzal believes Halitosis – the man who calls himself Mohammed Riaz, in reality one Dougal Kirk – was part of the gang beating up people. He's got other theories about that too.' I outlined them.

'He's got a record as long as your arm,' Tom put in. 'One of our so-called soccer-supporters that goes to matches simply to stir up trouble. I'd back your Afzal.'

Chris's eyes met mine for a fraction of a second. 'I'd say the stuff with Afzal was off his own bat. We shall soon find out.'

'Could be. And Dan looked furious when he heard about Carl's car fire. And I'd have thought the attack on Mike Appleyard might have been a bit of freelancing, too – simply to emphasize that he had the right to park where and as badly as he wanted. Which reminds me, Chris, did you find anything under my car?' I asked. 'And when can I have it back?'

'They may have to do a controlled explosion,' said Chris. And then he relented, and flipped the keys into my hands. 'I'd say you were a free woman, Sophie. What your governors choose to do about you—'

'That nasty sexual slur. The student who said I'd exposed myself – that's got to be retracted. And I don't like to be vindictive or even vengeful –' my eyes met Chris's – 'but I'd have thought he might profitably continue his studies at another college.'

'I'll have a discreet word with one or two of the old governors,' Worrall said, 'about both Sophie's reinstatement and the student's transfer. Incidentally, I telephoned my colleague at the Staffordshire college to which Sebastian Conrad was summoned post haste and he was notably evasive. Chief Inspector, perhaps one of your colleagues might like to engage him in conversation? Though I sincerely trust you will discover he was simply doing a colleague a favour, for reasons unspecified.'

'If you'll be kind enough to give me his name and address, sir – ah! Excuse me.' He answered his phone and rose to his feet in the same movement.

They all left together: I stayed where I was, though whether I sat and thought or merely sat I'd be hard put to tell, especially after Chris went to do a spot of interrogating and I was left alone.

Ian woke me with some of his most delicate Earl Grey tea and a salmon sandwich – tinned, but even he couldn't always work miracles.

I got in first. 'Ian, I was stupid last night. Plain stupid. I should have waited for you. I'm sorry.'

'I should have—'

'It'll only upset my stomach if you make me argue.' I'd have to use that excuse more often. I sipped the tea. 'Any news?'

'Plenty. I've been talking to that Sherringham of yours.

258

He insists he's nothing to do with our friends: that as a member of staff, he was just acting on their orders when he talked to you. Failure to do so would have resulted in his instant dismissal, though I find that hard to credit.'

'New contract,' I muttered.

'My guess is they've got something over him, too. He's not told us what, but I think he will, if we leave him to sweat long enough.'

The sandwiches were good: I could have done with twice as many. 'Go on.'

'We've got that Dave Clarke and his lads from Fraud in. But they're reasonably sure that the businesses Godfrey and Fairbairn's friends were associated with were legit. Up to a point.'

'So what does it all come down to? Racism?'

'Surely not. People wouldn't go to such lengths—'

I yawned, enormously.

'Tell you what, you have another bit of kip and I'll let you know what develops.'

'Just one thing: when you people searched Halitosis's room, did anyone have time to check over everything? Papers? That sort of thing?'

'I should think so ... All right, I'll check. I tell you, Sophie, you're a slave driver.'

I shook my head. 'If there's anything I can help with—'

I think I was asleep again when Chris bounded into the room, clutching a fistful of floppy disks. 'Strictly speaking, no one should be looking at these but our resident geek – but she's off getting married. I could ask you to act as a consultant ...'

'Gimme!' I was too stiff even to bend to switch on Chris's computer; but I wouldn't tell him that. I merely waited till the room was clear and I could get up and down as slowly as I needed. And as painfully.

And what did I find? A fully-fledged partner to the British National Party. EFE: England for Ever. Really imaginative. It had its own newspaper: I'd need a computer with more sophisticated software to see what that looked like. A set of accounts. A list of overseas contacts. All very interesting. But what I wanted was a membership list.

Agendas and minutes was the next disk – extremely systematic. In fact, frighteningly sophisticated. There was an articulate mind at work on the written documentation; I didn't know enough about book-keeping to evaluate the accounts, but I'd bet they'd stand scrutiny. Come on – members . . .

'How's things going? It's OK, Sophie – only me!' Chris laid a calming hand on my shoulder as I jumped out of my skin. And left it there.

'Well, as we say in the Black Country, I'll go to the foot of our stairs! I've just got to the best of all disks, Chris. Bring a chair so you can see the screen – you'll do your back damage if you stoop like that.' I must remind him about those Alexander Technique lessons . . .

He did as he was told.

'Now,' I said slowly, 'I always thought the crazy Right was the province of young men trying to show how hard they were. Football hooligans. And older men who liked the idea of exerting a bit of power. Terreblanche in South Africa, Le Pen in France. It's not something I'd ever imagined a woman would be associated with.'

'There was a Frenchwoman on TV the other day – one of Le Pen's right-hand people—'

'Who stuck out *because* she was a woman. Right?'

'Very smart. Attractive.'

'Fascist chic apart, no one would ever suspect a woman would be tangled up in anything really unpleasant, would they?'

'Are you telling me we've got fascist chic here in Brum?'

I pointed at the screen. 'I think they're grooming Barbara Fairbairn to be a parliamentary candidate. She's got all the respectable credentials. If you want a plausible candidate,' I said slowly, 'you could do a lot worse than select a high-profile woman with all the domestic virtues. And a decent salary, dollops of which could drop conveniently into party funds. *And* she's in a position to manipulate vulnerable black and Asian people – the people you hate most – into doing things that will bring them into disrepute.'

'Well, Sophie, to borrow another quaint old Black Country saying: this beats cock-fighting.'

'You've got enough here to talk to her about, surely? Whether she's actually done anything illegal—'

'Incitement to race hatred? That'll do for starters.'

I was woken by the sound of jeering, and the thud of missiles. Chris's window was too high above street level to be hit by a stone – and I must admit that even if I had thought it was a risk I should still have looked out.

So what in the name of goodness had brought this rabid accumulation of thugs to suburban Harborne? They looked like the worst sort of visitors' supporters in the most vicious days of football hooliganism. Then it slowly dawned. News of our Halitosis's incarceration must have mobilized his colleagues. From where I stood, the police seemed to be acting with commendable calm, but I could see film and still cameras scanning the mob. I opened the window. What were they yelling?

A hand reached around me to close it. 'Just in case we're forced to use CS sprays,' Chris said quietly.

'Did you get anything from Fairbairn?'

'What would you expect, with her solicitor sitting beside her? Actually, Sophie, I'm sure you were right when you said getting rid of you, but not killing you, was the name of the game. She really seems to like you. Admires your guts. And Godfrey says you were the best teacher he'd ever come across – says if it hadn't been for you he'd never have got to uni.'

'Can't get everything right, always,' I said.

We sat quietly, listening to the troubles down below.

'You've had a bad time,' he said finally, touching one of my bruises in much the same way as I'd touched Afzal's. 'And yet I suppose you'll hot-foot it back to work as soon as you get the all-clear from the governors.'

'Not this time. I've got a sick note, remember! I can spend a couple of weeks doing what I want – if I can only work out what that is. See Aggie, of course. Tidy up both our gardens: I'll do yours, while I'm at it. Go down to Andy's farm for a bit. Tell you what,' I said, his pallor and bruises impinging on me at last, 'why don't you come down too?'

'I'd like that,' he said.

Epilogue

I knew it was a dream, even while it was happening. Jim Ryan was in the lift with us for one thing: and Jim escaped from William Murdock a couple of years ago. Shahida was there; and Sean; and so was Carl, who kept on sidling up to me. We were all waiting for the lift to move from the ground floor. Then Dan got in – a young, sleek Dan, like he was when I first taught him. And he had a whippet under his arm.

We all stared. Somewhere the William Murdock rules must have said no dogs on college premises. Dan had clamped his hand like a muzzle round the dog's mouth; pity he hadn't covered the other end. Even as we watched, the dog defecated.

No one spoke. We were struck dumb in the presence of the boss, an illicit dog and a doggy dollop.

We'd reached the eighth floor. Dan stepped towards the lift doors.

'Aren't you going to clean it up?' I asked quietly.

The others looked at their feet, embarrassed.

I didn't want to yell, but he was leaving the lift with the little heap still steaming in the corner. 'Dan? What about the dog-shit?'

He didn't even turn.

The others stayed in the lift, staring. At their feet; at the dog-mess; at me.

'Right,' I said, pressing the button for down. 'I'm leaving this place. I'm not standing for this crap a moment longer!'

And I walked out, through the foyer, through the front doors, and out into the fresh air.

So it was quite easy, after all. As soon as I woke up – before I'd even had my breakfast – I'd typed my letter asking for a year's sabbatical. Yes, it was unpaid. Yes, it was a risk. But there'd got to be something better than William Murdock.

Hadn't there?